Damnificados

"*Damnificados* is a rich fictional creation inspired by legends of the past and visions of the future. The true magic of the novel is that it conjures a teeming, vigorous world that feels like an urgent version of now. Go on, live a little with the damned."
  —Richard Beard, author of *X20*

"JJ Amaworo Wilson is a terrific writer with a story that grabs you by the throat and never lets you go. Two-headed beasts, biblical floods, dragonflies to the rescue—magical realism threads through this authentic and compelling struggle of men and women—the damnificados—to make a home for themselves against all odds. As the crippled Nacho says, the refuge he helps create is 'always on the brink of chaos.' Yet into this modern, urban, politically familiar landscape of the 'have-nots' versus the 'haves,' Amaworo Wilson introduces archetypes of hope and redemption that are also deeply familiar—true love, vision quests, the hero's journey, even the remote possibility of a happy ending. These characters, this place, this dream will stay with you long after you've put this book down."
  —Sharman Apt Russell, author of *Hunger*

"Amaworo Wilson takes Nabokov's advice: In crisp sentences he fondles details. They close us in on a world we didn't know, and now won't forget."
  —A.C.H. Smith, author of *The Dark Crystal*

"A great novel. Amaworo Wilson's new Tower of Babel and its population really gripped me. An extraordinary story with unforgettable characters and fantastic scenes . . . a parable and memorial of the fate of the damnificados of this earth."
  —Ruth Weibel, Liepman AG literary agency

"JJ Amaworo Wilson writes with deep human sympathy and memorable descriptive powers. *Damnificados* is a story that needs to be heard."
  —Diran Adebayo, author of *Some Kind of Black*

Damnificados

Damnificados

JJ Amaworo Wilson

PM PRESS
2016

★

Damnificados
JJ Amaworo Wilson © 2016
This edition © 2016 PM Press

ISBN: 978-1-62963-117-2
LCCN: 2015930894

PM Press
P.O. Box 23912
Oakland, CA 94623
pmpress.org

10 9 8 7 6 5 4 3 2 1

Cover: John Yates/Stealworks.com
Layout: Jonathan Rowland

Printed by the Employee Owners of Thomson-Shore in Dexter,
Michigan. www.thomsonshore.com

For David Henry Wilson
and in memory of
Elizabeth Ayo Wilson

You'd better get a home in that rock, don't you see.
You'd better get a home in that rock, don't you see.
Between the earth and sky, thought I heard my savior cry,
You'd better get a home in that rock, don't you see.

God gave Noah the rainbow sign, don't you see.
God gave Noah the rainbow sign, don't you see.
God gave Noah the rainbow sign, no more water but fire
    next time.
You'd better get a home in that rock, don't you see.

Poor man Lazarus, poor as I, don't you see.
Poor man Lazarus, poor as I, don't you see.
Poor man Lazarus, poor as I, when he died he had a home on
    high.
You'd better get a home in that rock, don't you see.

Rich man Dives lived so well, don't you see.
Rich man Dives lived so well, don't you see.
Rich man Dives lived so well, when he died he had a home
    in Hell.
You'd better get a home in that rock, don't you see.

Negro spiritual

Blessed are the meek, for they shall inherit the earth.

Matthew 5:5

CHAPTER 1

The tower—Damnificados—The

invasion—Cerberus—Night fires—

Dogmeat—The beasts take a nap

THE SKYSCRAPER WAS THE THIRD-TALLEST BUILDING IN THE CITY AND FROM THE HIGHEST floor you could look down on the backs of birds gliding on air. One muggy August afternoon Rolo Torres tried to parachute from the fiftieth floor. The chute stayed shut and he landed face first in a refuse pile.

"At least we don't have to dig a hole to bury the dumb shit," said the mayor.

The building had stood empty for a decade, pockmarked by bullet holes, paint peeling in the sun, flaking away like a layer of skin, and a posse of graffiti artists had looped their messages in cartoon writing on the back of the building: libertad, torre de mierda, cojones, viva la revolución, and a fresco of soldiers in silhouette marching to Hell.

Surrounded as it was by low-rises, the monolith took on the aura of a bully. With its six hundred eyes it watched the world, and its shadow moved like the hands of a clock, blotting out the surrounding bodegas and wastelands and cinder block houses for minutes at a time. Over that decade the glass had fallen out the windows or been smashed by stray birds and bats till the building's eyes were hollows. And with the glass gone, the wind lassoed its ghost-whistles around and through the skyscraper's neck, shooting in and out of its arteries and whooshing down its lungs.

Some winter days the building would sway like a dancer. And when it did, the mayor, perched on a balcony sixty floors up, would cry, "It's gonna fall!" and his wife would tell him to shut the hell up because he was the mayor and he was supposed to be a leader but he was yellow as a streak of lemon and he knew it and his wife knew it and his kids knew it and when he died it was with the whimper of a wounded dog and he soiled his pants in front of his enemies, which by the end was everyone including his wife.

✳

And it is these same damnificados, twenty years on, who crawl out of the darkness one balmy midnight, a raggedy army of beards and grime, heading for the tower. They come from Agua Suja and Minhas and Fellahin and Bordello. They come from Sanguinosa and Blutig and Oameni Morti, cardboard cities and shantytowns on the hills, where the rain makes rivers of mud, where houses slide away. And they drag fraying baskets and polythene bags, soot-stained blankets, coats of crinoline and fake fur. A woman in her fifties pushes a wheelbarrow which carries a three-legged dog. And from out of a nook comes a cripple named Nacho, heaving his wasted body on bandaged crutches, his quick eyes scanning the streets for trouble. Krunk! Trouble! A four-hundred-pound Chinaman emerges foot first from a hole in a wall, kicking down the bricks. Another damnificado. He looks both ways and slings a scarred wooden club over his shoulder.

Some of the damnificados have wrapped their faces in cloths, like lepers, only eyes visible, and their steps are padded as a panther's because many have no shoes to walk in, just rags binding their feet. And others move barefoot, hunched and furtive, two by two, shifting in the shadows for safety.

Slowly and silently they converge on the tower block. And a cat spies them from its roof of corrugated iron and narrows its eyes and purrs its approval. There's nothing like a midnight rumpus to stir a cat. The distant music of sirens droops further and further into oblivion, and then there is no sound save the scampering of mice on stone.

The silence is broken by the roar of a bus as it swings its rump around a corner. A great gouge of smoke bursts out of its exhaust and then the bus convulses to a stop and two filthy, lanky teenagers exit, blond, wiry, carbon copies each of the other, each jumping the final step. Twin damnificados, men of the scarecrow army.

"Wo ist der Grosse? Where is that big bastard?" says the one.

"The tower or the Chinaman?" asks the other.

"Der Turm. Who's the Chinaman?"

"You'll know him when you see him. He's massive. He once killed an ox."

"Who hasn't killed an ox?"

"He strangled it with his bare hands."

Nacho the cripple turns a corner, sees the monolith and stops, thinking this is just as it was foretold all those years ago in Zerbera. He feels the damnificados around him, hears their breathing, recognizes the smells—a musky anthology of old food, sweat, piss, trash. Re-cognizes. Knows again, because he has dreamed of this time and this place. He crabs across the street, out of the shadow. Jaywalks with the wooden muletas under his arms, his lame leg dragging. Knows he is the first and has to be the first. Passes a gateway where Torre de Torres was inscribed on a plaque until the graffiti artists chiseled it down to rey de reyes. King of kings.

And once Nacho is past the sign, the others follow, first the Chinaman, then the twins.

"That's him. He's a bear."

"He's an elephant."

"He's a Chinaman."

"He's a bear."

Then the woman with the dog in the wheelbarrow. The wheel squeaks. She curses the world for her bad luck. Broken wheelbarrow, broken dog. It lies asleep, lulled by the journey from Sanguinosa, its long pale head tipped over the side.

The damnificados cross over. They stand ready. They gaze up at the towering monolith. Babel in black. Streaked concrete. Home from home. They surround it, milling. They wait. They glance at one another. Somewhere a clock chimes twelve.

"Now what?"

"We wait for Nacho. He'll give the word."

Nacho approaches. The doorway is boarded up, a criss-cross of wood hammered in with nails. He motions to the Chinaman, says something low. The Chinaman walks to the door and clasps his club in two hands. He swings once and a board explodes with a crack like a gunshot. Nails jump. With a final kick, it caves in. A small cheer goes up.

A woman's voice: "Now it's ours."

Nacho is overtaken by his army of damnificados. They approach the door and then they hear it. They stop. At first it's a whine but then it drops an octave and then another until it's a low growl. No one moves. The growl comes again. In the doorway, in the darkness, a shape shifts.

"It's a dog."

"It's wild."

They make out movements in the gloom. The creature begins to pace the dusty atrium behind the door. Growls low again. Moves forward. Then a shaft of moonlight breaks open the darkness, zeroing in on the splintered boards as the animal comes closer, bares its fangs. The damnificados stare. Something wrong. A breach of nature. The beast has two heads.

＊

There is a gasp and they shrink back. Dozens cross themselves and start to pray. A woman covers her son's eyes. The Chinaman, breathing heavily from breaking the door, stops panting and stares, a ghostly look in his eyes.

The animal lets out an unworldly howl from its double throat, both mouths stretched wide, two rows of fangs visible in each. The army does not move. The moon shimmies behind a veil of clouds, throwing a blanket of darkness over them all.

One of the damnificados turns to Nacho.

"It's a sign from God. We can't go in."

Another: "God? That thing came from hell. We need a priest."

A man in a raincoat stained black with oil turns and looks around. "We don't need a priest. We need a gun. Let's kill it."

Again the animal howls into the night, its jaws upraised. The beast is mangy but strong. Its heads move in unison, emanating from the same short, wiry neck.

Raincoat says to the Chinaman, "Beat it. Club it. Make it die."

The Chinaman does not move.

The woman with the wheelbarrow says, "We don't kill dogs. They are us."

"We have no choice," says Raincoat. "How do we get into the tower?"

"You call that a dog?" says another.

Nacho moves forward. He squints at the beast, and says in a whisper, "You're right. It isn't a dog. It's a wolf."

"It can't be a wolf," says Wheelbarrow. "Wolves don't live in cities."

"These do," says Nacho.

Raincoat turns to Nacho. "So it's a wolf. Then we kill it."

Nacho says, "It isn't *it*. It's *them*. There are more."

"How do you know?"

Behind the wolf there is movement, a gathering.

"Because it was calling for help."

A dozen other wolves pad into view. They are one-headed, sleek, ears erect, cold-eyed. They stare at the army as the army stares at them.

"We have guns," says one of the veiled damnificados. "We can fire warning shots."

Nacho shakes his dishevelled head. "You fire a gun, all hell breaks loose. They'll tear our throats out."

"We have to take the building. Let's kill them," says Raincoat. "Then we roast them."

Nobody moves. The two-headed wolf stares at Nacho. Nacho turns away and speaks.

"Build fires. There's debris everywhere, wood and paper. Build a fire every ten meters around the tower. Where are the twins?"

Hans and Dieter move forward.

"Come with me. We need your father's truck."

All around the tower is a river of debris and mud and newspapers, cardboard boxes turning to pulp, smashed wooden crates.

Half the damnificados stand on guard facing the door, weapons in hand—razors, cobra-neck flickknives, rifles from World War II, pistolas that look like water guns, clubs, hunks of metal, sticks, stones, bottles. The others half walk among the trash and pick out the flammables. Children squat, heads low, fingers exploring. A woman from a shantytown called Mundanzas pulls down her veil and says to Wheelbarrow,

"Why don't you take the dog out and let us use that wheelbarrow for wood?"

"Why don't you stick the wood where the sun don't shine?"

In groups they make piles of debris. One man finds a can of kerosene and moves to each pile and pours a little. In their fear they keep watching the doorway where the wolves mill and mingle. Then the damnificados ignite the piles with matches and lighters. Soon there is a circle of small fires surrounding the tower, and the wolves retreat into the shadows, and a few of the elders are reminded of the legend of Las Bestias de la Luz Perpetua, from an earlier time before sixty-story towers were erected in the heart of the city.

An hour passes. Children hide behind their parents' legs, peeping out and disappearing again, and the damnificados stand or sit or squat, waiting, while the flames make heroes of them, as flames always do. Their filth is gone in flamelight, their rags too. Their hunger. In the flickering, crackling light, they become ancient warriors, as still as marble gods.

A flatbed truck pulls up, and Nacho and the twins get out of the cab. Hans is carrying a heavy plastic bag. He puts it on a makeshift table of plywood and Nacho pulls out a mortar and pestle and a smaller bag. He and Dieter begin crushing white pills. Hans pulls out thin slabs of meat the size of a man's hand from the bigger bag and they thumb the powder into the meat, kneading it, folding and unfolding the raw steak.

When it is done, Dieter and Hans carry the meat in piles toward the door of the monolith. They toss the pieces into the doorway and the steak lands, slap, slap, slap.

Ten minutes pass before the first of the wolves slinks into view. It noses the meat, nuzzles it, raises its head. Some kind of offering. It does a full turn, a slow circle, breathing heavily. Suddenly it lurches its head downward. It tears at the meat with its incisors, and soon the other wolves follow. Hans and Dieter look at each other. The last wolf to appear is the two-headed beast. It takes its share.

Raincoat turns to Nacho, "What is this? Feeding time? We should be killing them, not feeding them."

The wolves have dragged the meat into the darkness, and as they tear into it, there is the sound of thrashing and the scraping of claws on stone.

Nacho nods to the twins.

Thirty minutes pass. The twins and the Chinaman move forward, fifteen, ten, five feet from the splintered door. Silence. Hans steps in. He disappears for a few seconds, then comes out.

"It worked," he says. "They're all asleep."

"Good," says Nacho. "Then we have to move fast. The drugs will only last for another hour or two."

The twins and some of the others go in gingerly, with the Chinaman close behind wielding his club, and they load the sleeping wolves onto the bed of the truck. They draw straws for the two-headed monster and the Chinaman loses and picks up the animal by its belly, so its heads drag at his feet. He throws the beast onto the pile.

Hans and Dieter get into the truck and Hans drives it away. He will keep driving until he reaches the outskirts of the city, where the woods are deep and rain-soaked, where a wolf can hide and run and live and die.

CHAPTER 2

THE NIGHT FIRES ARE NOW EMBERS. THE FIRST RAYS OF SUN BURN AN ELLIPSE INTO THE horizon, and the gathering light is blurred with the smoke and fog of the city. As the sun shines on the shantytowns of Slomljena Ruka, Fellahin, Dieux Morts, Sanguinosa, an explosion of light turns the hills into a mosaic of glistening mirrors. The crowing of cocks and the curdled yelps of dogs puncture the quiet. Somewhere a truck growls.

The damnificados are stirring. They have waited all night, seen hounds from hell that turned out to be wolves, warmed themselves by fires, eaten the food they carried—raw potatoes, a little bread—and now it's time to take the tower.

"The wolves are gone," says Nacho to a family huddling together. "We can go in."

He walks among them, his crutches leaving a trail of dots on the ground.

"The tower is ours," he says.

No one moves.

"It's cursed," says a woman. She stands up. Grimy forehead, riven by lines, her face a street map of Sanguinosa. She may be sixty-five, may be thirty. No one knows the age of a damnificado. Their faces are a collection of creases, valleys, craters, unexpected bursts of ugliness. "That animal is a sign from God. We can't go in."

Nacho stops, ruffles his hair, faces her.

"I understand you," he says.

"No you don't," she says. "There's worldly things and not-worldly things. Things we don't expect to see on this Earth. God sends them to warn us."

"Then what should we do?" asks Nacho. "Do we go back to our homes? Take our families back to our hovels, to our cardboard shacks under the bridges? Or do we pray to God to let us enter this damned place? Look. The sun's rising. That's also an act of God. Another day dawning."

Nacho stands in front of her as the light begins to cast her face in yellow, a mask of lines and hollows. "God brought us here too. Maybe for a reason."

Hans, newly returned from the woods, walks toward Nacho. Says, "Du musst hineingehen. Nacho, why don't you go first? Take the Chinaman with you."

And Nacho does. The giant and the cripple move together, one with the gait of a wrestler, the other a-hobble on worm-worn sticks.

"It's cursed," says the woman to herself. "We can't go in."

The Chinaman kicks again at the remains of the door he smashed, the splinters coming off in showers of dust. He and Nacho enter the atrium, where they'd picked up the sleeping wolves. In the sunlight they see all that was hidden at night: the floor dense with trash, bones, crumbling stone. The space a small cavern. On both sides a stairwell. At the back, a disused elevator shaft standing open. Rotting stacks of paper, mold climbing the walls.

Nacho and the Chinaman take the two different stairwells. The stairs are shallow, worn. Nacho heaves himself up to the floor above. A corridor. The Chinaman appears from the other side of the building. Small apartments. Ten on each floor. Already Nacho is counting, figuring the numbers of damnificados, who will go to the top floors and who to the bottom. How to house someone fifty floors in the sky in a building with a broken elevator. How to solve the conundrum: the elderly need the lower floors but it is the lower floors that will need the warriors because that is where the tower will be attacked.

How to use his contacts to get the water flowing once again through the rusted pipes. How to build a community in this upright tomb.

He maneuvers his way back down to the atrium and is about to call the damnificados when he sees them pouring slowly through the doors, like zombies. Families with sleeping children draped over their shoulders. Dreadlocked men as old as Methuselah.

Hunched shoulders, people lost in coats and bags and beanie hats incongruous in the morning heat.

And he thinks, 'This is it. This is the beginning.'

*

"Never doubt what a hundred souls can do, given the time and the need." Don Felipe Holguin stands before Nacho. A priest in sandals. Unshaven, gray. He is tall and stooped but with the nose of the boxer that he once was before he heard the call from Jesus.

"We have *six* hundred souls," says Nacho.

Damnificados. The lowest of the low, rising to the heights of the third-tallest building in the city. Sicarios. Knifemen. Assassins. Bandidos. Quick-handed, cold-eyed. The unholy, the unhoused, led by the lame. Nacho divides the damnificados into groups of six, keeping families together. He knows a quarter of them by name.

"Only small groups will accomplish anything," the priest says to him. "More than eight and you will get factions and everything will go to hell. I've seen it happen."

At first Nacho writes the tasks in three languages on large boards. Sweep rubble, remove trash, wash floors, plug leaks, rebuild walls, kill vermin. He sees incomprehension and remembers that most damnificados cannot read. He talks to them, learns who can do what. Finds among them a soldier, an engineer, a mechanic. He assigns task leaders among the groups. Calls the leaders together. Tells them what they must do and the tools they will need to do it. They return to their groups and lead. The physically stronger go higher up the building.

He sends a delegation to find brooms, brushes, wheelbar-rows, hammers and nails wherever they can. They trawl the gar-bage dumps, beg and borrow. A group of the older women sets up grills outside the building, where they cook corn and plantain and the discarded parts of chickens and pigs. Another group he sends on reconnaissance, to find land in the vicinity where they can grow food. Small plots.

"We'll become farmers," he says. "Carrots, potatoes, whatever will grow. And trees, too. There's no shade. We need trees for the old to sit under. And to attract birds."

"Why do we want birds? They'll steal our food," says Raincoat.

"Because birds sing. There's no music here."

"Then we'll start a choir," says the priest.

The engineer sets up a system of ropes and pulleys to get tools, water and food to the higher floors. But there are no ropes long enough to reach beyond the tenth floor. Nacho procures a moped. Then he gets the twins to lay wooden planks on the outer stairs leading to every floor, rising in long diagonals. An ex-army grease monkey rigs up the moped with reinforced tires, and now it roars up the planks day and night, loaded with goods.

The rooms of the monolith are littered with rubble and trash. Dried-out corpses of beetles and cockroaches freckle the floors. Nacho enters a room one story up, looking for his base, and comes across the remnants of tenants long gone: a chair falling to pieces, a moldy blanket covered with wolves' fur, six toppled wine bottles gently rolling and clinking in the breeze that blows through the windowless gap in the wall. He looks out of the hole. Thinks, 'One floor up, I can see the entrance, and the road that people will cross to get here.' But something nags him about the sight lines. He cannot see the bigger picture. I need to be higher, he says to himself. But then I'll need to climb stairs on my crutches. He wills himself up another floor, enters a room where a family is sweeping. They nod at him and make to leave.

"No, stay," he says.

He hobbles to the blown out window and again looks out to the street. Now the angle is better. He can see above the bodegas and the street vendors. But still he is not happy.

"What's on your mind?" asks the priest.

"Which room I should stay in."

"Why?"

"I need to see the surroundings."

"Why?"

"Because I like to know who's coming. When they hear we've taken the building, they'll come for us. Sooner or later."

"Who's *they*?"

"I don't know. The gangs. The police. The army. The politicos. I don't know, but someone will come for us."

"Nacho," says the priest, "what will you do? Stay awake all night every night watching for enemies? You have six hundred pairs of eyes here. They can keep watch for you. The world doesn't have to be on your shoulders. Frankly, you don't have the shoulders for it."

And so Nacho takes a room on the first floor and asks the ex-soldier to organize guards, a twenty-four-hour watch from three levels on all four sides: the sixtieth floor where a watcher can see for miles, spot a convoy or a tank coming half an hour before it makes its way through the traffic. Four pairs of eyes at all times, north, south, east, and west. The thirtieth floor, too, will have four watchers. And the first floor also, from where, without the need for binoculars, the watchers can see the expression on a man's face as he approaches the entrance, whether he's carrying a knife or a bomb or a basket of fruit. And of course there are the guards to the entrances on the ground floor, all four of them armed and each with a child's walkie-talkie retrieved from a dump.

The main entrance belongs to the Chinaman. There he will sit motionless for hours on end, arms folded. A Blutig carpenter makes a chair for him from objects found in the building: great hunks of wood from a broken dresser and the reclaimable springs of a mattress. The Chinaman has the gift of stillness. A visitor might think he's asleep because his chin touches his chest and under the broad peak of the baseball cap he sometimes wears, you cannot see his eyes. But, like Nacho, he is always watching.

The garbage piles outside the building are the toughest of all. They are inhabited by colonies of giant rats that shoot through the darkness of the trash tunnels. Some of the second and all of the third-generation vermin have mutated. They can now adapt to the color of the trash, like chameleons. Nacho calls a meeting with his leaders. They try a hunting mission, but the rats are too quick. They try poison but the rats adapt and eat it like bread. They concrete over a section of the trash pile to see if it will work, but the rats gnaw through the concrete and scamper the walkways at night, laughing.

"We must burn them out," says Nacho. "Even rats cannot survive fire."

He has seen controlled burns before, but never in the middle of a city. He understands it's the wind that matters, and natural breaks where a fire will stop. He walks the perimeter of the tower, calculating angles and the length of gullies.

One calm day shortly after, he tells the damnificados to stay inside and cover the window openings with boards, blankets, or cardboard, whatever they can find to keep the smoke out. He gets the mechanic to mix a canister of diesel and gasoline, molds a driptorch from an old coffee can, and rigs it up to the moped. One of the twins ignites the wick and rides around the perimeter, dropping fire on the largest of the garbage piles. A thousand rats scamper and the piles are leveled.

As the trash chars and turns to cinders, toxic fumes rise, black veils twisting up the sky. They curl toward the window openings of the monolith, but as these are covered, the fumes barely enter. Instead, they dissipate, swallowed up in the expanse of sunlit fog that blankets the city.

The twins' father's truck pulls up, orange embers crackling all around. Hans gets out of the cab and with two other men begins to unload huge sacks from the bed of the truck. The Chinaman unties the sacks and fifty wild cats bound out, teeth like knives. They follow the scent trails of the escaping rats, down holes, up drains, into all the dark spaces where a rat might hide. And when they are done with their massacre, the cats melt back into the alleyways and slinkholes of the city.

"Where did you get those cats?" asks the priest.

Dieter looks at him. He has never spoken to a priest before.

"From the cat-catcher in Estrellas Negras. We paid her with a table and chairs. They say she's a witch."

"La bruja de Estrellas Negras. She's real?" says the priest.

"She stank of cat piss and skunks. Hans nearly threw up."

*

They send for Lalloo. He knows how to steal electricity from the pylons and generators. But when he arrives he is drunk. Singing to himself, eyes blood-red. The twins support him on either side and leave him to sleep it off in the atrium.

He wakes up. Nacho welcomes him. He falls asleep again.

He wakes up an hour later. Nacho gives him a plate of food and a cup of wine. He ignores the food.

"We need electricity for this building," says Nacho.

That afternoon Lalloo is up a ladder, boltcutters and pliers hooked onto his belt. He puts the monolith on the grid, lamps buzzing bright, drawing mosquitoes at dusk as the call to prayer rises from a nearby mosque. Later he tries and fails to fix the elevator, tells Nacho the thing is busted for good.

*

The Chinaman raises Nacho onto his shoulders and walks up sixty flights of stairs. He is panting by the time he reaches the top. With the Chinaman, the priest, the twins and Raincoat by his side, Nacho looks out. He sees half the city, the skyline punctured with other towers—hotels and office blocks—and dozens of billboards half-obscured. The roads are jammed with taxis and a million cars, bicycle rickshaws, yellow buses blasting salsa, exhaust fumes pluming upward, people dawdling or scurrying.

He looks down at the land surrounding the tower, irregular, uneven, gullied like wounds, black patches still smoldering from the burn that drove out the rats.

"This was a wasteland," he says. "There are mountains of trash buried under the ground. Whatever happens, we must never see another trash pile. Not here. This tower has to be clean inside and out."

*

The families move in. Those with the elderly take the lower floors. They bring in furniture, lanterns, candles, everything reclaimed from the dumps. Some have stoves, and even refrigerators. They make beds from pallets and recycled planks. Old sofas come in from the dumpster at Minhas. A hotel burns down at Puertarota and the damnificados head out at 3:00 a.m. to salvage beds and wardrobes, loading them onto the twins' father's truck and hanging off the sides as it winds its way back to the tower.

They stalk the rich areas for abandoned TVs and pull them off the sidewalk. Lalloo fixes everything electrical after Nacho lets him stay in a room on the sixth floor. His hands shake but he can find his way around electrics in his sleep and for weeks he goes from floor to floor fixing everything in exchange for food and wine.

A riot breaks out south of Agua Suja and in the chaos six brothers somehow bring a baking oven home to the tower, marching it like a coffin in a cortege. It takes them all night to haul it to the tower and when they arrive their hands and shoulders are bleeding. They set it up the next day on the third floor and open a bakery.

On the sixth floor Maria Benedetti, an ex-beauty queen from Sanguinosa, sets up a salon. She uses pilfered combs and brushes, shampoo made from soap and goat's milk, and a hair dryer that was her mother's. A string of damnificadas, pouting preening girls, crowd into the salon, and soon women from Favelada and Fellahin begin coming to get their hair done and Maria puts up a street sign, 'Marias Beautty & Hare Salon.' Nacho gets wary when he realizes the visiting women arrive in the afternoon and don't leave till morning. He says to the priest, "They're prostitutes. They go to the salon, spend their earnings on their hair, and make the money back without even leaving the tower."

The priest says, "But who can pay them here? This tower is full of damnificados. Which of them has money for women?"

What the priest doesn't know is that the tower is home to working people. Many find jobs in factories, as guards, caretakers, sweepers and cleaners. Nacho does nothing about the hookers, reasoning that liberty is all, liberty to make a living, to have a home, to sleep with whores.

He opens three schools, one each on the fifth, the fifteenth and the twenty-fifth floors. He finds old desks and boards in a junkpile, and buys a supply of chalk. Behind the offices of an insurance firm in Amado he leads a raid on a dumpster and finds half a ton of used paper. He puts it in eight-foot cans from an abandoned factory, douses it with soapy water, and spreads the slurry on huge rollers. The sheets are hung up on the balconies of the first to the tenth floor and when they are dry, Nacho cuts them into rectangles with his good arm. Now they have paper. Meanwhile, the twins steal pens and pencils from every bank, business, post office, and library in a fifteen-mile radius.

At first no one attends. The children are all out making money. They clean car windows, pick up glass to recycle, sell candy or umbrellas in the rainy season, beg, juggle at traffic lights, do magic tricks. So Nacho starts with the parents in one hour sessions. He draws objects on the board and has the students do the same. They draw everything that is important to them and they name it. Then they write it together on the board, sounding out the letters. Children. C. H. I. L. D. R. E. N. They say what they want for their children. M. O. N. E. Y. O. P. P. O. R. T. U. N. I. T. Y. H. A. P. P. I. N. E. S. S. And Nacho asks, where are your children now? On the street. Cleaning cars. Begging. And Nacho asks, how will they get money, opportunity, happiness? And eventually the parents find their way to the word E. D. U. C. A. T. I. O. N.

Nacho takes them for walks and they make out the words on signs, begin to read the word and the world. They write communal stories on the boards, Nacho acting as scribe. Their family histories. Myths and legends from their towns. Half-heard tales. And when they are done, Nacho puts them into pairs and they 'read' the stories together, puzzling out the words.

Nacho brings in comic books: superheroes, men in tights saving cities, girls with twenty-foot rubber arms and supersight, clairvoyants and villains. They piece together the stories. They retell them and find meaning and write words from the tales.

Where did the tower come from? Who built it? What was it called? Why? Why was it empty? They write their answers on paper. Where did the desks they were sitting at come from? But before the carpenter took his saw to the wood, where did the wood come from? Who brought it to the city? How? Why?

And gradually the children of the damnificados begin to appear.

CHAPTER 3

NACHO MORALES. CRIPPLE. WITHERED LEFT SIDE. ARM AND LEG. GAMMY SINCE BIRTH. Mole under his right eye. Abandoned on a riverbank, swaddled in rags. His parents saying, "He'll die soon enough." The river stinks of human excrement, runs through Agua Suja shanty-town. The mother herself a child of twelve. The father sixteen, pushing dope. A year after he leaves Nacho to die, he hears of a deal with imported heroin, gets himself a gun and a bandana which he wraps around his mouth. Thinks he's Billy the Kid. Jumps from a scaffold. Steals from his own gang, the gun as big as his arm. Pockets the money. Realizes he forgot a getaway plan. Runs as far as the river where he abandoned his son. The gang following. Guns him down. Retrieves the money. Rolls him into the river. Floats down to Blutig. The longest journey he ever took. Bloated and stinking like a fish by the time a hook pulls him ashore.

And Nacho too, a year earlier, is hauled in by a stranger's hook. Samuel, a wanderer from Favelada, a teacher by day.

"What have we here?" he says and picks up the bundle. "Hello, small fry."

Squinty face, scrunched features, little pink tadpole. Samuel looks around. Surveys his options. Put child back, child dies. Vultures peck out his eyes. Take child to police, child goes straight onto trash pile. Take child home. No choice.

Catches a bus. Buys one ticket. Newborn wretches go free. The bus whines and lurches. The baby sleeps. A fat paisano woman sitting next to him, smelling of goats and chickens. Peers into the bundle. Thinks of cooing. Changes her mind.

Samuel, back seat of the bus, barely thirty, watching the streets go by, his unlined face as flat as cardboard in the window. Across the city, past Fellahin with its streets that smell of boiled sausage and falafel. A sheep crossing the road. An electronics workshop where everything is the color of oil. The back end of a protest march echoing down a side street, a white banner glimpsed from behind. Cramped shops squeezed together, clothes hanging out the upstairs windows, gyrating in the breeze. Schoolchildren in uniforms, loose gangs with stragglers breaking off, walking homeward, bent over by backpacks jammed with books. Then the long fence parallel to the road, tagged with hieroglyphs and runes and end-of-the-world messages.

Now the landscape opens out. Past Minhas, its great gashes in the ground and piles of black refuse, tiny workers in the distance. And here, groups of them caked in filth, waiting at bus stops, lighting smokes, slapping backs. Vendors with trays hanging from their necks, mingling in the traffic. And does the child just for a moment open its tiny eyes, see the blurred masses and their broken lives from out of that window? Does it harness its sixth sense and know it's being rescued from a riverbank to enter a world of endless suffering? Rescued by the teacher, Samuel, who was visiting his sick cousin in Agua Suja. Brought a cake. Strolled alone under trees, found himself following the river. Ignored the smell. Saw the bundle. Bent down. Reached out. The story of his life.

They live in the House of Flowers. It is tiny, cramped, made of reclaimed bricks, and the wind in winter slips through the cracks. But there are painted flowers in yellow and red on the outer walls and this makes the house stand out from all the others in Favelada. And there are many.

When he gets home he takes off the rags to bathe the child and sees the withered arm and leg. Two pale sticks attached to a body. Anna, his wife, walks in. Misses a breath, raises her hand to her mouth.

"This baby was by the river. Agua Suja. Abandoned. I brought him home."

Their son, Emil, comes in to look at the news. Glee. Poke and prod. Samuel lifts the child out of reach. Which is what he does for three years. With Anna, he keeps the child alive by warding off stray hands.

Nacho is a smudge. A hobo. A frog on the shore. His childhood is a blur of sickness: rashes, fevers, agues, poxes, sudden breakouts of nodules, bumps, pustules, pus.

He learns to speak. Quiet voice. At his father's side all evening every evening, and unable to run, walk, jump, swim, fight, he reads early and well.

School beckons. Samuel fashions a pair of crutches for Nacho, working on them at night, carving the wood with a chisel by the light of the moon till they are shaped and strong. Nacho tucks them under his arms and half-hobbles, half-vaults across the room. Wooden wings fit for angels.

He is too weak to make a good target so the bullies treat him as a freak. He plays dumb to avoid attention. Makes deliberate mistakes when he writes. Pretends he's a halfwit, till a teacher who is a friend of Samuel's keeps him behind after school.

"I know you're bright," she says. "Your father told me. Play stupid if you like but I'm giving you extra homework, extra reading. Book reports, some poetry, the philosophers. Write a journal. Write me stories. I'll read them, and we'll keep it a secret."

He nods.

When he's ten, a playground malandro stalks him, gets him in a headlock. Nacho begins choking. Suddenly there is a shudder and the arm around his scrawny neck goes limp. The thug crumples to the floor. Looming over him is a massive boy. Black hair. Slanted eyes. Turns and wanders away. The Chinaman.

The Chinaman is an island, a fortress no one can enter. They say he is mute or doesn't speak the language. He has a round, soft face and hands the size of frying pans. At ten he weighs two hundred pounds. At fifteen he will weigh three hundred. The school hires a carpenter to build a reinforced chair. It cracks first time. They give him a plank of wood between two concrete blocks. Sits in silence. Frowns.

Samuel walks Emil and Nacho to school every day. As they stride through the heart of Favelada, Nacho swinging big on his crutches to keep up, Samuel tells stories.

"This is where Odewoyo's Last Stand took place. Nigerian gangster. All his lieutenants dead. He came out blasting. Fifty police gunned him down. He was more holes than man. They put his gun in a museum. Look up. That's the balcony where Eugenia the Beautiful threw flowers to the masses. Gave her final speech. Look there. The bullring. Seems like wasteland, doesn't it? It was the place of the matadors, Guerrero, Zubayda, Hernandez, Ochoa, Davidovsky."

"What happened to it?" asks Emil, two years older and a head taller than Nacho.

"What happened to it? What happens to everything? Turns to dust. What birds are those? There! There! Keep your eyes open. You never know when you'll need them."

And this is how Nacho learns everything, sees everything. Wasted body, singing mind.

At first he sleeps on a mat in Anna and Samuel's room. They lie awake to check his breathing. When he turns six, he goes in with Emil in a bed fashioned from a broken table, the legs sawn down. Emil, at eight, runs wild, knows every corner of Favelada, every street. Takes Nacho to the butcher, the baker, the barber. Shows him off. Skims stones in the river while Nacho counts the bounces. They get chased out of the market for stealing apples. Nacho, as always, innocent, shuffling on his muletas.

One day Emil climbs up the wall of the whorehouse in Roppus Street, hangs on a window ledge and sees the butcher's fat ass bumping away on the bed, a woman called Lulu beneath him. Giggles. The butcher turns around in midgrind, hauls himself off Lulu, strides to the window, face red and puffed like a ham, erect penis leading him on. Emil scrambles down, laughing, as a shoe flies out the window, missing his head by inches. Joins Nacho, and off they walk, the butcher's invective following them down the street. Nacho doesn't know it now, but he will one day call upon a favor, ask the butcher for meat in the dead of night to feed a wolf pack, and the butcher will remember him because he knew his father and will say yes, and once again naked he will drag himself downstairs and pull out hunks of raw steak still wet with blood.

Emil sleeps long and deep every night, worn out by his daytime excursions. But Nacho is a nonsleeper. He reads where a strip of light pours through the window. Reads and reads into the small hours. By eight he knows the poets, Norse mythology, dinosaur etymology, biographies of queens and statesmen, the names of plant species, can follow a manual on engine building, nineteenth-century Russian sagas, theories of dead philosophers, art criticism, polemics, Marx and Freud, Dickens and Poe.

A friend of Anna's sometimes stops by and speaks to him in Spanish. Another in French. An aunt three times removed comes over and rattles away in Italian. The languages stick to him like mud to a boy's knee.

The winter he turns ten he breaks out in pustules and takes to his bed. Anna feeds him watery potato soup, brings library books to his room. After three days he gets weaker. They move Emil out of the room, put Nacho on a pallet on their floor, and call a healer. Her name is Haloubeyah. She sweeps into the room in a black kaftan, smiles, asks his name. Looks him in the eye, touches him once on his good arm, and boils a poultice in the tiny kitchen. Foul smelling broth. Sings as she works. Emil stares till his mother kicks him out of the room. Haloubeyah gives Nacho a root to chew on. Minutes later he is asleep and she applies the poultice.

The next day Nacho recovers. And his hair begins to grow like a madman's.

CHAPTER 4

The First Trash War—The House of

Flowers—Alberto Torres—A raft in the river

DECADES EARLIER, BEFORE NACHO WAS FOUND LIKE MOSES IN THE BULRUSHES, PEOPLE began to pour in from the countryside in search of work, and Favelada suddenly had four thousand damnificados with nowhere to live. So they found pieces of land and built on them using whatever was at hand: stones, bricks, wood, mud, iron. The houses began to spring up. Patchwork cubes with a hole in the roof for a chimney. A damnificado called Lalloo showed them how to steal electricity from the pylons to get light and heat, and some of the families found old television sets abandoned in the dumps or on the sidewalks and took them home and hooked them up, banged them around until they got a channel working. Thus did lives begin and end to a constant babble, a twenty-four-hour cycle of game shows and soccer and news and assassinations and telenovelas and white noise, parrot chatter, jibber-jabber, canned laughter.

The towns spread, but no governments recognized the new areas. Sanguinosa, Fellahin, Blutig, nonplaces for nonpeople. No roads were built, for why would you build a road to nowhere? Mountains of garbage appeared—rotting food, plastic, paper, broken glass—until the smell insinuated itself into the hems of the damnificados' clothes, the nooks of their rooms, their dreams. And one day the damnificados of Favelada rounded up their donkeys and carts, loaded up the trash with pitchforks and shovels, and took it to the wastelands. Some months later a group of men who had found work pooled their money and bought a truck. Every Saturday they would fill the bed of the truck and drive ten minutes south. They dug massive holes in the ground, threw in the garbage, and after some months covered the pile with soil.

But then other damnificados began to live in the wastelands. A small community of addicts, escaped convicts, and vagrants appeared. After a while they saw the truck was bringing piles of trash, so they moved the trash back, dumped it in the dead of night on the very doorsteps of the houses of Favelada. In retaliation, the truck brought more trash. And then an incident occurred. One day the driver of the truck and his crew unloaded the trash, as normal. On their return to the cab, they found a beheaded doll on the seat and in the doll's hollow plastic body, goat's blood still warm. A sign.

And this is how the Trash Wars began.

The truck from Favelada roared into the wasteland the following Saturday, its bed piled high with garbage. The place seemed deserted. Suddenly a woman's voice rang out:

"Kami ay labanan sa dulo!"

The truck driver applied the brakes but left the engine running. All around them, makeshift houses. In front of them, one woman, tiny, ancient, skin and bone, hair tied in a scarf. Her fierce eyes widened and she screamed it again, higher, almost ululating:

"Kami ay labanan sa dulo!"

The driver turned to the parrot on his shoulder.

"What the hell is that?"

"Filipino."

"I don't give a fuck what language it is. What does it mean?"

"'I will fight you to the end.'"

The driver smiled, turned the key, killed the engine.

Suddenly, figures emerged from the wasteland as from hell. Dirt-smeared rag-men waving sharpened sticks and tomahawks. Youths with helmets made of chicken bones and wire. Madwomen in filth-encrusted aprons, yelling in Arabic, Latvian, Tagalog, French. A swamp pirate, lank hair down to his hips, open waistcoat revealing a necklace of six blackened human ears on a string.

The driver, an ex-farmer with a vicious streak, opened his door, got down, reached back into the cab, and pulled from the floor a metal chain.

"Kami ay labanan sa dulo!"

"Be my guest, little lady," said the driver, and suddenly the mound of trash on the bed of the truck flew up in piles. Twenty men burst out of the junk, stinking like the devil's latrine, vaulting the side of the truck, armed to the teeth with chains, belts, bottles, whips, clubs.

There on that desolate plain, damnificado slaughtered damnificado. Hand-to-hand thrashings, medieval batterings, skulls pulverized, ribs smithereened, arms lopped off. The groans lasted long and loud till a freak storm exploded through the clouds and drenched the battlefield, damping down the dust, tamping the blood, ringing a tattoo on the tin roofs of the houses.

The truck driver lay dead in a shallow grave of rain-spattered plastic bags and fraying ropes, his arm sliced off at the elbow ten feet away, the hand at the end of it still gripping the key to the truck. One of the six survivors on the trash-bringers' side now prized open the dead fingers, took the key, and ran through the rain. Jumping into the cab, he sparked the engine and sped home to Favelada, the driver's parrot squawking in his ear.

*

The House of Flowers sat on the edge of the township. Neighbors and near-neighbors sprang up overnight—half-built concrete walls, scavenged wooden boards, roofs of corrugated tin with slate lined on top. Palettes for beds. Plastic washing buckets for everything that could be washed—cutlery, clothes, faces, bodies. Nails driven into walls, from which hung towels, pots, pans. In the rainy season these makeshift houses sank slowly into rivers of mud. The leaks in the roofs turned to holes the size of plates, and buckets sat collecting the stream of rain that drummed down. Sometimes a house got washed away in a day or night, the family disappearing to higher ground.

Up on the hills the lights of the shantytowns glowed at night like wary eyes. The ramshackle houses crowded together, climbing upon one another as if for comfort. The street snaking up the hill was cobbled and stank of crushed fruit, bloated vermin lying dead in puddles. Slicks of oily water conjured fragments of rainbows. The streets themselves were fetid, rotting, and sunbrowned children ran wild in oversized T-shirts, shoes with holes where laces should be, chasing madly after skeletal dogs.

But here on the plain where the House of Flowers was found, no trash piles were visible. Order had long reigned in Favelada. Samuel and Anna and a thousand other migrants had brought the most precious things Favelada had ever seen: peace and family. And while the chattering of the televisions continued in the scratched up houses and The Bickering never left the vicinity for long, the days of destruction—the Trash Wars—seemed over. Yes, Favelada was poor, but there were teachers like Samuel. There was a library one mile away. A doctor from Zerbera and a dentist from Oameni Morti were building free clinics on the edge of town. Schools opened up.

As for the wasteland where the residents of Favelada dumped their trash, it was taken over by a man named Alberto Torres. A businessman. He built housing nearby and moved the residents there, and in a fit of madness that lasted five years, built a tower sixty floors into the sky. Torre de Torres. The monolith. He lived there and so did his sons and daughters and the sons and daughters of his sons and daughters and his distant cousins twice removed and people called Torres who claimed ancestral kinship and people not called Torres who didn't. And it was the son of Alberto Torres, Alberto Torres II, also prone to bouts of syphilitic madness, who later pronounced himself mayor of the tower and watched as his cousin fifteen times removed, and crazy as a cuckoo in a jar, hurled himself from the fiftieth floor with a parachute that wouldn't open.

But that was long after the Trash Wars and long before the rise and rise of the shrimp called Nacho, squirming in his wooden bed, a book jammed close to his face, his hair all askitter, sprouting in clumps like weeds in a field. His mother takes to sitting him on her lap and combing it from behind, untangling the hairs that grow together and giving it a semblance of evenness, a pretense that these rogue outcrops are at least growing in one direction.

At least they are growing. The rest of his body isn't. At twelve he reaches five feet and that is where he will remain for the rest of his life, though on windy days his hair might take him to five feet five. It has its advantages. He wins at hide-and-seek, curling himself into a laundry basket in the corner of a room. And he masters the habit of going unseen, watching from the shadows, fitting himself into the cracks and crevices where no one looks. He has an indio complexion, a little browned, but Caucasian features—a straight, full nose, thin lips, blue-gray eyes. Though his body is curled and stunted, his face is cherubic. He will always look younger than his age. Only the cares of later life, facing down armies and despots and bureaucrats, will wear away his angelic countenance, bring him the lines and creases of manhood.

*

Emil the tearaway has begun to take things apart and fix them. On his wanderings he finds an abandoned car half covered over with weeds. He climbs into the rusting body, then out again. He opens the hood and starts playing with the engine, trying to get something to spark.

Another day he finds a broken radio in a skip and takes it home to fix. He pulls it apart on the family table, Samuel standing over him, and digs and twists and sticks nails where they don't belong.

"What are you doing?" asks his father.

"Building a robot."

When Nacho is thirteen, he and Emil take a bus to the river. The sun is glowing and they pull off their shoes and dip their feet in the water. Emil wanders over to a pile of twigs and reeds by the shore and begins nosing around, picking up small branches. They walk again and find a pileup of junk at the edge of the water, scrap wood and board jammed together on a bed of filthy brown foam. Nacho sits on a boulder, rolls up his pants and catches the sun, his withered leg dangling off the side. Emil begins to build a raft, pulling the sticks together and roping them with bits of twine. He floats it into the water but it sinks till just a scrap of rag that was the sail is visible. Then that too goes down in a silent descent, leaving rings in the water.

They will go back many times to this river, build many boats that list and shake and finally sink. And Emil will go on building boats that will one day save the masses and lead him to the love of his life.

CHAPTER 5

Rain—Flood refugees enter the

tower—Broken psychologist—

Susana—The image of Jesus

THE RAINS COME LATE. BUT WHEN THEY COME THEY HIT THE HILLSIDE SHANTYTOWNS OF Agua Suja and Oameni Morti hard, sending the walls of lean-tos and shebeens sliding down the mud. Agua Suja's makeshift roads turn to streams, and a car slaloms drunkenly, driverless, down the hill, as if on skates. The water gathers pace and picks up debris. Bicycles come skidding down, rocks, chunks of concrete, wooden crates, tires, a canary in a cage, shrubs ripped from their roots. A dead, bloated sheep bounces down the hill like a punctured ball. A river of mud, upending everything in its wake, cleaving a trough between houses. A boy clings to a roof. A dog is sent tumbling a hundred feet and somehow survives by gripping the slats of a disintegrating barrel. Whole houses are wiped out.

In Oameni Morti alone, there are another six hundred homeless. A third of them head for the nearest city and find, in Favelada, the tower they have heard about. Torre de Torres. Where a cripple reigns and a giant Chinaman keeps order. Bedraggled and broken, they come in groups, still drenched. The rain is knifing down, angling in on the hot wind. The damnificados of Oameni Morti cross the road and one calls Nacho's name, but his voice is drowned out by the beating of the rain. Nacho appears at the door and beckons them into the atrium. He has seen these faces before. And these rags. And these children in dirty T-shirts and knee-length shorts.

"We're sending for food now," he says. "You can stay on the sixteenth, seventeenth, and eighteenth floors. There's nothing there, but we're working on it. And the rooms are clean."

Without a word, the new damnificados make their way up the stairs. Some lie down immediately and drift into sleep on the concrete floors. Others sit by the window openings looking out into the dark where the rain catches strips of light from the neon city, floods the roads, and makes a swamp of the old wasteland around the tower.

Minutes later another hundred arrive from Agua Suja.

"Es gibt zu viele," says Hans, looking down from his balcony on the fifteenth floor. Dieter smiles.

"Too many? Können wir nicht wegschicken."

"You're right. Nacho would never send them away. What is it the lady says about her dog?"

"What lady?"

"Wheelbarrow."

"They are us."

"They are us. Dogs are us. And these people, too. Willkommen."

Fifteen floors down, Nacho says to the priest, "These floods are just the beginning."

And the priest replies, "Build an ark. For a thousand people."

Nacho looks at the sky and at the priest. "We're already in it."

What they don't know is that the rain will soon become a flood, an inundation unseen here for a hundred years.

*

The Agua Suja crowd brings treasures: two qualified teachers, a mechanic, a psychologist, and a woman who smiles with her eyes at Nacho. Her name is Susana.

The teachers are young, and unlike Nacho, they both teach children. He installs them on the fifteenth and the twenty-fifth floors and sends the Chinaman up with huge rolls of paper, blackboards, and armfuls of stolen pens. He hears term is ending at one of the regular schools in the area and the twins go to raid the dumpster. They bring home a truckload of dog-eared, torn books which are still readable: a class set of a poetry anthology, twenty-five history books published three decades earlier, a box of assorted novels with scrawls in the margins, ABC books, mathematics primers, and two mold-damp encyclopedias from a set of five: A–E and K–N. The rest of the alphabet they would live without.

Nacho invites the psychologist, Dewald, to his bare room. He needs men and women to help him lead. He is about to offer the man a drink when he realizes this is the last thing Dewald needs. Nacho sees the man has left his life at the bottom of a bottle, sees a tan mark where a wedding ring once was. Watches Dewald's tired eyes, underhung by sagging pouches, the skin almost blue. The shaggy beard flecked with gray. Here is a man, he thinks, who has probably seen too much, though Nacho senses that Dewald is little older than himself, perhaps forty, perhaps forty-five. They talk awhile about Agua Suja and then Nacho feigns tiredness and bids the man goodnight.

The woman is different. He smiles at her and she returns his gaze. When he examines himself in the mirror, which he rarely does, he sees a careworn face with the boyishness gone, hair like a tornado, half his body withered, the other half wiry. The only remnant is the mole under his eye, a perfect dark brown circle. He's all skin and bone and cords of thick green veins running up his arms, over his forehead. He has never expected to know the feel of a woman, her smell, her aura. Has never been close to one in adulthood. Yet he is not without desire. In his life before the damnificados he has seen beautiful women, talked to them on occasion in many languages. He once made a woman laugh and saw her close her eyes and throw her head back, and it is an image that has always stuck with him.

It was Emil who had made women swoon or totter away to unknown pleasures. Emil with his dash, his quick wit, his fearlessness. Emil who had once cracked a big joke while sitting with a circle of friends around a bonfire. Before the laughter had died down he got up, walked ten meters and sprung to the top of a high wall in one leap to watch the sun rise. He landed, without using his hands, flush on the narrow wall. Nacho sat quietly in the glow of the flame and looked on as every girl in the group watched his brother silhouetted against the rising sun.

But at least he has exchanged glances with Susana. From afar it is impossible to tell her age. Once, he sees her washing clothes with a group of the other women and he comes closer with the pretense of asking if the pump is working. From behind and then from the side he guesses that she is older than him by maybe ten years and his heart sinks a little, but she is a handsome woman. Small with high cheekbones, a brown complexion, and always clean. He asks his question and another of the women answers yes, the pump is fine, and he turns away quickly and walks back to the tower's interior.

*

A few days after the arrival of the men and women from Agua Suja, a commotion comes from upstairs. Whooping and the sound of bells rising above the rat-tat-tat of the rain. Someone singing a hymn in an *a cappella* baritone, and doing it again louder the second time. Nacho wakes up, staggers off his pallet, rubs his eyes, and pulls on a pair of brown pants. He closes the belt and throws on a T-shirt. Grabs his muletas leaning against the wall. The noise has turned to a hum of people. He negotiates three flights of stairs, and sees a line of people on the stairwell, hunched against the rain.

"It's a miracle," says a woman in a red dress.

"God visited us," says a hunchback in pajamas.

Nacho sees Raincoat in the line.

"What happened?" he asks.

"The image of Jesus appeared on a loaf of bread. Sounds like a scam to me. I've heard this bullshit before. But thought I'd see for myself. The fuckers are charging one libro per minute. Fifty corazons for kids. Babies get in free."

The line buzzes with children, dogs, old women, drunks, ex-miners, the bereaved, the battered. Damnificados one and all.

Nacho wanders forward, sees a makeshift sign on the bakery door: "Imige of 'Jesus Christ' 1 libro 1 minute Under 12 50 crzn Baby's free."

A Brazilian farmworker recognizes him and says, "Entra, Nachinho. Pode entrar. Voce nao precisa 'sperar com' a gente."

Nacho thanks him and says he'll wait in line like everyone else. He wanders to the back of the queue. A family comes next, the children bright-eyed, one of them carrying a plastic doll that she talks to in French. Then a straggle of loners, a man with a spider's web tattooed on his face, a junkie with the jitters, a middle-aged woman propped up on a stick. Nacho thinks, I don't know these people. Reach a certain number, a certain mass, and you lose connection.

The line moves forward slowly, one turn per minute. Nacho sees the clouds gathering, readying themselves for the day's storm. There in the iron light they wait, a fresco of the damned, shuffling onward to behold their salvation. As he nears the door, Nacho gets to see the visitors exit after their one minute. A fat black woman walks by, crossing herself. A drunk follows her a minute later, telling everyone, "It's Jesus! It's Jesus!" before he breaks into a coughing fit.

Nacho can now see the entrance to the bakery. The doorway is covered by a black veil in front of which sits one of the bakers on a stool. His brother stands next to him, a large paint can in his hand. The can is full of money. They see Nacho.

"You don't have to pay. Come in."

The line parts as they let him forward.

They pull open the veil and Nacho enters. He has been here a hundred times. The familiar smell of baked bread, the shelves honed from milk crates, the counter of linoleum and glass. He is ushered into the back area where the oven takes up half the wall space. Two other brothers still in their white aprons beckon him forward. Nacho stops at a table, leans over and sees a large light brown oval loaf placed on paper. Imprinted on it a darker shade of brown is the exact shape of Christ on the cross, arms diagonal, knees bent, head tilted. The cross stretches the length of the loaf.

"We baked it this morning," says one of the brothers. "Came out like this. I saw it immediately. Called Harry here."

"He woke me up," says Harry.

"Had to check it wasn't just me seeing things."

"Bastard woke me up, says Jesus is on the bread."

"Woke him up I did. He looks at it."

"I looks at it."

"Says it's Jesus on the cross. I finished baking the other loaves. People still have to eat, Jesus or no Jesus."

"I rings a bell, starts singing, tells everyone I see."

"That was Harry singing. Got a voice on 'im. Dad says make a sign, charge people."

"I makes a sign."

Nacho says, "What are you going to do with the bread?"

Harry and the other man look at each other.

Harry: "We don't know. We haven't got that far. We's put it in a museum maybe?"

The other man: "Put a frame on it. Put it on one of them platforms."

Nacho: "A pedestal. It'll go moldy."

Harry: "Maybe it won't, see. It's a miracle loaf."

Harry nods at his own observation. "Miracle loaf."

There was to be no frame or pedestal. No museum.

Five minutes after Nacho leaves, a madman pays his libro, picks up the loaf and takes a huge bite out of Jesus's head. The brothers pin him to the floor and Harry half-strangles him before two of his other brothers—the minders at the door—hear the noise, go in, and restrain him. A whisper goes around the crowd waiting outside.

"He fuckin' ate it," says a ten-year-old.

"He ate Jesus?" says a drunk stewing against the bakery wall.

"He bit off his head," says a cleaner from Agua Suja.

"He killed the Lord," says a hooker, her bottom lip trembling.

"He's a devil worshipper," says a devil worshipper from Fellahin.

Inside the bakery, Harry is wrestling to get free of his brothers. He turns to the madman. "You're gonna pay for this!"

"I already did," says the bread-biter. "One. Fucking. Libro." He swallows the doughy remains of Jesus and walks out the door into the spearing rain.

*

Susana spends her time with another woman of a similar build and look. Nacho thinks they may be sisters, but he doesn't ask. They live together on the sixteenth floor in a room divided by hardwood walls. Every morning he sees them leave the tower together to go to work cleaning the houses of the rich over on Cadenza Street. It's a long walk, but they go by foot, even in the rain, to save on bus fare. Sometimes Nacho watches them from his window opening until they turn out of sight on Rottweiler Avenue.

Once, Susana turns around and looks back at the tower and Nacho moves as fast as he can from the window bracket and regrets it immediately, feeling like a child caught in midfelony. Then he reasons with himself: this tower has six hundred windows. She could have been looking at any one of about a hundred and fifty in her sight. And she probably can't see anything anyway because there's a sheet of rain blurring everything. And even if she saw me, I'm just a man looking out the window. It doesn't mean I'm spying on her.

In any case, Nacho soon has bigger things to worry about— a gathering storm and a swarm coming out of the sky to make wrecks of them all.

CHAPTER 6

THE RAIN POUNDS THE LAND. IT COMES DOWN IN SWEEPING SHEETS, EACH DROP DETONATING onto the walls of the monolith and the old wastelands now reclaimed. The roads are awash with skaggy water, mud-browned and pocked with the million droplets that pepper it. Stick figures run sloshing through the streets, holding covers of plastic or polythene above their heads. Cars get marooned, engines coughing like old men.

Those first rains that flooded Agua Suja and Oameni Morti were an hors d'oeuvre, a little taster.

Across Mundanzas, Sanguinosa, Blutig, where the cities border fertile lands and rainforest, massive leaves grow overnight. Plants shoot to the height of a man and flowers splay open with anthers of violet and yellow. All the animals are gone already, flown or leapt or galloped or crawled to higher ground. Two days before the rains came there were reports of snakes seen in dozens sliding up the creeks, wild pigs on the run, mules gnawing through their tethers and bolting to the hills.

Just a few settlements remain in Gudsland and Balaal, where the water was once sweet, where you could grow anything: yams, corn, beans, rice. From behind the plastic sheeting of their wooden houses or under rain-drummed awnings of banana leaf, the faces of the damnificados peer out. They are far from anywhere. They see in the distance their roads washed away. The ground beneath their feet begins to move.

On the edge of Favelada, the waters rise. The new door of the tower is already half under, and the Chinaman moves his reinforced chair to Nacho's room on the first floor and looks down on the deluge. He hunches forward, squinting against the rain that lashes in through the window opening.

Nacho is with the bakers upstairs.

"Harry, how much dough do you have?"

Harry is on his stool in the main part of the store, the oven in the back room behind him.

"Why?"

"The roads are gone. We may not be able to get out for days. That means we can't get supplies. How much bread can you make?"

"I'm a baker, me. I ain't Jesus Christ. I don't do miracles with bread."

"I didn't ask for miracles. I asked you how much dough you have."

Harry shuffles his beefy body on the stool, scratches at his sideburns. "We ain't got dough. We got flour, yeast, salt and water. That's what you make bread with. You can live without the salt. We make two hundred and fifty loaves a day, three hundred if we're up for it. We got about three days' worth of ingredients in the pantry. Means I can do you about eight hundred loaves, and each one feeds a family. Take it or leave it."

"Eight hundred," says Nacho. "We have about eight hundred people living here."

"You don't say. Listen, it's rainy season, right? Rains every year. Then it dries up, right? And everything goes back to normal."

"Look outside."

Harry glances out the window. Sees a car sailing by.

✳

The rain rages on. Nacho gets the leaders on each floor to do a head count.

"Why bother?" says Raincoat. "Anyone not here is somewhere else. And what are we gonna do? Go out with a lifeboat? If you're out there you're either in someone's house or you're dead."

But he does it all the same. In the building there are thirty to forty missing, but some are itinerants who spend their lives missing. Another dozen clean hotels or malls and got caught, unable to return home.

Nacho sits in his room. He has a bookcase that the carpenter made for him, a couple of crates for chairs, a desk. He reads while the rain blasts down. He lies on his wooden pallet. He has slept on pallets most of his life. Once, when he was in his twenties, he was put up in a hotel. It was an interpreting job for a group of businessmen. He lay down and felt as if he were sinking. With his good arm he tried to remove the culprit—a ridiculously fat mattress—but it was too heavy. He picked up the hotel phone and asked for help. Thirty minutes later a waiter arrived with an omelet. He called again and said he needed someone to help him with the bed. He waited ten minutes, heard a gentle rap on the door, opened it, and a prostitute walked in, six foot in her heels.

"Will you help me move the mattress?" said Nacho.

The woman obliged without batting a four-inch eyelash. Together they pulled the thing onto the floor revealing just the hardboard slats and a thin foam pad.

"Now what?" said the lady.

"Thank you!" said Nacho.

The monolith succumbs to The Chattering. Families gather around the TV, the children sitting cross-legged on the floor. But on day three of the flood, the building seems to groan and suddenly all the power shuts out. The lamps flicker and die and the televisions crackle briefly before turning to black. Nacho immediately hauls himself upstairs to the bakery. The six brothers are crouched or stood in front of their oven. A layer of half-baked bread lies inside. They turn and look as Nacho enters the room.

Harry says: "No power, no bread."

Nacho hollers to the twins.

"How many gas burners are in the building?"

Hans shrugs his shoulders, turns to Dieter. "Ich weiss nicht."

Dieter: "Warum stellt er solche Fragen? Is it a quiz? Ask us an easier one."

Nacho: "We have no power. I want you to ask the leaders how many gas burners are on each floor so we have something to cook with."

"Ah, OK."

Back in his room he turns on the faucet and a brackish ooze comes out. He sits down on one of the crates. The static hiss of the rain is unceasing. He hobbles to the window. All he can see is a lake of water, fifteen feet below the first floor and rising fast. The bodegas are almost all gone, either washed away or underwater; the huts and hovels, too. The current leads past the tower, carrying lumps of debris, and a lone electricity pylon freelancing down the deluge, turning and turning in the slow confusion.

Nacho puts his head in his hands, scratches at his mop of hair. He thinks, 'First the electricity goes, then the water, then the sanitation. How long can we hold out?' The words of an old woman come back to him. "That animal is a sign from God. We can't go in." 'But we went in,' he thinks, 'and now we can't get out.'

He remembers the House of Flowers. A butterfly the size of a book, floating past his face. Yellow wings. Nights lying awake, reading by the light of the moon, the same moon that's all but blotted out, a smudge of white wax.

✳

There is a knock on Nacho's door. A small boy.

"My father wants to know if there's school today."

"Oh! Yes! I'm late!"

He gets up to the fifth floor in the dark and can at first make out nothing, but then as his eyes adjust to the candlelight he sees that the room is packed with men, women, and children. Some stand at the back, others sit on the chairs at the center, on the floor between the chairs, and around the walls.

"Well well well," he says. "The rains arrive, the electricity dies, the water goes off, and everyone comes to school."

No sound. They wait. Nacho makes his way to the front of the class. Right in front of him, seated on the floor, is Susana, the woman who looks at him in a way he cannot read—admiration or affection or just respect for the leader, the teacher. He scratches at his hair, drags himself onto a chair in front of everyone, and clears his throat.

"Truth be told, with all the rain I kind of forgot about school today. Stupid of me as I should have known you would be here. But I can tell you a few things about rain."

He pauses again, looks around, tries not to catch Susana's eye.

"Throughout history Man has lived in fear of floods. They're as ancient as any story ever told. The Epic of Gilgamesh was written on stone tablets. Tells the story of a flood that drowned everything. Or almost everything. Of course there was a hero and his name was Utnapishtim. And he was commanded in a dream by one of the gods, who said to him, 'O man of Shurrupak, son of Ubar-Tutu, tear down your house. Build a ship. Abandon wealth. Abjure possessions. Save your life.' And that's what he did. He built a ship six floors high and brought his family on board and as many animals as he could find. And when the flood came, he was ready. And he sailed for six days and six nights. Then he released a dove, a swallow, and a raven, and sailed to dry land, which he found on top of a mountain. Of course, this is like the story of Noah, who built the ark. And some say the stories are one and the same, although the epic of Gilgamesh came a lot earlier, before man had invented paper."

He stops again. Thinks, 'I am my father.' Telling stories to understand the world, and to while away the time.

The rain is coming down in massive diagonals, wiping across the sky like vines, the droplets riddling the walls of the monolith. Bulbous clouds hang in the air, big puffers, gray blowfish. Nacho watches for a moment and all he can think of is hunger, disease, darkness, eight hundred people in an upright ark that does not move, no land to stand on. He turns back to his class. People shuffle. A child yawns.

"Vishnu was a Hindu god with four arms and a thousand names. His body was blue because he existed when water was everywhere, before the universe was created. Now one day a devout citizen named Manu was washing his hands in a river. Vishnu appeared to Manu as a tiny fish. And Vishnu asked Manu to save him from the roiling water, and Manu did, and he put the fish in a jar. But the little fish kept growing and growing until he was bigger than any whale, and eventually he revealed himself as the god Vishnu. And because of Manu's kindness in rescuing him, Vishnu warned Manu of a great flood that was coming. And he told him to build a boat big enough for the animals of the world. And the deluge came and the boat swirled around and was thrown from sea to sea for seven days and nights until eventually it bumped against the very tip of the Malaya Mountains, where there was dry land, and Manu's friends and family were saved. And they began again. They planted the seeds and released the animals into the wild and built homes. And Manu, the savior of the earth, became a great king."

A child's voice: "Are we going to build a boat?"

*

In the following days, Nacho meets again with the leaders on each floor and tells them they need to ration out their food and keep one another alive in case the waters don't recede. He tells them to make an inventory of all the food that is on their floor and to work out how to get families to share. He asks for gas cookers so the bakers can bake bread because the electricity hasn't come back. He tells them to put together a supply of candles, matches, lighters, torches, and batteries.

But the days and nights are hard. The rain begins to make pools on some of the exposed floors where no boarding has been put over the windows. Food runs short on some floors, and on others, where alcoholics or junkies live, things begin to get desperate. Banging on doors. Rolling on floors. Fights break out between families.

On the sixth day of the rains, a plague of mosquitoes arrives and the damnificados are struck by a mystery virus. Their eyeballs go blue and they begin to shake. Six hundred of them sweat and tremble and take to their beds, and Nacho cancels school and all other gatherings because of the fear of contagion.

"It's borne on the wind," says a windbag.

"There's no hope," says a no-hoper.

"We're all doomed," says a doom-monger.

With everyone shaking, the crash of broken crockery rings out from all floors followed by 'shit!', 'mierda!', 'Scheisse!', 'merde!' 'kak!' People go unbuttoned for days, zips hang open, no one dares shave. Marias Beautty & Hare Salon closes down until further notice as Maria cannot hold a hairbrush let alone a pair of tongs or tweezers.

Among all the shaking, however, the junkies and alcoholics turn out to be the exception. Those who have spent their lives trembling, going cold turkey, fighting off the jitters, find that once infected by the mosquitoes they cease to shake altogether. They are steady as the great rocks of Balaal. In wonder, they come together and hold up their hands on a miraculous horizontal and do imaginary card tricks, juggle imaginary knives, play imaginary piano sonatas, do imaginary scientific experiments involving test tubes and microscopes and lethal doses of arsenic.

Meanwhile, the mosquitoes take up residence in the pools on the walkways of the tower, in the stairwells and on the roof. They lay their larvae, which writhe and squirm and grow fat on the blood of the damnificados. And in the incessant rain and heat, the creatures mutate and a new übermosquito is born with two-inch legs and seven senses, that can squeeze itself through the tiniest of holes and move silently at twice the speed of other mosquitoes. It attacks at all times of day, lying in wait on boards and walls, feeding on the living. It has a serrated three-pronged proboscis so sharp that a human cannot feel its prick. Its antennae contain receptors that detect carbon dioxide in a breath from one mile away, and its brain is able to calculate who that breath belongs to—young or old, healthy or sick, man or woman.

Some of the damnificados put up mosquito nets, but the new species flies right through them, puncturing the cotton mesh as if it were air. The men and women try polyethylene, polyester, nylon, and ask the nonshakers to stitch clothes together and hang them fast against the window openings, but the predators find a way in. The damnificados burn candles and incense, but the übermosquitoes wait it out, watching the smoke dwindle from their perch, and swoop down when the air clears.

Whole families get the shakes and sweat like dogs. The whites of their eyes cloud over and their skin is marked by tiny red blotches where the mosquitoes bit.

Then, mysteriously, the mosquito attacks stop. At first, the damnificados say it was their doing.

"They couldn't get past my underpants on the window!"

"I told you I killed two of them yesterday!"

"I burned camphor. That's what did it!"

But what happened was this: the übermosquitoes began to eat the mosquitoes. The mosquitoes then defended themselves by operating in gangs. A war ensued. The übermosquitoes won. But while the war was raging, an army of dragonflies came in from Fellahin and attacked the übermosquitoes. Even with their seventh sense telling them they were in danger, the übermosquitoes, wounded and weakened from their war, were easy prey. And thus were they wiped out.

Within twenty-four hours the eyeballs of the infected damnificados, previously dark blue at the height of their sickness, turn white again. The shakers wake up to find they are no longer shaking. With wide eyes, they fasten the buttons on their clothes, pick up cups of steaming coffee, touch their loved ones with a steady hand.

The junkies and alcoholics suddenly begin to shake again. While in the middle of imaginary harpsichord recitals or defusing imaginary bombs, they look down and see their digits trembling in a blur.

*

The rain keeps falling. Nacho looks out of his window and sees the walkway is covered. He knows he must move to a higher floor. But he also knows he is close to despair. Every day he tries to listen to the news and weather reports on the radio. But the reception is bad and the reports turn to a crackle. He fiddles with the radio knobs but gets a channel of Azerbaijani folk songs, a coffee ad in Swahili, a tennis commentary in Gujarati, a sketch show in Icelandic.

In his desperation he consults a medium on the forty-fifth floor, the Chinaman heaving him onto his shoulders before clambering up the sodden stairs. The woman, dressed in a dirty pink nightgown, opens the door and says, "Excuse my clothes. I wasn't expecting anyone." She invites them in, looks at Nacho's palm and says, "You will live a long and happy life," and he replies, "Thanks, but I need a weather report." She stirs some tea leaves in a mug of water, looks into them and says, "rain."

The Chinaman takes Nacho up the final fifteen floors to the roof and Nacho looks out over the surrounding waterscape. The rain has turned into a thick drizzle, a gray veil that blocks out the sky. He can just about make out a handful of other towers and skyscrapers in the city, still standing.

He says, "We have to get a message out. We need help. Food. Water. But how? We are nonpeople. Damnificados. No one will help us because we don't exist."

The Chinaman, standing next to Nacho and looking down into the abyss, seems to move his eyelids in acknowledgement. Nacho, the rain conjuring translucent beads in his hair, suddenly turns to his friend. He has an idea.

"We need carrier pigeons."

A survey of the building finds that of the sixteen pigeons kept by the damnificados, ten have been eaten, two haven't been the same since the übermosquitoes bit them and gave them the shakes, one dropped dead of natural causes, and three have escaped. Nacho abandons his idea and instead commandeers a dozen white sheets.

"What the fuck is this—a ghost party?" says Raincoat as his finest rayon sheet gets whisked away by Hans, while Dieter puts the foam mattress back in place.

"Woooooooooooooooooooo!" says Hans in Raincoat's face.

"Verpiss dich," says Raincoat. "Hear me?"

"He speaks German!" says Dieter to Hans.

"Yeah, and I want my sheet back tonight or I'll kick you two scrawny Krauts into next week. Verstehst du?"

"Ja, mein Herr!" says Dieter, feet already hitting the outside steps.

After stitching the sheets together so there are four large rectangles, Nacho paints 'Help!' in eight languages on each sheet and hangs them, one on every side of the building, thirty floors up. The rain lashes the sheets, soaks them until the words turn to soup, and Nacho takes them down and starts again. This he does six times in a week. But he knows the city is blind. He has not seen a soul outside the tower in twelve days. He has watched cars floating down the street, pylons, a cinchona tree, mosquitoes and dragonflies dueling in the broken light, but no one from the outside world.

✳

And what's this?

In the mass of turbid water, under the spears of gray rain, a shape is moving across the city, advancing on the tower, small, resolute. Nacho makes it out. It slaloms between the roofs of the few remaining bodegas, the tops of still-standing pylons, the floating garbage. Grows bigger and bigger as it approaches, though no more than a few feet high.

A voice singing in a smooth baritone, slightly out of tune: "Row row row your boat gently down the stream! Merrily merrily merrily merrily, life is but a dream!"

The voice is muffled in the downpour but repeats its refrain.

A boat comes into view. A haggard rust-jug made of tin and balsa wood, with a sheet of corrugated plastic for a roof. Tires slung to the sides, held by binding rope. A limp flag atop the roof, a patchwork of rags in yellow, black, and green. At the front of the boat a dapper pirate, impervious to the rain, decked out with bandanna and two weeks' beard, one foot on a box as he steers with his hands. The boat is weighed down with sacks, crates, polythene bags. He's almost at the tower's entrance.

"Row row row your boat gently down the stream! Merrily merrily merrily merrily, life is but a dream!"

Nacho shouts, "Emil! Emil!"

Other faces come to the windows of the north side. They begin to cheer. At that moment, Maria the hairdresser looks out and falls in love.

CHAPTER 7

EMIL THROWS A ROPE. HANS, SENT DOWN BY NACHO, GRABS IT, TIES IT TO AN IRON BAN-nister on the first floor stairwell, and hauls in Emil's boat so it bumps gently against the west wall of the tower.

"Thank you, my friend," Emil calls out above the roaring of the rain. He stands a moment and gazes up at the height of the tower, squinting against the downpour. He cannot see the top floors. They merge with the sky in a sweep of gray, an impressionist's daub. He is soaked through, barefoot and wild as a wolf, his white shirt clinging to his chest, his jeans darkened and rolled up to the knees. He climbs out the front of the boat, places two hands on the stairwell, and pulls himself up. A welcoming party has gathered—Nacho, the priest, the Chinaman, the twins. Nacho lets his muletas fall and embraces his brother.

"Dammit, Emil. Another mouth to feed."

"Heard you were trapped."

"Aren't I always?"

They stand back, look at each other.

Nacho says, "You need a shave."

"You need a haircut. I'm bringing gifts," says Emil.

He turns to the boat and jumps back in, lands like a cat, two feet, knees bent. Picks up a sack, brings it to the front of the boat.

"Rice! Seven sacks."

He turns and bends over, pulls up a large bag.

"Coffee!"

Keeps going. Beans! Corn! Biscuits! Sugar! Water! Wine! Kale! Bananas!

He shouts to Nacho, "Can your men help me carry this stuff in?"

"What?!"

"Can your men . . . ach. Hey you!"

He gestures and the twins climb aboard and the Chinaman stands at the stairs and takes the sacks in one hand and moves them on.

"Who's the big guy?" says Emil to Dieter.

"The Chinaman."

"Kidding me. I knew him years ago, when he was the size of a *baby* elephant."

"Don't tell us—he's grown."

"He's grown."

"Who are you?" asked Dieter.

"Nacho's brother. You mean he doesn't talk about me every day?"

"Never mentioned you."

"And who are you two? There are two of you, right? It's not just one of you moving extremely fast."

"I can't hear you."

"I said, take this sack."

The sacks go to the floor of Nacho's room. They pile up until there is no more floor space. Sweat from the lifting mingles with the rainwater on the twins' foreheads and makes damp blond swipes of their hair.

Emil and Nacho sit on the floor, surrounded by sacks.

"So, brother, where did you get all this food? And how did you find me?" asks Nacho.

"News travels fast. Everyone knows you took over the Torres building. Word is out. The police, the army, the malandro bastard traficantes, everyone knows. You can't hide a thousand damnificados. As for the food, I trawled everywhere. There were stocks in a warehouse in Oameni Morti. They put them there for the rich. A Turkish importer in Bordello let me have the coffee for a pittance—his storehouse was flooded and he needed to offload everything. I found the sugar in an abandoned pantry in Balaal. Eight sacks of it. When the rains came I knew you'd be trapped."

"Do you remember this building?"

"I remember our father telling stories about it. It's built on a trash heap, isn't it?"

"Yeah. Several generations' worth."

"Why here?"

"What do you mean?"

"Why this building? Why did you bring them here?"

"Look at the size of it. The location. We can see for miles."

"See your enemies coming."

"And it was empty."

"Who are all these people? Are they all damnificados? Drunks and junkies?"

"I don't know. They just needed somewhere to live. I brought the Chinaman with me, and the twins. And some others I knew before. We're always on the brink of chaos."

Emil smiles. They are sitting against the sacks. A pool of water has gathered under Emil, dripping off his clothes and his skin.

"You want to get changed? I can find you some dry clothes."

"Do you have rules? Laws?"

"We live by a code."

"What does that mean?"

"Each floor has a leader or a group of leaders. They organize everyone so the place gets cleaned, and they keep out the malandros, settle disputes, make sure no one starves. We have schoolrooms. Shops. A bakery."

"How do they make money?"

"Some of them work. They're cleaners, maids, caretakers. Others sell trinkets or bottled water, candy, that kind of thing. Some of them beg."

"How do you keep the gangs out?"

"Look at the inhabitants of this place," says Nacho. "They aren't gang material. We're all misfits. Ex-addicts. Ex-drunks. Mental cases. Indigents. Cripples. That's us. The gangs haven't come for us and I don't know if they will."

"They'll come for the building, not the inhabitants. You're sitting on a piece of prime real estate."

"What can I do? We have lookouts, a few weapons. The Chinaman. Anyway, why don't you tell me about you?"

"The Chinaman? What, he can deflect a bullet?"

"No one's come shooting at us yet."

"He's good for lifting a sack of flour. But if someone wants to invade, the Chinaman won't stop them."

"What can I do? Why don't I find you some dry clothes? You're dripping all over the place."

Nacho gives Emil a towel and makes a call for dry clothes. Maria, the hairdresser, has been lurking glamorously nearby in full makeup and red summer dress, six-inch heels, hair tied back.

"I can get him some clothes," she says. "We have some in the back of the store." And she skips up the steps.

Emil strips off and dries himself and asks Nacho, "How are you going to divide the food?"

"We'll do it by floor. Each floor gets its ration. The leaders divide it up."

"You're building Utopia, brother."

"Have to start somewhere. Where did you get the boat?"

"I built it. Got all the pieces from a scrapyard in Balaal. I was finishing it when the rains came. Knew it would come in handy. I rescued a bunch of hookers from a flooded whorehouse last week. They were screaming from the windows. Waving their knickers. They offered to pay me on the boat. All at the same time. I said someone has to steer. Took them to a safe house in Sanguinosa. They promised me a lifetime of free love."

"You've already had a lifetime of free love."

"The following day I found a family on a roof in Fellahin. They were sheltering under tarpaulin. Four kids and a parrot in a cage. They were shouting at me in Arabic. I couldn't understand a word, but I let them onto the boat. They kept shouting, all four of them. At me, at each other, at the rain. We passed a body bloated in the water and they went silent. Then the parrot started talking. It knew five languages. Didn't make sense in any. I dropped them off in Slomljena Ruka, found a makeshift bridge that led to a mosque. They wouldn't get off the boat. I had to wave my machete at them. The father said 'shukran' but the mother spat at me."

Maria knocks on the door.

"Come in," says Nacho.

Emil has the towel wrapped around him. Maria walks in like a princess.

"I brought you some dry clothes. I'm Maria, from the sixth floor. Marias Beautty and Hare Salon?"

"Ah," says Emil. "Thank you, ma'am."

"We're always open if you need a haircut."

"Thank you. I'll bear that in mind. I appreciate the clothes. I'll return them to you just as soon as mine dry out."

"Be seeing you."

She exits. Slowly. A little wave of four ringed fingers.

Outside, the rain comes lashing down, strips of mercury battering the land.

"Then there were the pirates," Emil goes on. "Gangs of Somalis in stripped-down shikaras. They were rescuing people for a thousand libros a head, and pillaging everything they could find. I saw them slit an old man's throat 'cause they wanted his shoes."

"Where have you been in this boat of yours?"

"All over the region. Oameni Morti, Sanguinosa, Dieux Morts, Agua Suja. It's all under water. I must have seen a hundred corpses floating down the streets. I went as far as Blutig. I was collecting provisions all along and hiding them in the hull. When I had too much to hide, I came straight here. I'd already had to evade the pirates and the police boats. They go out at night, cover up the police sign, wear masks, rob everything in sight. I paid a bribe in Fellahin. They wanted my papers. I told them it was my boat and they put a gun in my face. So I gave them four hundred libros, said it was all I had. They kicked my boat into a spin and shot a hole in the flag. But they let me go. I don't know why."

Nacho nods, surveys his room, the worm-shredded furniture, the handful of books, the surfaces covered with sacks.

"Things are desperate here," says Nacho. "We're almost out of food. The water pipes clogged up a week ago and the electricity flickers on and off. Families are cooped up in one room, tearing each other to pieces. We try to get them to come to the school or the church, but it's hard. The walkways are turning into pools. We had an infestation of mosquitoes. God knows what's under the water down there." Nacho gestures with his head to the outside world.

"Under the water?" says Emil. "Death. Dead rats, people, dogs, dead everything. This tower has saved a lot of lives, brother. That's another reason they'll come for you."

✳

The provisions are shared among the inhabitants of the building. Emil is a hero. Moves into the tower. Takes a room. Sleeps for forty-eight hours on a bed of newspapers, covered by an old bear-skin blanket he brought from Sanguinosa. Likes the feel of it on his skin. Wakes once only to eat. Opens his eyes and sees Maria with a bowl of soup and plates of bread and rice. Doesn't stop to wonder how long she's been there. Eats. Sleeps again, curled fetus. Watery dreams.

Nacho comes in. Stays at the doorway. Remembers Emil sleeping in the House of Flowers. His snuffled snore. His turning and turning.

When Emil wakes, he sits up, dazed. Evening. The sun going down, a blur on the horizon. Stands at his window watching the rain. Looks down at the flooded streets, debris sliding in the brown eddy that swallows the world.

Maria comes again with food. Then guests bringing gifts. Children's drawings, a wax figurine of a naked woman, a dish with painted flowers. Sees his room has gained furniture. A borrowed chair. A small chest of drawers.

After two days Maria invites him over. Emil declines. Says he needs to be alone. Feels awry. Goes to check on his boat. Hears the roof peppered with rain. Cleans gunk from the transom. Bails out water with a bucket. Sits at the tiller and looks out as far as he can see, the boat in the giant shadow of the monolith.

Remembers.

*

After he left home, with a departing grin for his adopted brother and a wave and a kiss for Samuel and Anna, Emil wandered. He wandered on foot, on horseback, by bicycle, on cargo trains, sometimes squeezed between crates, sleeping on his feet. One train took him all over the land. From a tiny slit of a window, he saw green fields and mountains and rivers go by. Later he climbed on top of a carriage and lay flat on the roof and felt the spray of a waterfall in Cascavel. His hair turned yellow, bleached by the sun, grew lank and stringy. He scavenged food at stations, walked into cornfields and ate his fill, once stole a chicken, slaughtered it in the night and cooked it on an open fire, eating, living like an animal.

He hid out in a scrap-wood boxcar that trundled across the countryside. Took refuge in an abandoned rail station in Hoffnungslos, where the weeds had burst through the floor and a colony of bats dangled from the rafters. In Lixo he met a hobo blackened with rail soot, hair down to her thighs. She wore dungarees and a wild look in her eye. Spoke to him in a language he didn't understand. He made love to her on the floor of a forest, and afterward they skewered scarabs and goliath beetles with a stick and ate them over a fire.

In Mordende he found work constructing a courthouse. They fed him well and the job was easy. He slept in a flophouse off the premises, fifteen other men snoring and grunting and stepping over bodies to piss outside. A passing harem of whores visited on the first Tuesday of every month. They wore bustiers and fishnet stockings and carried fans like eighteenth-century socialites, and the men blew their wages for fifteen minutes of pleasure in the half-built anterooms of the courthouse, returning sweaty and red-faced, grinning like children.

When the courthouse work was finished he boarded a train going south, clinging onto the outside of a freight wagon. Villages went by, one-horse towns, an abandoned fort on a hill, church steeples and ramshackle barns; farmhands chopping wood, suspended in midswing, and the sound of children's cries in the distance. From afar he saw a twister rise from the earth, a gray cloud shaped like a funnel unspooling into the sky. He saw a man hanging lifeless from a tree, the noose around his neck as still as iron.

He didn't know where he was going, nor did he care. He was alive and wandering, just as his father had wandered.

He made it to the coast and walked the sea-lashed docks at Ferrido, eyes wide at the giant ships. All of life teemed there. He saw a crew of sailors disembarking, square-jawed, hard-eyed. And a shirtless fisherman, lean as a paddle, dragging a net to the shore. In the seafront food stalls, he saw lobsters jostling in a tank, octopus tentacles dangling from hooks, and seal meat carved into sleek fillets. He asked around, lied about his past, found work on a trawler. Learned about winches and nets and cables from watching the other men. Kept his head down and didn't flinch in a storm. Worked sixteen hours a day and slept with nine others in a cabin.

After a month they returned to shore for six days. He and a Ghanaian he had befriended went to the bars, spent every night with a girl from a different province—Sheol, Zerbera, Milarepa, Gudsland. Emil did another month on a trawler. This time the storms were larger, thirty-foot waves hammering the ship and keeping the men below deck for days at a time.

On his return to land, he met a fifty-year-old shipbuilder in a bar. The man was being held up against a wall by a tattooed Serb. Emil, drunk and bored, kicked the Serb in the back of the knees and broke his nose with a billiards cue. His reward was a job.

The shipbuilder, a ratty white Namibian with most of his teeth missing, let Emil sleep in the warehouse and apprenticed him in the art of making boats. There he learned about lofting and framing, about stems, sterns and keels, planking, epoxy and caulk. His body learned the positions, how to move in the making of the thing, so that within six months he had surpassed the Namibian. Soon he began sleeping in a battered Bermuda-rigged ketch the Namibian couldn't sell. The swaying of the water rocked him to sleep and he learned to read the fluttering of the sails, to comprehend the wind just by listening.

One day a client was in the warehouse and asked Emil where he was from.

"Favelada," he said.

"In the north? Oh my God."

"What?"

"It's all over the news. They're burning it up."

"Who?"

"The soldiers. Where have you been? They're sending in troops, killing everyone. You have family still there?"

Emil took the first train home. With his savings, he bought a ticket and had a seat for the first time in his life. He couldn't get comfortable so at Hilketa Station he climbed into a stock car and sat on the floor with a gaggle of chickens.

When he arrived, he saw plumes of smoke peeling into the sky. Chaos. Buildings flattened. He walked to the House of Flowers. It was still standing. The neighbor, a woman of sixty, intercepted him.

"Emil! You returned. I'm sorry."

"What? What happened?"

"Your parents."

"What happened?"

"No one told you? The soldiers came and they . . . that was it . . . they . . . we . . . we removed the bodies yesterday. I'm sorry."

Emil stood still a moment.

"What are you saying?"

"The soldiers killed your parents. I thought you'd know. They came yesterday. They killed so many."

"Where's Nacho?"

"We don't know. The house is empty."

Emil burst in. The door was still ajar. He clambered over upturned furniture, papers, books. Went straight to the laundry basket in the corner of the room. Pulled off the lid. Nacho was curled inside, trembling. Emil picked him up, held him.

"You're safe now."

Emil took Nacho to a disused barn on the outskirts of Oameni Morti and there they camped out. Back in Favelada, the bodies were buried next to the trash, stones marking their names. There was no more land left. After the purge, so many were dead that corpses had littered the earth, blood tainted the river. Among the gravediggers was the Chinaman. He could dig a grave at twice the speed of the others and he worked without pause for twenty hours. One day, while he was digging, a shout went up. The soldiers had returned and were firing indiscriminately. The Chinaman threw down his shovel, the hole unfinished, and ran. Huge target though he was, the soldiers missed, and he took refuge with Emil and Nacho in the barn. Emil looked after them, scavenging food at night and warding off the wild dogs with a wave of a sharpened stick.

The grave the Chinaman had been digging soon filled up with rainwater and when the rainwater subsided, it became yet another trash pit in the heart of the city.

A few days after Emil, Nacho and the Chinaman had escaped to the barn, three of Samuel's students snuck out at dusk and threw plastic roses on the graves of their old teacher and his wife. No funeral took place. Almost everyone who had known them was dead.

CHAPTER 8

EMIL FINALLY SUCCUMBS TO MARIA AND TAKES HER TO HIS BOAT, WHERE THEY LIE TOGETHER listening to the rain drumming on the plastic roof. She climbs on top of him and they make love all day and night, pausing only to eat their meager rations side by side—bowls of rice, steaming potatoes, breadcrumbs.

Accustomed again to the rocking of the boat, its lapping on the floodwaters and the gentle bumps against the side of the tower, Emil abandons the building and takes to sleeping in the boat under the bearskin cover.

"I have a bed upstairs," says Maria. "Sheets! The floor doesn't move! Why are we sleeping here?"

"I can't sleep if the floor doesn't move."

"Course you can! Stronzo! You're just stubborn as a donkey."

"Ah, baby. I like the boat. It sways when we make love."

"Yeah and the rain gets in, and the water stinks. And look at my clothes. And are you sure no one can see through this plastic thing?"

"The roof? Oh, I'm sure. Watch out for that bucket behind you. Whoah."

But the tower's inhabitants soon turn against its new favorite son. They wonder why no more food is coming. Why the boat lies rocking against the wall while its navigator copulates with the local hairdresser, sleeps all day, fiddles with his engine while the people starve. The twins go down to talk to him, ask to borrow the boat to go in search of more food, but he refuses, saying the boat isn't ready. The soothsayer says he's a fake and Raincoat rails against his indolence. The priest makes barely veiled references to saviors in boats bringing loaves and fishes, while the congregation groans in hunger and assent.

Eventually Nacho sends Hans down to the boat with a message for Emil: 'Come and see your little brother. He'll be waiting in his room.' Where else?

Emil has been digging away with a knife at a canker of mold between the boards of the boat. He wears a dirty white shirt and a bandanna, jeans rolled to the knees. His beard is now full and black as a pirate's. He climbs onto the tower barefooted and knocks on Nacho's door.

"No need to knock, brother. Haven't seen you in days."

"Maria just wants to make love all day. I can't get anything done. I need to clean the boat."

"That's what I wanted to talk to you about."

"Maria or the boat?"

"The boat. Can you go out again? Look for food?"

"I don't know where else to look. I combed the area last time. I brought everything I could. That was weeks ago. Now there'll be nothing left or whatever's left will be moldy."

"Emil, I have no right to ask this of you, but the people here need hope, something to latch onto. That's how they keep going. There are families here who are starving. They're ready to tear each other apart. If you go, at least they'll have something to wait for. At least until the damned rain stops."

"You want to send me out on a wild goose chase. So the damnificados can have some pipe dream that I'll bring them a meal."

"If you can't do it, then let the twins borrow the boat."

"No. The boat wasn't built for them. They don't fit in it."

"Then let me go in it."

"You?"

"You show me how to sail it, I'll go."

"You can't go. You told me yourself. The people here live on the edge of madness. You're the only thing keeping them from killing each other."

"Then you go."

Emil looks around his brother's room, sees traces of the sacks of food that he brought—stray grains of escaped rice, a black patch on the floor where a handful of ground coffee was spilt. He scratches behind his ear.

"Tell you the truth, Nacho, I'm thinking of going anyway. Just I wasn't planning on the wild goose chase and the hero's return. I like to roam. Even in a storm, I'm not really looking for a port. There's a lot out there. Places. People. Here there's a tower and too much water."

"And a woman."

"I've never stayed anywhere for a woman. Even a good one."

"We need food, brother. We can't get out. Help us. Or teach us how to build a boat. We'll do it ourselves."

"No. Take too long. And you don't have the tools. I'll do it. I'll leave today. Go over all the old places. The warehouses. Pantries. Kitchens. I'm doing it for you, not them. I never had your zeal, you know that. Or our father's. That 'man of the people' stuff. It wasn't me and it still isn't. But I'll do it."

He doesn't look back before he vaults out of the gap where a window should be, onto the rain-slick stairwell and into his boat.

"What do I tell Maria?" shouts Nacho.

"Tell her I've gone to get some food."

"The truth. Why didn't I think of that?"

＊

The day Emil leaves, the weather turns cold. The nonstop hiss of the rain becomes a clatter, and eight hundred faces peer out of the window openings of the tower to see hailstones as big as tennis balls rattling off the outer walls. In the briny water below, a pattern of rings appears, detonating into circles again and again.

Meanwhile, the hail raps on the roof of Emil's boat as he steers between two high rises on Salamurhaaja Street. He docks under a stairwell off Boondoggle Avenue, throwing a rope with a hook around the metal banister. He is moving fast, reaching for the bucket first and then the hand pump because he already knows he's been hit and there's a hole in his boat and if it's big, the thing will sink.

＊

"He could have said goodbye," says Maria, applying lipstick in front of a mirror. Outside, the hailstones have given way to a blustery sleet.

"He didn't know how to," says Nacho, at the doorway of Maria's salon. "He's better at action than words. He's trying to find food for us all."

"Men always have to be the heroes, right?"

Nacho shrugs. He has other things on his mind. Besides thinking about how the walk up five flights of stairs on his muletas nearly killed him and now he has to go back down, he reimagines the people he saw on his way up. In each window he saw the faces of damnificados. He saw their hollow eyes. The lethargy. He has seen it before. This is what happens when people begin to starve.

✳

The night passes. Nacho wakes. Groggy. Something is different. He hears the call to prayer. The muezzin's throaty tenor rises and breaks open the silence. Allahu akbar! God is great! In a voice that could raise the dead. Land of bandy legs, crooked teeth, chain-smokers, roundbellies. The voice pauses and comes again. A flock of birds reels in telepathy, hangs on a curve to the right, to the left, ducks under a bridge out of sight. The city, too, is waking. Cranes everywhere, half-finished high-rises, metal skeletons. Minarets like gold-nibbed fountain pens fifty feet high, the domes of the mosques gigantic upturned soup bowls. Everything half under water.

Silence.

The rain has stopped.

Nacho goes to his window and sees an azure sky. He looks down and sees that the murky water has begun to subside. From upstairs, the voice of Harry the baker, a grubby baritone, jaunty tune, words indecipherable except for the high note on 'rain' which sounds like raeeeeeeeen.

Over the next twenty-four hours, the water recedes yet more until the earth is again visible. Weeds erupt from fields of sodden trash. Tide marks stain the buildings. Layers of silt clog the roads. The people, like animals awakening from a long hibernation, begin to walk the streets again, seeing the world anew, with fresh eyes. Miracles abound. A family of damnificados has survived in an attic on Beggarcat Street, living off a supply of tinned ravioli. When the rains abate, the parents walk out pushing a shopping cart lined with blankets. Inside it, two skeletal children are woken by the burst of sunlight.

A pit bull emerges from a bodega. It survived by climbing onto the outside of the building, and during the heaviest rains kept its nose above the water, and gripped the wooden slats of the roof to stop being swept away. It caught a bird in its massive jaws, gnawed the thing to death, and lived off it for a week, crushing the bones between its teeth.

A flower long believed extinct blooms from a shallow mound of mud, announcing itself in a shock of red and yellow.

But just as the damnificados prepare gleefully to escape the tower in search of food and water, news comes that there are crocodiles in the atrium.

"Saw 'em wiv me own eyes," says Harry the baker to a throng gathered on the stairwell of the first floor.

"How many?" asks Raincoat.

"Two."

"Big 'uns?"

"Large."

"Then we need guns."

The twins emerge from nowhere carrying broom handles sharpened by the carpenter from Blutig.

Hans turns to his brother. "Ready for some fun?"

"Ja, ja," says Dieter. "Wo sind sie?"

"In the atrium somewhere."

They climb down the steps gingerly and look around. There in the corner of the room, two fat crocs, eight foot nose to tail, leathery beasts the color of mud. Crouching, languid. Hans and Dieter jump down the final steps, wielding their sticks like swords. The boys are rangy, lined with lean muscle on their skinny shoulders, bare-chested and sweating in the heat. They wear jeans cut off at the knees and no shoes. All the better for maneuvering around a pair of rain-drenched beasts twice their size.

"Hallo, meine Damen!" says Dieter, and begins a quickstep around them. He prods one of them in the side. The animal stirs.

"They're twins!" he announces to Hans, laughing.

One of the crocs raises its head.

"Jump on its back!" says Hans.

"*You* jump on its back!"

"Go for the eyes!"

"*You* go for the eyes!"

They do a sideways shuffle as the crocodile swaggers into their orbit. As it moves, its thick tail waves side to side.

Nacho appears at the staircase.

"What the hell!" he says. "Get out of there!"

The twins pause and reluctantly walk to the stairwell. Nacho leans on his crutches, disbelieving.

"What were you planning?" he says. "Kill them with broom-sticks?"

Hans looks at him. "We have to get them out of the atrium if we want to leave the building."

"No," says Nacho. "Where will they go?"

"We don't know."

"Exactly. You want two crocodiles on the loose?"

"So what do we do? Tranquillize them like we did with those dogs?"

"They were wolves," says Dieter.

Nacho scratches at his unkempt hair. "Incapacitate them."

Hans turns to his brother. "Was bedeutet das Wort?"

"Ich weiss nicht. What does this word mean?"

Nacho has already turned to the people crowding behind him. "Does anyone have a tranquillizer gun?"

Raincoat says, "This ain't a fuckin safari. Tranquillizer gun my ass. Put some holes in the fuckers. Kill them and sell the skins. I'll do it. Who's got a gun?"

Just then the crocodiles trundle over the debris blocking the atrium doorway and walk into the sunlight, shoulders rotating like a big cat's as their tails wallop the trash behind them. The twins scramble down from the stairwell to follow them, but in the wreckage of the ground floor they lose the beasts.

"Hey, where did they go?"

"What?" says Raincoat. "You lost two crocodiles."

The animals have slid underground, noses foraging in the mulch. They won't be seen again for eight months, and when they *are* seen, no one will come for them with sharpened sticks and teenage bravado.

*

Across the city the nightmare unfolds. When water goes down, something else comes up. In Favelada and the surrounding zones, dead bodies are found floating. Looters emerge, stealing food and water wherever they can until some of them morph into armed gangs, and a black market opens up. The police officers who did not escape the city join the gangs, ripping off their badges, stockpiling their ammunition.

In Minhas, hundreds of miners and their families walk across a bridge at the edge of the city to escape their gutted homes, but are turned back by armed militias wearing hoods and jackboots. An outbreak of typhoid occurs in Agua Suja. Six die of hepatitis A in Fellahin. In Balaal, there are reports of tuberculosis. In Favelada, four teenage sisters succumb to malaria. The hospitals are helpless. Their first floors are flooded, and on the second floor stacks of bodies pile up, crammed into operating rooms or doctors' offices. The stench draws the rats, who spring through the windows and grow fat on bloated corpses. Disease spreads.

Eventually, teams of workers, along with the army, come to clean up the city. They bring bulldozers and other heavy equipment, clattering and banging all day long. Half the streets are closed—sealed off with orange tape and traffic cones—while the cleanup takes place. Trucks arrive full of chemicals to wash away the stink of the sewer that now occupies the city. Families begin to return, sweeping piles of debris from their porches, nosing around their homes like strangers, picking up broken remains, digging through the muck to find some old photo or toy.

Also as the water recedes, a mystery is gradually revealed that brings crowds in their hundreds. At the city gates, five giant stone heads become visible. At first, all that can be seen are the gently curving tops of the five heads. But the water goes down, and over days the features of carved faces become exposed. First, the foreheads, then the unmistakable hollows of eyes. Short noses protruding. Mouths in the rictus grin of a Greek kouros. Finally, the rounded chins. Something between Easter Island moai and statues of the Buddha's head, each four meters high and each weighing twenty tons. They have been placed there, blocking off the street between the giant iron gates of the city. The heads are arranged in a gentle semicircle but facing in alternate directions, three facing outward, two facing in.

While the inhabitants look on, astounded, the city's archaeologists and anthropologists are brought in to examine the heads. They take samples of the rock and consult textbooks and ancient writings. Then the city authorities decree that the heads must be moved to unblock the streets, but it's no use; there's no machinery to do it. The only machines big enough have been sold off for illegal profit or broken down for spare parts—engines, loaders, hydraulic winches.

An archaeologist from Kotemoyoye pronounces, "Three of the heads are watching for enemies beyond the city walls and two are watching for internal enemies. This tells us there are invaders waiting, and traitors among us."

Another says, "They were placed there by living gods."

Footage from surveillance cameras is acquired by the investigators. They play it back again and again, sitting in darkened rooms, watching every movement at the city gates, but nothing shows how the heads arrived. It is as if they appeared by magic. Or took root on the streets under the water and carved themselves.

"It would've taken five hundred men twenty days working day and night to bring the stones from the river. And that's assuming they were brought here by some kind of enormous boat," says the archaeologist from Kotemoyoye.

But there is no enormous boat, and there aren't five hundred men who melted into thin air once the deed was done under the flood water.

"They were brought here by aliens! Extraterrestrials!" says a journalist. "This is not the work of human hands."

"It's a message from God," says a priest.

The type of stone remains unidentified, a substance malleable enough to be carved but strong enough to survive unscathed underwater for two weeks. They look all over, at the granophyre rocks in Minhas, the disused porphyry quarry in Dieux Morts, the charnockite mountains north of Blutig, the scoria surrounding Agua Suja. Nothing matches. They go further afield, testing quartzes, pumices, phonolites, troctolites, hacking up the mountain rocks of Zaurituak and Mrtva Zemlja, drilling into the basalt beds of Nista Zivote, the obsidian mines of Hajja Xejn. Nothing.

Soon the reporters and the cartoonists get to work. In a newspaper called *The Hour*, the heads are turned into caricatures of local politicians, with the caption: 'the government: five heads, no brain.' Then the stones are taken over by a group called the Cincocabezas, a posse of damnificados who take up residence on top of the rocks, shouting slogans and waving anti-government banners. They build fires on the heads, perform satanic rituals, slaughter goats. It takes the army four minutes to blast them away with water cannons. The damnificados topple and slide off the heads, somersaulting like harlequins.

Meanwhile, in Favelada the denizens of the tower wend their way to an End of Flood street party close to the city gates. The women are dressed to the nines, hair dyed with henna and indigo, eyes lined with crushed galena and burnt almond powder, toenails painted strawberry red, waists wrapped in multicolored silks. The men's faces, too, have been scrubbed clean and among them walk damnificado cowboys in fraying Stetsons and mismatched boots, dreadlocked elders, sicarios with knives in their belts, mad-eyed swamp-men in patchwork dungarees.

A band has set up on the corner of Hadassah Street on a makeshift stage of pallets and crates: a singer, two guitarists and a phalanx of percussionists crouched over or holding found objects: upturned trash cans, plastic bottles half filled with gravel, tin buckets, and a timpani of pigskin stretched over a copper bowl. The young singer gyrates, whirls. She is lithe as a cat. Her kohl-rimmed eyes scan the audience as she waves a hand bangled at the wrist like a Romany medium. Her voice—amplified by the microphone she holds in her other hand—dominates above the bass and the percussion, her mouth wide and red. She sings in many languages, always culminating in a Turkish chorus that brings the crowd to a frenzy, and four drag queens from Fellahin come flouncing out of nowhere and perform a line dance so perfect they look like mechanized puppets.

Up on a second-story window ledge, the twins, shirtless, are doing a dance routine side by side, their faces contorted in concentration. Nacho looks on from his seat on the edge of a wall, the Chinaman below him watching the people like a nightclub bouncer.

A song finishes and a roar goes up. The singer says something in Arabic, pauses for a subdued cheer, then switches to Turkish. More cheers. She grins and raises her arms, lifts her head to the sky and closes her eyes like a child swallowing rain. Then she lets out an unworldly note—an ahhhh at top C, somewhere between a scream and the sustained plaint of an opera diva. The note resolves into a sequence, sliding down the arpeggio as the percussionists ram home the beat. They are themselves damnificados, men in rags, taut jaws, loose white shirts or none at all. They are made of wiry muscle tissue with veins like ropes.

The twins move in perfect unison, moonwalking, shrugging, krumping, turfing, freestyling in telepathy, their faces coordinated in mock pain or joy or wonder. Below them at street level, Maria the beauty queen and her girls are dancing in a tight circle, arms rising and falling, feet twisting in their cork-lined heels.

Whole families dance together on the edge of the melee, holding hands, the parents, with gap-toothed smiles, encouraging the children.

The band goes on well into the night, the singer now draped in strips of black chiffon. She sings a solo while the band members stand like statues, silhouetted in the fading light. The song speaks of the dead, and when she is finished the transfixed crowd roars once again before the guitar begins anew.

Nacho turns to the Chinaman.

"I want to see the stone heads," he says. "We're about a mile away from the city gates. Come with me."

As the Chinaman helps Nacho off the wall, a voice calls to them above the music.

"Where are you going?"

It's Don Felipe, the priest.

"What are you doing here?" asks Nacho.

"The same as you. Watching. I asked you a question."

"We're going to the city gates." Nacho has to shout it. "I want to see the stone heads."

"Can I join you?"

"Yes. Come on."

The priest leads them to a rickshaw driver, and says, "We can go with Ahmed," but Ahmed takes one look at the size of the Chinaman and waves his finger from side to side. They walk instead.

They pass dozens of gutted shacks still damp with mold side by side with the daunting skyscrapers that line the city like sentinels. In every corner, piles of debris—rocks and stones, planks of wood—clog the spaces. Wild dogs prowl. Though the water has receded, the city has an eerie sense of displacement, things out of joint: doors no longer fit their hinges, trees stand at unnatural angles, electricity pylons cough up bunches of random wire. On every wall there are horizontal marks where the water reached and stayed for a while, leaving its brown imprint, before it found new levels, like the rings of a tree commemorating itself.

The stone heads come into view and Nacho stops, lets out a small gasp, and tries to get the measure of them, to see their size. The Chinaman stops, too, frowns.

"My God," says Nacho.

The priest raises an eyebrow.

"Or *your gods*," he says. "People are worshipping here. That's what I heard. Laying out little shrines, like pagans. Look."

They walk closer, Nacho on his wooden muletas.

At the foot of the stones, small fires are burning. Groups of sitting damnificados glow by the lights of the flames, and it reminds Nacho of the day they got into the tower. He remembers the bloodshot eyes of his comrades, sleeping children slung over shoulders, the looks of fear when the wolf emerged. The wolf—like him, like the Chinaman—a freak of nature, something gone wrong in the genes, out there alone in a crowd.

Slowly Nacho walks around the giant heads. The damnificados call out to him in greeting, offer him whisky and cigarettes. He declines. The acrid smell of smoke drifting on the night air. The music from a mile away has ended, and now the only sounds are the distant rumblings of faraway buses and the buzz of insects.

A commotion. The people sitting around their fires stop and stare. Seventy or eighty damnificados from the street party are heading toward the gates of the city. Again Nacho is reminded of his own little army that took the tower, but there's something different about the revelers. Shouts go up. They are carrying hammers and spray cans. They are high on adrenaline. At the front is a black man in his thirties, six and a half feet tall, hair shaven to the skull. He is wearing a necklace of snake's teeth and a wild look in his eye. Nacho has seen him before, knows him as a graffiti artist.

"They're coming to destroy these heads. They'll either smash them or spray them," Nacho says to the priest. "This is the after-party."

But as the mob comes closer, something in their demeanor changes. The black man's expression turns quizzical. They slow down. The spray cans are lowered. Like Nacho, the mob is awed. Some of them crouch. Others sit. Yet others make a slow circle around the heads, like visitors to an art gallery. They are wordless, and the violence, the pent-up smashing and hammering that was in their hearts just moments before, is gone. What do they see? Religious symbols? Things that were crafted for *them*? Gifts? An act of retaliation for all the oppression they and their ancestors have faced, every invasion, every massacre, pogrom, bloodbath, assassination? Their villages have been ransacked, their homes burned down, and then floods come to drown out their cries. So what is this at the gates of the city? Five giant heads, watching out for them, warning the government that the people will prevail. In the unknowable mystery of the heads, the damnificados see defiance.

The black man says, "Come on. Let's go find a drink." And he leads his gang away, spray cans pocketed, hammers slipped into belts.

Nacho stays in shadow, the Chinaman and the priest beside him.

"What would we have done?" asks Don Felipe. "They were going to destroy everything here."

"I don't know," says Nacho. "But some day we may need those men. And their weapons."

CHAPTER 9

SLOWLY LIFE RETURNS TO NORMAL IN THE TOWER. THE DAMNIFICADOS FIND PROVISIONS AT the outer reaches of the city, close to the farmlands. Many are employed cleaning up the city, and head off every morning on the yellow buses that hiss black fumes and roar through red lights, piped salsa blasting all day. Nacho uses his contacts to get running water back, and three days later, electricity. The bakery reopens. Maria's salon, too, and her old clients return.

As for Maria herself, she takes on the role of scorned lover, but sheds no tears. Every day she dresses majestically. Not a morning passes when she doesn't expect to see Emil's handsome head at her door, his hair drenched, his hands bearing coffee or rice or a pocketful of gold, and she needs to be ready to seduce him once again. She commissions a seamstress to make her a red dress, as hot as embers, and wears it like a second skin. She becomes magnificent, a teenager again, her face glowing from oils and ointments made of Palestinian beeswax, Egyptian kelp, arnica and althaea, capsicum and myrrh. She dyes her hair jet black and lets it hang below her shoulders and orders fresh flowers daily to put behind her ear—a zinnia, a rose, a lotus, an iris.

In her private room she puts up wall hangings from the holy city of Kairouan, keeps vanilla-scented candles burning and lavender water in jars. She floats petals from her flowers over the bedspread every evening and sleeps in their aroma, dreaming of Emil. Before sunset she stares out of her window on the sixth floor, expecting to see him shirtless riding toward her on a painted elephant. For she remembers him as heroic and exotic and barely of this befouled Earth.

As the sun gives way to darkness, she closes her shutters and reclines on a chaise longue rescued from a tip in Sanguinosa and feeds herself tiny scraps to maintain her figure. Then she goes to her mirror to check that her backside bulges to just the right proportion, to see that her breasts are full and round. She examines her thirty-five-year-old skin and vows never to smile again for she sees crows' feet fanning from the corners of her eyes. She sees creases in her neck and says, "I will wear scarves from now on, whatever the weather" and goes hunting for chiffon and cotton, linen and silk.

"Where is he?" she says to Nacho. They are outside, at the foot of the tower. The sun beats down.

"I have no idea, Maria. I wish I could tell you."

"It's been two weeks. The rain has stopped. Why isn't he here?"

"He left when it was still torrential. Remember? He was looking for food for us. He probably had to go far away because everything was under water here. Then who knows what happened? It's dangerous out there. People are desperate. No food, no water. I don't know."

"What are you hiding from me?"

"He's my brother, Maria. I've known him all my life. You knew him two weeks. There's no one who wants to see him more than I do."

"You're wrong. And I will see him again, whatever you think of me. I'm not like all the others. I was never a drunk or an addict. I can read and write. My father spoke out against the corrupt politicos and he was killed for it and we were cast out. My mother died of grief soon after and I had to fend for myself, but I'm not a vagabond like these people."

Nacho looks at her, says nothing. He has spent much of his life defending and protecting 'these people.' Maria goes on.

"I employ eight women in my salon. They are nothing without me. People visit from all over and spend their money. I put it back into the community, if that's what you want to call it, this shithole of a tower. I make . . ."

"OK, enough!" says Nacho. "I know who you are. I see you every day. I don't know where my brother is. If he returns, he returns. If he doesn't, then we'll find him."

He hobbles away on his muletas, leaving Maria fuming and radiant in the sun, Cleopatra in a red dress. She walks to the shade of the tower, chiffon scarf fluttering in the breeze.

✳

The Second Trash War was altogether more brutal than the first. It involved a massive catapult on wheels, pellets of trash recycled into bombs, and a sixty-foot dragon made of iron and asbestos that shot fireballs from its gut.

It was Naboo Lalloo, father of the very same Lalloo who could fix electrics with his silver hand and who knew everything about wires and springs and volts and hinges, who reinvented the art of war. On cold days the father would sit in his shed dreaming up new ways to massacre and maim. His wife would bring him plates of spiced kofta and falafel in that shed while he scribbled diagrams on yellow pages torn from a notebook. In his gallibaya of white linen, he would sit motionless until with a casual cock of the head he would begin sketching a plan. He took his inspiration from nature. It was nothing to him to watch a bee stinging his hand in order to learn how the penetration occurred, how the creature hovered and honed in, driving home the lancets and the stylus. He watched curiously as a mantis in the wilds of Fellahin ensnared a lizard, gripping it at the thorax in its spiked forelegs, and bit off the head.

But it was technology he loved. Naboo Lalloo read up on medieval catapults, nzappa zaps of wood and iron, cannons of all kinds, guns. He used the materials around him and conjured up ballistics with an added twist: a bomb might disseminate poison gas, a grenade could spray an acid shower, a bullet would explode. With the softest of smiles for his loving wife and his three children, his mind would roam the horrors of the past and invent the horrors of the future. But for him it was all an exercise, a mind game, for Naboo Lalloo lived in a dream world in which others did the doing and he did the imagining. He had never fired a weapon. Never seen a corpse. Never drawn blood. In truth, he had never killed a living creature, nor even struck one. For a man ensconced in a land of endless trash, this was a rare thing. He relied on the flying cockroaches to kill the mosquitoes. For the cockroaches he relied on lizards. For the lizards he relied on rats. For the rats he gathered a troupe of sharp-toothed Bengal cats.

"Let nature do its work," he said to his girls and to little Lalloo, already a dreamer, too, at five.

The leaders of the Trash-bringers soon learned of his skills: the simple tradesman, a maker of household tools, who could also devise weapons. They visited his house. His wife pointed to the shed and they trooped in and shook his hand and looked over his designs. The military leader, a fat paisano called Torres, marched in, grinning, and slapped Naboo Lalloo in the face.

"This is so you'll always remember whose side you're on."

He slapped him again.

"And this is in case you'd forgotten already. We'll take these now."

And he picked up Naboo Lalloo's beloved designs, folded them into quarters and put them in his breast pocket below the quintet of shiny medals he had awarded himself six months earlier.

Within two weeks Naboo Lalloo's designs were built. And just days later, his fifty-foot catapult came rolling down the hillside toward the wastelands of Favelada, with its missiles, pellets of packed trash, cooked and hardened as rock. His spinning leg-chopper was hitched up to an armored truck, and his exploding spears were poised on the back of a wagon, lined up on a diagonal like the bristles of a hedgehog.

But the key weapon was the dragon.

They'd trussed up a munitions truck. For the dragon's body, a painted canopy was attached to an iron exoskeleton. They hired a sculptor to carve a dragon's head, and cast it in iron and asbestos. They hung green rubber legs in front of the wheels. Then they positioned a flamethrower on a hinge so that the flames would shoot from the dragon's mouth, operated by a pair of soldiers sweltering in the dragon's ribcage.

It was only later, much later, when Naboo Lalloo was taken to the fields that he saw the carnage his inventions had wrought. Scores of bodies lay strewn on the wastelands as pockets of smoke drifted up from the embers. The wounded, too, sprawled out across the landscape, groaning and retching, their limbs akimbo like dolls left in the rain. The blood mingled with the garbage, dark globules of spray-spatter from the hand-to-hand hackings, and coated the mounds of molding cardboard and paper. His catapult had softened them up, blasting down the barricades where the wretched army of damnificados had taken refuge. The spinning leg-chopper had then mown down the first line of resistance, shredding a phalanx of retreating soldiers.

An Alsatian dog, handsome as a lion, had had its foreleg severed but the creature had managed to scramble into a ditch. There it was rescued by a small girl, who put it in a wheelbarrow, ran home bumping on the uneven ground, and using all the courage she could muster, saved the animal with a linen tourniquet.

When Naboo Lalloo's exploding spears then decimated the shelters where the damnificados lived, the girl ran, pushing the dog in the wheelbarrow. Her mother shouted at her to leave it behind, but she wouldn't. They made it to the trees and vanished into the woods.

At night, the final resisters had been nursing the wounded and gathering themselves for another day when the dragon reared out of the darkness, breathing fire. It climbed over the trash mounds, swaying like a drunk, righted itself, and let out another burst of flame that massed yellow in the night sky. The heat could be felt from three hundred yards away. The remaining damnificados turned and ran, for they knew finally that—home or no home—this place was cursed.

In the aftermath of the battle, Torres—khaki-clad and sweating in the heat—snarled at Naboo Lalloo, "See what we did with your toys?" And Naboo Lalloo returned to his shed and drank himself to oblivion. His wife took over the running of the house and ushered the children around, avoiding their father where possible. The man became morose, grew old before his time. Whisperings were heard all over Favelada: "What has happened to Naboo Lalloo?"

He built a waist-high pyre and burned what remained of the designs in his shed. Then he burned down the shed. A small crowd came out to witness the scene. Naboo Lalloo, tradesman turned madman, hair thinning and gray, eyes encircled by black rings, moved about his yard, hurling paraffin from a can and talking to himself in Arabic and Persian. As the flame took, with a *whoosh!*, gangs of street urchins came running, hands gripping the chain-link fence that enclosed Naboo Lalloo's property. His wife and the children had long since fled to Balaal to stay with an uncle, but word reached them of the spectacle.

When months later they returned, they found Naboo Lalloo sitting alone in a chair in the middle of the bare living room, reading by candlelight a book about pig farming. The ceiling was hung with a canopy of cobwebs and the shutters were jammed closed so that even in daytime it was dark. Naboo Lalloo was dressed in a filthy gallibaya and had not eaten for days. He turned as he heard the door open, and saw his children but did not recognize them, or his wife. So he carried on reading while they walked toward him through the layer of dust and mouse droppings that coated the floor. In the corner of the room lay a dozen empty whisky bottles with the labels still on, and one standing, half-full.

The mother guided the children out of the room and told them to wait. She went back in and called his name. Nothing registered. She walked around to face him. He had put the book down onto his lap, but his eyes were full of nothingness. Truth be told, all he could see were the bodies of the dead that littered the trashlands of Favelada.

*

The monolith gleams in the sunlight. Its eastern side is in deepest shadow, a blackness that always seems deeper when the sun is shining on its western face. The place is abuzz with activity. On the ground floor, the men and women are still removing debris left by the flood. Nervously they prod at pieces of wood, half expecting a crocodile to slide out from underneath and muscle its way across the stone floor.

Built on a base of compacted trash, long ago concreted and planted over, the tower is never far from an unholy stench. The older damnificados remember the days when the wind was up and the smell would travel as far as Blutig and Oameni Morti. Now, the dregs of the flood carry their own stench. During the last days of the cataclysm the sanitation had failed; rotten food and excrement had washed up in the deluge; dead bodies were floating down the streets.

Those who had lived there for years said you got used to the smell. But the newcomers—even those from other shantytowns with no refuse service—cover their faces, burn candles, gasp and splutter. They wear masks of cotton and gauze and scurry away from the monolith to their places of work. At Nacho's suggestion, the twins bring two live pigs on the bed of their father's truck. These they borrowed from a Nista Zivote farmer drunk and dozing in his slippers. The beasts spend a day nosing around the atrium and the entrance, rootling in the muck and gobbling up refuse. But it soon becomes clear that their shit smells as bad as the trash they are eating and that pigs are not, after all, a first-class cleaning device made by nature. Nacho tells the twins to return the pigs. They drive off in a gust of fumes. They dump the pigs and on their way out, the farmer's wife stands in the middle of the road and unleashes a volley of buckshot at the departing truck. Hans hits the floor and Dieter accelerates as the figure in the rear mirror, wild-haired and stumpy as a barrel, vanishes out of sight, shotgun jumping at her shoulder.

The priest's services throughout the flood attracted the largest congregations since he arrived. But when the flood ends, the numbers dwindle.

"These are a godless people," he says to Nacho, perched on a crate in the cripple's room. "They only attended because they were trapped and needed salvation. As soon as the rain stops, they disappear. Until the next crisis. Now they're all at the city gates worshipping idols of stone."

"Isn't it always this way?" says Nacho. "Some are devout. Others come and go."

"No, it isn't. When I was in Hajja Xejn, I saw the same faces every week for two years. They gave alms. They lived righteous lives. No matter what happened in the outside world, they came every Sunday and prayed to God. The people here don't care about anything except their next meal."

"Yes. They need to feed their children."

"What about their souls?"

"I don't know, father. But I can tell you this much. At the schools the attendance grows week on week. We now have nearly as many literates as illiterates among the adults. They can read signs on the streets. They get better jobs because they can read instructions. It took time, but it's working."

"Reading and writing are important. I have to read the Bible to them like children. But you know where literacy leads."

"What do you mean?"

"They'll read books. They'll read the constitution. They'll read their rights. They'll learn they have been exploited throughout history. And then there'll be only one end." The priest lowered his head, but didn't take his eyes off Nacho.

"Which is?"

"Revolution. More bloodshed. More slaughtering. That's if the government doesn't come for us first. And they will. They'll come to shut us down. You, your schools, the tower. They know we're here."

Nacho strikes a match to light a candle. The sun has dipped below the blurred horizon.

"Yes. My brother said the same thing. They'll come for us."

"And then what?" says the priest.

"We begin again."

"Find another tower?"

"Find another tower. Or a piece of land. Build a commune."

The priest laughs. "A commune? The last of the great idealists! If the government comes for us, we'll all be dead."

"I doubt that. Someone always survives. That's why the stories are never told only from the victor's side. There's always some poor wretch who gets out alive and spreads the word. That poor wretch was me once, many years ago. I haven't trusted a man or woman in uniform since."

"Ha! Does that include me?"

"Yes. You wear the uniform of God. I would've liked you to help me lead these people. I thought you had experience of the world. You can write and you speak well. But you're an outsider. You aren't a damnificado and you can never be. In fact, you're the opposite—a beatificado. You're blessed by your faith. The people here are blessed with nothing. And you don't understand them because you aren't one of them. I respect you, Don Felipe, but I don't trust you with the damnificados because you don't love them."

The priest is shocked into a momentary silence. Then he says, "That isn't true. I love all of mankind. I'm here because I want to help these people. That's the only reason."

"Then help them. Comfort the sick and the needy. Give them hope."

"I'm trying. That's what I'm telling you. But they don't come to the service."

"Then go to them," says Nacho. "Go to them in their stinking homes. Drink their foul coffee. Sit on their stolen furniture, like you're sitting on mine. Who cares if you get a splinter in your ass? Look them in the eye and listen to their stories. You can't love them if you don't know them. And stop thinking of them as *them*. They aren't another species. They are us."

"You sound like the woman with the dog in the wheelbarrow. The crazy one."

"She isn't crazy, father. She's cared for that dog since she was a child. She rescued it from a battlefield and saved its life. It's lived longer than most humans."

A silence passes between them and then the priest gets up to leave, his stooped gait stretching slowly, like something prehistoric.

"I thank you for your company, Nacho. And I'll think about your words."

"I hope you do. Good night, father. And let me know when you have time for another game of chess."

The priest closes the door softly and pads up the stairs.

＊

The aftermath of the flood brings yet more tenants to the monolith beyond the men and women from Agua Suja. A group of untouchables arrives, haunted and weather-beaten. The youngest child among them was born in the flood. She has spent her life soaked to the skin, sweating in and out of fevers, blinded by rain and now she spits up rainwater the color of mud.

Another group—more bedraggled still—emerges from the forests of Dahomey-Krill, furtive and panicked. Nacho attempts to welcome them, but their leader, a dreadlocked man in his seventies holding a stick that could be a spear, says, "Ki gen segonde ki ou sou?"

Nacho understands the creole and says, "I'm on your side. But why do you ask me this?"

The leader calls another man of a similar age, who comes forward.

"You speak English?" says the man.

"Yes."

"Who side? Who side you on?"

Nacho looks at him for a moment. "We're all damnificados. We live here. You and your people are welcome."

"How we know you not kill us?"

"Why would we kill you?"

The man speaks to his leader in creole. The leader's eyes dart nervously. He looks at the Chinaman looming behind Nacho. He says something. His accomplice turns to Nacho again.

"Sa a se Favelada? Here? This Favelada, yes?"

"Yes," says Nacho.

"War! Begin here."

Nacho looks him in the eye, uncomprehending.

"War!" the man says again. "Fatra lagé! Fatra lagé! You kill us!"

Nacho says, "My God. Fatra lagé? The Trash Wars? They ended forty years ago. Where have you been?"

"We hide in Dahomey-Krill. Forest. We live there. But water come up." He points to neck height. "We escape forest. Come here."

"There is no war here. Tell him to put down his stick." Nacho looks around. "They don't need the knives. There is no war. It ended. Finished. Fini! Li nan fini!"

The leader nods. He gestures with his head toward his people, says something in creole.

Later, once they are given a high floor, the newcomers tell him they have been hiding in the forest for forty years with no outside contact. There they built homes and cleared out a patch of land, farmed it, and owned chickens. They say the rains destroyed everything and they had nowhere to go. Some of the elders still remembered the way to the city and so they trekked back—to the scene from which they had fled four decades earlier, believing the Trash Wars still raged.

At first, those of them who were born in the forest are afraid of everything—television, telephones, even the honking of car horns. They shun other people, scared of the alien dress and manners. But soon they begin to blend in because they have no choice. Like all who dwell there, they are at the mercy of the monolith. They sway when it sways, hear the wind's songs that blow in and out of the stairwells, and smell the last dregs of the trash left over from the flood—fumes that crawl up the sky even as far as the fortieth floor, where they now live. Nacho fears for them. The city is no place for forest dwellers, but the leader tells him that soon they will leave, find new forests to live in.

Nacho looks at them, and though they say they are farmers, he sees warriors, men of discipline. They are lean-muscled and broad-chested, and not compromised by the junk of city life—fast food, drugs, alcohol. They are already an army. And he knows he may need their strength.

CHAPTER 10

THE MONDAY AFTER THE ARRIVAL OF THE FOREST-DWELLERS FROM DAHOMEY-KRILL, THERE is an unwelcome visit. A black sedan pulls up across the street on the north side of the tower. Three men emerge, one in a suit, two in khakis, each wearing sunglasses. The lookout on the thirtieth floor sees them first and picks up his child's walkie-talkie, souped up by Lalloo to spread its coverage. He contacts the lookout on the first floor.

"Twelve o'clock," he says. "Black car. Military."

The word gets to Nacho immediately, who tells the Chinaman, "Visitors."

The man in a suit is burly with a florid moustache and lavishly ringed fingers. He smells of money but there is something earthbound about him, as if he worked half his life on a farm or chopping wood or breaking heads. As the three visitors approach, the Chinaman stands. The suited man does not hesitate. He breaks into a grin.

"You must be the famous Chinaman! Thank you for guarding my tower so well! The name is Torres. Where's the little cripple?"

Nacho hobbles down the stairs and into the sunlight.

"Are you referring to me?"

"Well, hello. Mr. Morales, I believe. I'm Torres. These here are my acquaintances Colonel Bandero and Colonel Hafeez."

"What can I do for you, Mr. Torres?"

"You can get out of my tower is what you can do for me. You're sitting in a piece of real estate that belongs to me and belonged to my father before that, and I want it back."

Nacho, unflinching, pauses to calculate the scene. Two soldiers, unarmed, one civilian in a suit, looks like he could swallow a cow. It's not a death squad. Not yet.

Nacho says, "I believe the land was taken by force, illegally. And then the tower was built illegally without the required permits."

"You must be mistaken."

"Then the tower was abandoned. By law, when a building has been abandoned for three years it becomes government property. And when government property lies empty for more than two years it can be legally occupied by those in need. And we are those in need."

"You are squatters. And you're squatting in my house. Mind if we take a walk?"

"Not at all. Though I may struggle to keep up," replies Nacho.

"I walk slowly. Colonel Bandero and Colonel Hafeez, please wait here. I'm sure the Chinaman will entertain you with his charming banter."

Torres clasps his hands behind his back and begins a slow stroll around the building, Nacho in his shadow.

"Mr. Morales, you've made a name for yourself. Congratulations. They tell me you're teaching these people to be good little boys and girls. A model society."

"I don't know about that. There are certain things we don't tolerate here, but we have our problems the same as anywhere else."

"Your people can read and write."

"Some of them."

"They go to work instead of selling drugs or stealing. And I heard something else. When the rest of the city was kicking sixteen bales of shit out of each other for a scrap of food during the flood, I'm told you shared provisions here. Not a single riot! No murders! You're like the fucking boy scouts! That's a remarkable achievement considering the animals you keep in your zoo. Do you smoke?"

"No."

"I have a cigar habit. Shameful. I picked it up in Hagr El-Malesh when I was running a commando unit there. We confiscated six tons of Honduran tobacco and got the POWs to hand-roll them. When I left, they gave me a box of two hundred."

He lights one up and the acrid fumes rise and vanish in the sun-fuzzed air.

Torres goes on. "I'm not a monster. I'm a businessman. So I'll make you a deal. You have one week to leave peacefully. After that, if you're still here, you and your tenants will be massacred. I will hang your flayed corpses on the city gates and let the vultures eat your insides. Not because I'm a monster but because I intend to run for office, and as you know, there's nothing like a show of strength to keep the voters happy. You do know that, don't you? How was it you became the leader of these animals?"

"I'm not their leader."

"Really? Then why am I speaking to you?"

"And they're not animals. I was never elected. I have no title."

"So anarchy reins in the Torres tower. And el pequeño lisiado is a nobody. You have any other fairy tales for me?"

Torres stops and looks upward at the outer walls of the tower. He sees clothing hanging out to dry, flapping in the breeze. Satellite dishes perched on the stairwell like giant coins. Figures moving in orderly silence. He sees signs: the salon, the bakery, a tattoo parlor, a barber.

"You know," Torres goes on, "I've seen so many nasty things in my life."

He nods at Nacho, scratches his moustache, looks as if he's about to burst into tears.

"When I was five years old my grandfather made me watch him sacrifice a sheep. He cut its throat and the blood was supposed to drip into a bucket but the old man fucked it up and the blood flew all over me and this stupid sheep was gurgling and its legs gave way like it's slipping on ice. I've always disliked killing since that day, but you see I had a family and my reputation to take care of, so I killed. I killed maybe a hundred men. A few women. But it was never a pleasure for me. Not like these crazy people, these monsters. That's why you're still alive. You see, I'm a humanitarian at heart."

They walk a little further. Torres pauses to tap the ground with his toes.

"They say there's fifty feet of garbage under the surface. Garbage living on garbage. My great-grandfather was a hero in the Trash Wars, and my grandfather acquired the land and built this tower. Then my beloved father, God rest his soul, they gave him the title of mayor."

"He named himself mayor," says Nacho. "A building doesn't have a mayor."

"They worshipped the man."

"They were scared of him."

"Same thing when it comes down to it. You seem like a civilized man, Mr. Morales. You're well respected in the city. You have big balls. They say you speak a dozen languages. Why don't you leave and earn an honest living? Go find yourself a desk job or teach little children. Buy a house in the country, settle down with your childhood sweetheart. Spend your weekends growing roses and walking the dog. Well maybe not the last part. Walking isn't your strong point."

"Funny, I was thinking the same about you. The bit about earning an honest living."

"Those two colonels I came with. Bandero and Hafeez. Imbeciles. They don't know their tits from their tonsils. But they command a battalion of two hundred men. Professional soldiers. Killers. Bang bang bang! They're on my payroll. I click my fingers, everyone dies. So that presents you with a tickly fucking dilemma, Mr. Morales. Either you get out of my tower or I'll kill you all."

He blows a cone of smoke and swivels sharply, striding away from Nacho. Turns a corner and gestures to the colonels to get in the car. Doesn't look back.

The car pulls away and melts into the traffic. It slides in and out of packed lanes, narrowly missing street vendors wandering in the roads. It pulls up at lights, where impromptu shows take place—ten-year-olds juggling plastic balls for change, window-cleaners with buckets of water and squeegee bottles—before accelerating away with a muffled roar to the wide-gated parts of the city damnificados never see.

✳

Alone in his room, Nacho perches birdlike on a chair and tries to remember.

He would stand on a box to help his mother cook. There was nothing Anna couldn't make. Somehow when the pantry seemed to contain nothing but potato rinds and a clove of garlic, she would produce a stew bubbling in a pot, the odors drifting into every corner of the House of Flowers. He must have been four or five, already lopsided, balancing on his stronger leg.

The four of them would sit and eat together, a little cramped but happy around a makeshift dining table reclaimed from floorboards and packing crates. All of their furniture was like this—things made from other things. Uneven, cobbled together, ill-fitting. Bits of wood sticking out, sharp edges, loose screws. He remembers picking splinters out of his thighs in the days before he even knew his legs were not made the same way.

Wherever you sat, wherever you looked, the house was made of leftovers and extras and found objects. Cushions of patchwork: rags and skirts and ripped upholstery. The tablecloth was a curtain and the curtain was a tablecloth. Beds that were pallets. A desk that was a bench. As a child, he never noticed. That was just the way things were.

An improvised house bore witness to his father's improvised life: garbage man, busboy, laborer, teacher. To Nacho, the world was out of kilter, not his house or his family. Later, as he grew and saw more, he wondered why the Morales household didn't just have the right things in the right place: a door where a door should be, chairs of mahogany and oak, like the downtown libraries he visited and the churches he hid in when the weather turned cold.

He remembers Samuel's wandering mind. The head so full of stories he might walk to work in mismatched shoes and not notice or care. The man was simply dazzled by life. Anna was Samuel's salvation, his guide in the world of real things. She found him a watch in a used goods store in Fellahin and told him he should wear it so his hours would not pass by without him knowing. She kept him fed and cleanly clothed and instructed him on how to live in the realm of normal human needs. She taught him about bills, running water, shopping, electricity, and the falling-apart of furniture, clothes, and walls. With infinite patience she told Samuel what needed doing, and when, and what it would cost. She was his adviser.

These thoughts come to Nacho now because, alone in his room in the Torres tower, all he can think of is the fate of the damnificados, men and women he barely knows. They are from all over: Favelada and Fellahin, Agua Suja, Minhas and Balaal, the forests of Dahomey-Krill. Some speak Creole, others Spanish, others Arabic, Afrikaans, Gujarati, Tagalog, Urdu, Lao. They are carpenters and cleaners, beauty queens, fixers, ex-junkies, glue-heads, hobos. Uniting them is impossible, but saving them . . . he has no choice.

The tower has seen too much death already. The bullet holes in the walls are a testament to its history. On that island of junk ringed by potholed roads, firstly the Trash Wars had ripped apart families, then the tower itself had been built on the graves of the dead. A dying shaman once told him, "This land is sacred. The blood of the ancestors flows here, under the earth." Yet others told him the place was cursed, an island of the misbegotten, where people lived and died in trash, drowned in a mountain of cast-off plastic and cardboard.

Hundreds had fought to stop the tower from going up. They had watched as the surveyors came in and took measurements. Seen the digging machines come clanking down the street. Torres the Elder had made arrangements to relocate the people. He handed them contracts, which they were unable to read, and forced them to sign with fingerprints, giving away their homes. Those who did not want to leave fought with all they had: firstly words, and then knives, chains, bricks. Their blood had watered the trash piles, mingling with the blood of the fallen in the earlier Trash Wars.

Maybe Torres was right. They were the refuse of the city living on top of the city's trash.

Nacho looks out of his window and sees it is late. He imagines Don Felipe is sleeping at this hour, dreaming up sermons for his empty church. With no one else to turn to, Nacho makes his way up the outside stairwell. One of the motorboys sees him, helps him onto the back of the motorbike, and gives him a ride to the sixth floor. Maria's salon is closed but he knows she is in there. He knocks on the door. No answer. He rings the bell. Maria opens the door, hair up, dressed in a silk gown and full face paint.

"Ugh. Wrong brother. The barber's two floors up. And you're a lost cause anyway." She lets him in. "Do you have news for me?"

"Emil?"

"Emil."

"No. Sorry. Something happened today. We were threatened."

"You want some tea?"

"No thanks."

"Who's we?"

Maria beckons Nacho into the back room. He sits on a deep sofa and momentarily imagines his brother lying there being hand-fed grapes by a perfumed harem.

"All of us," says Nacho. "The tower itself. What do you know about the history of this building?"

"What do you know about the history of hairdressing?"

"The tower used to belong to a man called Torres. He's a psychopath. Now he wants it back, and he's threatening to kill us all if we're not out in a week."

"He can't do that. Can he?"

"What, kill us all?"

"Kick us out."

"Not legally. But he's in with the government. His family *owns* the government. I don't know what to do."

"So you come to *me*? You want me to offer to do his nails? Or I could give him a discount on one of the girls from Fellahin. Maybe he'll drop dead of syphilis."

"We need help, but I don't know where to look."

"Look here."

"Here?"

"Not in my salon, you fool. In the building. There are ex-soldiers, those men from the forest. Some of the others have guns. Organize resistance. What's Torres going to do—blow up his own tower? We fight him."

"We fight him? He has two hundred professional soldiers. They're armed to the teeth, probably have tanks," says Nacho.

"Well, can't you call in some favors? You seem to know every-one. How did you get electricity and water into this place? Make some calls. Bang some heads together."

"If it comes to banging heads, we're going to lose. Torres is the number one head-banger in the city. His family invented head-banging. The bureaucrats are either in his pocket or in his family. But I don't see how we can fight."

"What's the choice?"

"Leave and go somewhere else."

"Then how will Emil find me?"

"He'll find you or *we'll* find *him*. And that's not my main concern at the moment."

"You know we can't go somewhere else. The tower is ours. We have the rule of law here, schools, businesses. Some people spent their lives trying to find a home, and now they have one. We lived through floods and disease and goddamned monsters in the entranceway. We've half starved in this building. And now you want to leave."

"But then we'll all die. The building is just bricks and mortar."

"No it isn't. We have to fight. Build an army. Use that big Chinaman."

Nacho leans back on the sofa and closes his eyes.

Maria says, "You can sleep on the sofa if you like. It's a long way down."

"No, I'll make it. Thank you. I'll talk to the leaders on each floor tomorrow."

He gets up to leave and says, "Good night."

"Good night. Tell your brother I'm waiting."

Nacho smiles, lets himself out, and waves with the back of his hand. "Yeah. Where is that brother of mine?"

Nacho curls up on his bed and dreams of something wrapping itself around him. At first he squirms. He is being crushed by an anaconda, the colossal body squeezing his chest until he cannot breathe. The pressure slackens until he feels nothing but an embrace, two huge arms comforting him. He turns and sees the face of Samuel, his adoptive father, as large as the stone heads at the gates of the city. The enormous eyes open and his father says, "You'll be OK. Everything will be OK."

CHAPTER 11

With a slow trot, the saddled Andalusian is pulling a cart on which lie fifteen sacks made of thick burlap. It is early. The sun is playing peekaboo behind the city's towers and minarets and the traffic has not yet reached its morning crescendo. But still the horse and cart slow down the flow and incite the drivers to honk their horns and shout abuse through their wound-down windows.

Emil barely hears a word. He hasn't slept for seventy-six hours. He sags in the saddle, eyes drooping, black matted hair pasted to his forehead. His feet, shod in boots two sizes too big, keep slipping out of the stirrups and it is all he can do to keep his grip on the reins.

The horse trots reluctantly. Big and hefty as the beast is, it's struggling with its load and its flanks are coated in a sheen of sweat. Emil talks to the animal, leaning in to its ear, pats its neck, and slumps again. They negotiate the rubble of the road leading to the entrance of the monolith and come to a stop twenty feet away. By now the Chinaman has heard the hoofbeats and the two spoked iron wheels of the cart scratching and creaking, and in moments he is up and dressed. By the time he gets to the entrance Emil has disappeared. The horse stands there like a megalith, only its tail moving, swishing at a cluster of flies. The Chinaman looks into the bed of the cart. There he sees Emil lying flat out on the burlap sacks in his boots of Spanish leather, snoring like a bear.

This time there is no celebration. No gifts or gestures of gratitude. He brings them rice, sugar, coffee, raisins, almonds, salt, beans, dried meat, and flour. But among the damnificados, the whisperers grouch and whine.

"Where was he when we were starving?"

"Shacked up with the hussy."

"It took him two weeks to bring groceries."

"Look at him riding in on a donkey. Thinks he's Jesus."

"He brought the same stuff as last time. But less of it."

"One measly cart. And there are more mouths to feed."

"That food will be gone in hours. And so will he."

"And good riddance."

"He's a fornicating pirate."

"He's a piratical fornicator."

"He's a hobo."

"He's a drifter."

"Comes and goes as he pleases."

"Doesn't wash behind his ears."

"Mistreats his horse."

"Look at those boots. Disgraceful."

Maria puts on her red dress and fishnets, six-inch heels, a smear of cobalt eye shadow and two lines of mascara; pouts in the mirror and applies lipstick. She is ready for this moment. She hitches a ride with one of the motorboys down the six floors and prances to the cart, ignoring the magnificent horse. And in full view of the inhabitants of the monolith she climbs up on this farmers' cart with its lingering stench of hay and manure, straddles Emil, and attempts to slap him awake.

"Stronzo!" she shouts, in her mother's Italian. "You keep me waiting two weeks without a word, then you show up *asleep*! You come stinking of animal shit and wearing peasants' rags. Stronzo di merda!"

Emil snores his way through her tirade, arms spread wide, face to the sky like a dead man, and Maria asks the Chinaman to carry Emil to her room. He does so without a word, heaving him over his shoulder like a sack of wheat. Emil's head sways and bounces as the Chinaman climbs each step, but nothing at this moment can wake him. Not the sirens that scream through the city or, later, the midmorning call to prayer that echoes, amplified from the minaret.

Nacho finds a group of volunteers to unload the sacks, and once again they are stored in his room, to be shared out and distributed by the leaders on each floor. Nacho goes up to the salon.

Maria is seated, watching over Emil, who lies on her bed, his boots removed and placed neatly at the door, revealing a pair of flat flippery feet encrusted in filth.

"You knew, didn't you?" she says. "Knew he was coming back today."

"No," says Nacho. "I had no idea."

"Where has he been?"

"You'll have to ask him when he wakes up. He's an epic sleeper. Always was. As a kid he would run and run and leap off walls and go wherever his feet took him always at a hundred miles an hour until finally the batteries would run out and he'd sleep so long and deep you thought he'd never wake up. Treat him gently when he does."

"Why? He should never have left."

"He's been through something," says Nacho.

"What do you mean?"

"There's blood on his hands. He has a cut under his chin that wasn't there before. However he got all that food, he paid for it one way or another."

"I can see all that," says Maria.

"And as for that horse. It's an Andalusian. I just hope he didn't take it from one of the Iberian cartels, because if he did they'll be coming after him. As if one psychopath on our tail isn't enough."

Maria gets to her feet.

"I need to open up the salon," she says.

"And I should go, too. We have to divide the food. Let me know when Emil wakes up. I need to speak to him."

There is no motorboy in sight, so Nacho begins the slow descent down six floors on his muletas. As he negotiates the stairs, he bumps into Susana, the woman who has smiled at him ever since she arrived from Agua Suja. Nacho mutters, "Good morning." She nods and smiles. And disappears.

*

On the first night, Maria climbs into bed with Emil and lies on her stomach, hands under her chin, regarding him like a curiosity. She tries to undress him, expecting him to wake up ready for love, but he is so inert, so damned heavy in his sleep, she cannot take off his pants and she only gets his shirt off by rolling him onto his front and unbuttoning it. She drapes a smooth brown leg over his flanks and strokes his thighs through his rough jeans. He doesn't stir. She grips him from behind, first in an embrace, then after ten minutes of his snoring she digs in her lacquered fingernails wondering how long it would take to draw blood. He sleeps on.

She turns him onto his back and straddles him. She is naked now and with the shutters closed, the heat of the windless night is upon them. She looks down on his bearded face and rests her hands on his shoulders.

"Emil," she whispers.

Nothing.

"Emil." She says it louder.

His dreams continue undisturbed.

"Emil!" she snaps. "Emil! Wake up!"

He snorts a moment and turns unstoppably, flipping her off the bed. She lands with a thud on the floor, managing to cushion herself with her hands, and rasps, "Goddamn it!"

She climbs back into bed as noisily and violently as she can and turns her back on him. She changes her mind, turns around, and pulls the sheet from under him, yanks at it with both hands. He acquiesces, adjusting his position in his sleep, and she covers herself. Eventually she too drifts off to sleep as her haze of black-eyed fury dissipates.

A new day dawns and Emil sleeps through it. Occasionally he grunts and lurches or curls up in fetal position, and when that burst of commotion is over he is back to the deepest of slumbers. He lets out a groan and Maria imagines him dreaming of the nights spent in some hell-hole without her. He stretches out a hairy hand and Maria puts it to her face, comforting him in his sleep. She has forgiven him his nighttime performance and she now throws rose petals onto the sheets. She relights the vanilla candles which have grown lumpy at their base. In front of the mirror she readies herself for the day, glancing back at Emil every few seconds, wanting him to see her.

She works all day in the salon but returns to her bedroom every thirty minutes to check on him and she sees that he changes with the hours so that she can barely believe it is the same Emil by daylight, with the sun blaring across his jaw, as the Emil she sees at night, the dark hero in shadow, a swath of chiaroscuro shaping the nape of his neck.

At midmorning, she wipes a patina of sweat from his brow using a cloth dipped in lavender water as the sunlight angles in. She tries to cover him, but he kicks off the sheets in a flurry of writhing before settling again, his breaths turning regular as the ticking of a clock. He opens his eyes, tells a joke, mumbles about the House of Flowers, and falls straight back to sleep.

Nacho visits twice and sees his brother, conked out as a rock. He stops by the salon and reminds Maria to tell him when Emil wakes up and she says, "*If* he wakes up. He hasn't moved for days. How did you wake him when he was younger—stick a bazooka down his throat? I'll tell you when he wakes up all right. You'll hear me shouting at him from Blutig."

In the evening she hand-rolls a dish of pasta and bakes it in a sauce of tomato, fennel, and almonds, lays out two plates and two wine glasses. She goes to the bedroom and attempts to stroke him awake. He sleeps through every touch.

"Goddamn it. Wake up!"

She eats alone and makes casual conversation to the empty chair.

"How was your day, honey? Fantastic. I gave a couple of straight cuts, did a perm for an old lady from Sanguinosa, one manicure and three pedicures. How was yours? Fine. I brought a boatload of food for the rabble, killed a few despots, and rescued some babies from a fire. Oh and here's a bunch of flowers for you, darling. A token of my undying love. How are our wedding plans going?"

When Emil finally wakes up, he leaps out of bed in a blind panic. He's alone.

"Where's the horse? Shit!"

He looks around and sees dozens of candles, jars and vases, holy wall hangings, and a fluttering of rose petals settling on the bed.

"Shit! Where am I? Have I died?"

He sees his boots in the corner of the room with the socks hanging out like tongues and puts them on. Shirtless, he hurtles through the salon. Maria sees him but she has her hands full of hair. He arrives on the stairwell and bounds down the steps three at a time with the voice of Maria ringing in his ears: "Emil! Emil!"

"I'll be back in a minute!" he shouts, and then says to himself, "Where's the horse? I lose that thing, they'll string me up by the balls."

He sees the Chinaman at the entrance.

"Chinaman, where's the horse? Big white thing. Andalusian."

The Chinaman points and Emil follows his fingers. At the back of the tower there is a small area of fenced-in pasture where they had planted vegetables before the flood. The horse now roams there, tied loosely to a fence pole.

"Thank God for that," says Emil. He strokes the horse's neck, pats it on its flanks. "Good boy."

*

Emil is backed up against a cushion on Nacho's floor.

"I need to return the horse," he says. "It's a day's ride away. And then I need to escape. If they catch me, I don't know what'll happen."

Nacho sips his coffee.

"Don't tell me you borrowed it from one of the cartels."

"I borrowed it from one of the cartels."

"What happened out there? You were gone two weeks."

"My boat got a leak. I tried bailing out the water but it was no use. I had to leave it there, tied to a shack. I was stranded. I hitched a ride with another guy in a boat, but he turned out to be a madman. The guy was looting everything in sight so I got off in Constantinides. It was waist-deep but I managed to find an attic in an abandoned house. It was full of boxes and chests. After two days in there my food ran out and I couldn't escape because the water had risen. I managed to smash open one of the chests, hoping to find some canned food, but all I found was gold. Huge ingots and crucifixes and goblets. It was like pirates' treasure. But you can't eat gold."

"This sounds like one of Dad's stories," says Nacho.

"So I put some of the gold in a sack, broke out of the skylight and made my way across the roofs of Constantinides. I made it to a tower where a bunch of hippies were sheltering and bought myself a ride on a raft built by an ex-sailor. He was making his way to Balaal, where the water was lower and there was food. He was good company until he realized what was in my sack. After that I couldn't trust him. He kept reaching for his knife and I had to keep reaching for mine. If he'd had a gun I'd be dead now. Once the water was low enough I jumped off. I was starving. I soon realized we weren't in Balaal. We were in Sangre Fría. The cartels had taken over the streets so I had to creep around in the shadows. The water was up to my knees by this point. I guess Sangre Fría's on higher ground. But someone saw me and started shooting and that's when I stole the horse. I rode all night to Uccidere and exchanged the last of my gold for the cart and provisions. I didn't know how I would get back—it was still raining. I was exhausted but I had so much food and provisions I couldn't sleep and I was scared the cartels would catch me with their horse. I rode on to Puscagol, where I met a holy man who told me to surrender all my worldly goods. Then in Hjertesorg I met an unholy man who told me the same thing. Except he had a gun. I managed to disarm him and escaped with a few cuts and bruises. Before I left I chained the guy to a post. He's probably still there. And I still have his gun. By then the rain had stopped so I rode all the way here."

"Why do you need to return the horse?"

"They saw my face. One day they'll find me. If I return the horse, they may forgive me. The cartels are like that. They have long memories."

"It's not safe to go back to Sangre Fría. If they see you with the horse, they'll kill you. You should sell it or something."

"No, Nacho. I know these people. To them, a horse is like a woman. She can be borrowed, but never stolen. That's how it works. If I return the horse with an offering and then I leave, I may be OK. If I don't, I'll be looking over my shoulder for the rest of my life."

"There's something I need to tell you," says Nacho. "Torres was here."

"Which Torres?"

"What does it matter? They're all the same. He wants his tower back within a week. We have five days and then he'll send in his army."

"What army?"

"He has two colonels and two hundred trained killers. Maria says we should fight."

"What do the others say?"

"What others?"

"You mean you haven't told anyone else?"

"Like who? I didn't know who to turn to."

"So you asked a hairdresser? There's a soldier here somewhere, you told me. The Chinaman. Those German twins. They're kind of handy. The priest. Those brothers who run the bakery. You need to get organized. See what weapons you have."

"We'll be massacred. And the Trash Wars will start all over again, only they'll be the Tower Wars, and everyone will die."

"What do you propose?"

"We leave."

"You need to ask the people. Call a meeting. I can't believe you haven't done this already. Call the floor leaders. If they want to fight, then you fight. If they want to leave, then you leave."

"*We.*"

"What?"

"*We* leave. You said *you.*"

"Brother, I'm just passing through. You know me. Our father's son."

"I have one more thing to say to you."

"What is it? Don't tell me about Maria. She's been hollering at me since I woke up."

"No, it's not Maria. You brought us provisions again. So I'm saying thank you."

Emil leans back, looks down the length of his handsome nose, half-smiles, and says, "You're welcome."

*

Nacho spends the next three days getting organized. Once the damnificados vote to fight, he goes about developing battle plans. He knows the history of Favelada, knows the story of Naboo Lalloo, so he asks Lalloo the Younger about war tactics and surprise weapons. Lalloo, wallowing in a Force 10 hangover, says, "I can steal electricity for you. I can fix your car. If your coffeemaker blows up, I can repair it. But I don't know anything about killing people. I'm not my father."

Then Nacho goes to the ex-soldier's room on the thirtieth floor.

"How do we fight a guerrilla war?"

The man starts shaking.

Nacho goes on, "We're in the middle of the city. We have the tower. What do we do to defend ourselves?"

But the man's left eye is blinking involuntarily and his breathing has changed.

"I- I- I- I- I don't know. I'm a ci-ci-ci-civilian now. No more f-f-f-f-fighting."

Later Nacho tells Emil, "There's a reason these men and women are damnificados. Their lives have gone wrong. Or they've been unlucky. They aren't built for war."

Maria emerges in a microskirt and black halter top. She looks like a panther.

"Do what your enemy least expects," she says. "Torres thinks he'll walk into the tower and take over. What if he never gets that far? Why don't you go to him? Kill him and all his soldiers in their sleep. Attack first."

They pause. She looks hard-eyed at them both.

Nacho says, "Because we aren't killers."

"Then become killers! You think Torres is going to roll over and let you tickle his tummy? Stick a knife in him. Then see how much he wants his tower."

Once she goes back to the salon, Emil says, "I have to return that horse. I'll be gone a couple of days."

"No, you don't," said Nacho.

"We've already talked about this."

"The twins took it on the back of their father's truck. They left at five o'clock this morning. They'll be driving into Sangre Fría about now."

"Christ. They're teenagers. The cartels will rip them to shreds."

"They're smarter than you think. And braver. They'll leave the horse in plain sight plus an offering in a sack and then take off."

CHAPTER 12

Sniper—Raincoat—Waiting for Torres—

Maria plans her escape—The army arrives—

Carnage—Repentance—Aftermath

THE DAMNIFICADOS DECIDE AGAINST ASSASSINATING TORRES, AND FOUR DAYS LATER NACHO is face down on a bed jammed next to an open window, five floors up. Raincoat, turned sniper, is by his side, looking through the scope of a long-range rifle. Nacho glances at the plaza down below. Deserted. Further off, the traffic winds and honks its way through the day.

Behind Nacho, milling aimlessly, are the six brothers who run the bakery. They are rough-edged, broken-nosed, lavishly tattooed. "We likes a rumble," Harry had said at the meeting. "We're a bit punchy, us boys." "But can you use a gun?" Emil had asked. "Use a gun? I can roll you fifteen French doughnuts in sixty seconds flat. Guns is easy, my friend."

Awaiting eviction orders in the form of two hundred soldiers and a bully-boy, Nacho sits up and looks around the room. He sees leaning against the wall a collection of World War II rifles and a nineteenth-century Chinese musket. Heaped on the floor is an arsenal consisting of a Zapatista bullet belt full of empty cartridges, a handful of rusty-looking grenades, three revolvers, and a machete. He scratches his head, sees butchers, bakers, teachers, drunks, a hairdresser, and thinks, 'We're going to be slaughtered.'

As the waiting continues, Nacho ponders: was Torres bluffing? He lies there in sniper position, eyes peering through a pair of Abbe-Koenig binoculars pilfered from an army surplus store in Bordello. 'What if there are no soldiers? What if those two colonels were actors dressed in khakis?' Maybe Torres wanted to scare us away and that was his big bluff.

He looks to the side. Raincoat without his raincoat. Seeing the man in his shirt sleeves for the first time, Nacho thinks, 'He may be a cantankerous idiot, but at least he's here, holding a gun.' He talks to the man and finds out that Raincoat spent six years in prison for stealing chickens. The other inmates nicknamed him

Rooster. On his release, Raincoat traveled north to the wastelands of Izoztu, where it rains nine months of the year. He worked on the land but fought daily with everyone in sight. He said he was born angry. He fought with the boss about food rations, toilet breaks, lousy equipment, and moldy bedding, and he fought with his coworkers about card cheats, loud snorers, hat thieves, and bad debts. After a few months he got into one fight too many and, bleeding from the gut, hitched a ride to Favelada. The only thing he'd kept from his time in Izoztu was his dirty raincoat and a scar the shape of a Christmas tree on his stomach.

Nacho checks the time. 10:00 a.m. and no sign of Torres.

The tower braces itself. After the morning shift, the bakery has closed early, and Marias Beautty and Hare Salon sees off its final customer for the day at barely 11:00 a.m. before shutting its doors. The girls sweep the floor, hang up their aprons, and go home. It is a still day. Not a breath of wind disturbs the sheets and pants and skirts hanging from wooden pegs on clotheslines and draped over the iron railings of stairwells. A coven of crows gathers on the roof, black-caped witches craning their necks, and they wonder in crow telepathy if today will bring blood.

At 11:10, the tattooist shuts his parlor, bidding goodbye to the day's one customer, a woman who asked for the names of her children to be tattooed onto her leg, four talismans to keep her safe. She leaves the parlor wincing in pain as the wounds congeal, and prepares to load the six-shooter her wastrel husband left her.

Shortly after midday, the muezzin's voice rings out above the sounds of the traffic, calling the faithful to prayer. To Nacho it sounds like a plaint, a lamentation for the truncated lives of the damnificados. He thinks of those he has loved and tries to picture what his life could have been: traveling to distant lands, reeling off translations of great works, interpreting for heads of state. Finding love, a house on a cliff with white walls and a thatched roof where an owl periodically visits and hoots a simple song, raising children to be honest and wise. He thinks of all this and then looks again through the binoculars at the plaza that opens out beyond the atrium. An old lady walking. A student passing through. A cyclist wobbling drunkenly, zigzagging out of sight. But no Torres.

At 1:00 p.m. Harry and his brothers bring bread with a hunk of gouda and olives from Balaal. They present it on a platter like the last supper of a condemned man, but Nacho can barely eat. He picks at the food, feeling no pleasure in the salty tang of the olives, spitting out the stones and leaving the bread untouched.

Above all, he curses himself for having no plan but to fire down on the assassins. He invokes the great generals—Alexander, the child warrior, Hannibal, Belisarius, Suvorov—and imagines them conjuring elephants and flaming missiles to rout the enemy. He imagines troop movements and ground tactics, thinking in four dimensions, inventing weaponry not yet dreamed of. His mind takes him to the carnage of earlier Trash Wars, the legend of Naboo Lalloo, catapults and dragons, and the Trojan horse, a garbage truck full of hidden warriors, Las Bestias de la Luz Perpetua, a hall of mirrors to confuse attackers, and the images on the Zeffekat tapestry depicting every sorry tale of the wars. What, he thinks, will *this* war bring to the history books? A tower riddled with bullets. A tide of blood. The Little Cripple who led his troops to annihilation.

He thinks of the lineage of Torres—grandfathers, fathers, uncles—killers one and all, grasping for power and land and riches, bashing their way through history. The very tower he lies in now—built on stolen land, built on the bones of damnificados, desperados, desaparecidos. The Torres men—commanders of armies and robber gangs, which end up being the same thing, corrupt from their toes to the ends of their fat cigars. He whispers to himself, "Will justice ever reach this godforsaken city?" and Raincoat, lying next to him, hears it but says nothing, looking through the sights of the rifle, itchy finger twitching.

Nacho scratches at his hair, gets up and wanders the room, sits on a chair, lies back down, looks through the binoculars, listens to his own breathing.

At 2:00 he checks on his soldiers. A motorboy takes him up and down the flights of stairs. Nacho asks his fighters if everything is OK, if they are ready. He asks the priest to go around making sure no shutters are open except the ones they'll fire from.

"Again?" says Don Felipe. "I've done this four times already."

"Please do it again," says Nacho. "And make sure the children are inside."

Early afternoon ticks slowly into midafternoon, the shadows growing longer, beginning to cover the plaza below. Silence descends on the monolith. Some of the inhabitants begin returning to the tower warily after a day at work in other parts of the city. They approach carefully, quietly. They pass the Chinaman, proffer their usual nods, and go upstairs to their homes.

Up on the sixth floor, Maria is barricading her windows and doors, and Emil, lounging louche and shirtless on the bed, wonders if she's doing it to keep Torres out or to keep himself in.

"Emil," says Maria, her black hair wild and wet, for if she is going to die she will die glamorously, "why don't we mount that white horse and escape the city?"

"Well the thing is . . ." starts Emil.

"What's a white horse for, if not escaping? I know you only have one saddle, but we can ride bareback and go to the woods. There's a place in Gudsland, a patch of earth. My grandfather lived near there. It has shade."

"Wait, Maria."

"It has four apple trees and a view of the sea. There's nothing there but the ocean. The wind blows in off the water."

"Maria, the thing is . . ."

"We can start a family. Buy a goat and some chickens. Live a simple life. You aren't a city boy. You pretend you are, but I can tell. You just want a quiet life. And the children will be able to . . ."

"Maria, shut up! The horse has gone! The twins returned it to the cartel! I'm staying here to help my brother! I'm not going to Gudsland or anywhere else. Take the shelves from in front of the door and put them back where they were. If you don't, I will. Then I'm going to get my gun and stand and fight side by side with Nacho. The end. Credits roll. Music and lights. Get it?"

Maria stares at him. She's in her underwear and heels. She prowls over to the bed and raises her hand as if to slap him. He doesn't flinch. Instead she gets onto the bed, makes to kiss him and bites his lip so it draws blood.

"Stronzo di merda," she says. "Make love to me!"

As evening approaches, a boy comes to the fifth floor, looking for Nacho.

"Mr. Morales," he says.

"What are you doing here? You need to go home! Children can't be out here!"

"But Mr. Morales. We'd like to know if there's school today. There are ten of us waiting in the classroom."

Nacho puts his hand to his head.

"Dammit! I'm an idiot. I'm sorry. School is cancelled today. All of you go home. Cover your windows and don't go outside. I must have forgotten to give the message. I'm sorry. We'll have class tomorrow."

The boy says, "Yes, sir," and is gone.

The sun begins its descent. The sky is stained a cadmium orange and streaked with clouds like vapor trails ghosting across the horizon. An eerie quiet reigns in the tower. Some families hold hands and pray. Others are seated for dinner. Every five or six floors a shutter remains open, a telltale gunbarrel or binoculars or telescope protruding from the gap. The men and women from Dahomey-Krill sharpen their knives. The ex-soldier prepares himself to die a good death. Don Felipe, the priest, has been holed up in his makeshift church all day, listening to confessions, giving benedictions, improvising sermons to his ancestors, should he meet them some time soon. Dewald, the psychologist, drinks himself to sleep, figuring that if he's going to die a violent death, he may as well not be there to witness it.

It is just past 7:00 p.m. when the lookout on the sixtieth floor sees them. He rings a bell. The ringing is taken up by the lower floors until it gets all the way down to the fifth floor.

A convoy. An armored car and ten military trucks. They spread around the plaza and pull up on its edges in a semicircle. From out of the armored car the figure of Torres emerges, red-faced and rotund, trussed up in khakis and medals and a dark green beret. Ten soldiers with rifles clamber out of the back of one of the trucks and accompany him across the square toward the entrance of the tower.

"Knock knock!" he bellows, still walking.

Silence. Nacho looks on. Two beads of sweat race one another down his forehead, nestling in his eyebrows. He wipes them with the back of his good hand and lies still, watching through the binoculars. When Torres gets closer to the entrance, Nacho can no longer see him because of the angle.

"Anybody home?" shouts Torres.

Torres pushes at the door. It is locked. Then he backs up, heading for the middle of the plaza, and raises his head. He sees instantly the closed shutters and the open ones, and pulls out a cigar from his top pocket. He lights it and puffs contentedly.

"Hello!" he shouts. "Daddy, I forgot my keys! Can someone let me in?"

From the room on the fifth floor, Raincoat is trembling.

"He's in my sights!" he says. "One shot and he's dead. I can kill him now!"

"Wait," says Nacho.

"Why? What the fuck am I waiting for? I can kill him!"

"No! That's murder. We have to wait."

Torres calls again. "Oh, Naaaaaaaaaacho! Let me in! By the hair of my chinny-chin-chin! Or I'll huff and I'll puff and I'll blow your house down! I give you thirty seconds!"

Nacho's mind is racing. 'Do I sacrifice myself? But that won't solve anything. It's the tower he wants. Do I surrender? But then we'll all be driven out and homeless and we lose our dignity. And maybe we'll lose our lives anyway.'

Torres, cigar in hand, ambles back to the armored car. Moments later, the troops jump from the backs of the trucks and begin setting up their weapons: Uzis and Kalashnikovs and Puckle Guns on tripods. Beside them a host of infantrymen gets down on one knee, aiming rifles at the monolith.

At that moment the muezzin's call to prayer rises above the city, and a flock of birds appears, arcing above the tower like bits of burnt paper on string. This is it, thinks Nacho. He hears the clanking of metal, the machinery of war being inched into place. The two colonels, Bandero and Hafeez, are barking orders in Spanish, English, Arabic, Gujarati, but the muezzin's call drowns them out so Nacho cannot hear the colonels' words.

The first volley of gunfire rips through the lower floors of the tower like a typhoon, lacerating wooden shutters, exploding through windows and ricocheting off walls. Screams go up as the inhabitants hit the floor. A pause. A cloud of smoke rises and the smell of cordite drifts on the air. At the center of the plaza, not twenty feet from where the infantrymen kneel, a figure rises both from the dust and of the dust, the ghost of an old woman, shouting at the top of her voice, "Kami ay labanan sa dulo!" but then the apparition is gone and the soldiers look at one another as if to say "Did you see it? What was it?" And a machine gunner growls at his comrades, "This place is cursed. Let's finish the job and get out of here."

And Nacho, who also sees the apparition and hears the cry, realizes that, ghost or no ghost, Torres's firepower is one hundred times superior to the damnificados'.

He looks around the room. All hands are on heads or over ears, all eyes closed, barely a soul still holding a gun let alone able to shoot straight under fire. Butchers, bakers, teachers, drunks. Harry and his brothers are on the floor curled up like babies. One of them is weeping and asking for his mother. Raincoat fell off the bed at the first sound of bullets hitting brick and has now crawled under it. Nacho says, "Where's Emil?"

As if on cue, Emil bursts into the room. The others cringe and shrink as the door crashes open, thinking he's Torres or some dread killer with a Kalashnikov.

Emil dives onto the bed, revolver in hand.

"We need to shoot back," he says.

"Do it," says Nacho.

A voice from the floor says, "No!"

Nacho turns and sees Harry on his elbows, in doggy position, hands over his head, eyes looking up.

"They're too strong for us," says Harry.

"Shut up," says Emil. "Fight like a man."

Emil lifts his head to glance quickly through the space where the window should be. He raises the gun and pulls the trigger but nothing happens.

"Shit. The fucker jammed on me."

He ditches the revolver and reaches down to get Raincoat's rifle, which is on the floor. He takes aim and fires. The barrel's kick sends him rocking back onto the bed.

"Aaagh! I think I broke my shoulder!"

Another volley of shots blasts through the air, the clean clinical rattle of machine guns and the bullets cracking against the tower's walls. More screams go up amid the chorus of glass breaking, wood splintering, brick shattering. In the hiatus that ensues, shouts are heard: "Give in!" "Stop!" and the staccato rattle of feet shuffling. Smaller bangs of pots and pans. And Nacho thinks, 'What next? What next?'

Emil is covered in sweat. He clambers back into position on the bed, gets ready to fire.

"You broke your shoulder?" says Nacho.

"I have two of them."

He fires again, rubs his shoulder, turns to Nacho.

"Goddamn it. We have to shoot back. What are the others doing?"

They look around the room. Everyone is cowering on the floor.

The voice of Torres from the plaza: "Nachiiiiiiiiiiito! Come on out and I'll spare you all!"

Then voices from the tower.

"Go, Nacho!"

"Tell him we surrender!"

"We give up!"

What happens next, thinks Nacho an hour later, is a scene that will go down in history. Of all the blood-soaked episodes, the litany of destruction here on the plains of Favelada that have seen dragons, limb-choppers, warriors dredged up from air and fire, none could possibly be stranger. No man alive could have predicted it and no man alive will ever understand it, and whatever gods walk this Earth, they too are struck dumb by what happens. And after it happens, Nacho says to his brother, "They will sing of this for a thousand years." Neither the miracle-makers of Hajja Xejn nor the bruja of Estrellas Negras have ever seen or heard of such a thing. Even the shamans who walk the ice fields of Zaledenom Jezeru are stunned into silence when they learn what takes place here on this warm Favelada night.

And what happens is this:

On the sixtieth floor, the lookout peers down, but the thing that catches his eye is not the soldiers reloading. Instead, with the sun dipping low and the sky a saffron orange, he sees a pack of animals hurtling toward the tower. At first he cannot make them out, cannot identify the shapes haring in the semidark through broken streets and stalled traffic.

And as Nacho unlocks the door to the entrance and prepares himself to die in a hail of bullets or beg a deal from Torres, he too catches a glimpse of the blur of movement heading from the city center.

From behind the soldiers the animals approach at full speed. Torres's eyes and the eyes of his men are on the door opening slowly in front of them and so they see their attackers too late and by the time they turn around the wolves are upon them, led by a massive two-headed beast, leaping into their faces and gnashing at their arms. The pack has grown. They are eighty strong, rippling and sleek like tigers, and they rip into the soldiers, tearing at their limbs, mangling and mauling sinew and bone. The drivers of the military trucks see what is happening and most in an instant turn yellow, igniting their engines and accelerating away into the gloom, chased by their own soldiers, who have abandoned their weapons.

Torres, standing to the side, looks on, transfixed by the massacre, mouth open in a gape of incomprehension. He does not even try to flee. The call to prayer having finished, there are now just the sounds of gnashing and the screams of the soldiers.

From the door, Nacho watches. Like Torres, he stands dumb, his face a mask of white like a figure in a Greek tragedy.

On the fifth floor, Emil says, "Look."

Harry and his brothers and Raincoat remain prone on the floor.

"Look!" Emil shouts it this time, barely believing his eyes.

Harry and the others get to their feet and peer out the window.

On the higher floors, men and women stand and stare in disbelief at the rout below them. At first they cannot read the scene. This is nothing like the wars of legend or on the chattering box. They shield the eyes of their children and no one cheers.

Torres eventually comes to his senses, fully understands what is happening to his men, and begins to back away. The two-headed wolf turns toward him, its mouths covered in blood. At this sight, Torres runs. He runs through Ubijanje Street, and Carneficina Avenue, sprints under a bridge at Mortus Creek, wades across the garbage-clogged river at Basura, never looking back, bounds up Lixo Hill, runs into Fellahin, finds a church, bangs on the door until a priest lets him in, slams the door shut, bolts it, runs up the aisle to a statue of Jesus, kneels down, panting and trembling, and begins to pray.

He repents all of his sins and will now fly to the bosom of the Lord. He tells the Lord he will gladly sit on a hill in the wilderness for the rest of his life, cross-legged, in meditation, eat nothing but leaves and bugs, crave no worldly things IF THE LORD WILL KEEP THE GODDAMNED—oops, sorry, Lord—WOLVES AWAY FROM HIM.

He vows never to go near the tower again, never to sin again. He will mingle with the poor and wretched of the Earth, feel their sorrows, devote his life to good deeds. And he goes on praying alone, his military garb dripping in sweat mingled with the mudwater from his dash across the river, the blood of the soldiers staining his boots.

Back on the battlefield, at some invisible signal the wolves cease their attack. Only the two-headed beast pauses and turns to face Nacho, who stands at the entranceway, the spot where the wolf stood when the damnificados took the tower. The beast stares. Nacho looks back. Two guardians. Suddenly the animal lets out an unworldly howl from its two mouths and the wolfpack turns and hurtles through the city center and into the outskirts and all the way to the forest from where it came.

Slowly the inhabitants of the tower come down until there are hundreds of them at the entrance and on the land where the massacre occurred. The last rays of sun wash the plaza in sepulchral light. The damnificados are dazed, unsure of whether to cheer or weep.

Nacho organizes the cleanup, the gathering of the weapons left on the killing field. As a hose is brought out, the twins arrive in their father's truck and get out of the cab and stretch. Nacho is stood in front of them.

"Hi!" shouts Hans. "We were delayed, but we dropped off the horse. Hey, did something happen here today?"

CHAPTER 13

NACHO PONDERING IN HIS ROOM. THE LAST REMNANTS OF THE FOOD BROUGHT BY EMIL ARE scattered about the place—coffee beans staining the stone floor, grains of rice, a tiny pile of sugar morphing into an ant colony behind the door. We're like the first men, holed up in caves, he thinks. Pawns in a game. We can't explain anything: where our thoughts come from, how we became what we are, the origins of the beasts and the plants and the mountains that surround us. We know nothing. We're helpless as newborns.

The Little Cripple, twice orphaned, lame in one leg and one arm, with a head of hair like an electric shock, and nothing but his wits to lean on, sits against a box of books, exhausted from the day's exertions, and keeps pondering.

He remembers a statesman telling him, in an off-guard, off-the-record moment, "Your enemies are like an onion. One layer peels off only to reveal another thicker, stronger layer beneath. Your enemies grow from the inside. Don't ever think you are safe."

He was at a conference in Gao Deng years before, interpreting for this same statesman. In the evening they would go their separate ways, Nacho to a room in a hotel, the statesman to some informal gathering or party. But one evening the statesman called Nacho late at night and told him to go to the bar of the hotel. He found the statesman drunk and in need of company, an ear for his ramblings. So Nacho listened, for once not needing to translate the man's views.

It was then the statesman had told him about enemies and onions. Cursing his luck, almost spitting out the names of his rivals, the man once thumped the table, and the bourbon glass jumped, and the barman stared. But Nacho simply nodded and listened.

He had always been a listener. From his schooldays spent pretending to be a halfwit, he had cultivated the art of sitting still, not reacting, simply taking in with all his senses what was occurring around him. As others chattered and prattled, he sat in silence, occasionally nodding, deliberately fighting the urge to interrupt, to talk, to disagree, to become a participant in the game.

Interpreting suited him. The interpreter, he thought, gave nothing of himself, simply transposed the message into a different code. It didn't matter to him whether the speaker was arguing over the price of beans or advocating genocide; Nacho was just a conduit, a mindless machine, invisible, neutral, colorless as water.

His grasp of languages, of idiom and nuance, was treasured by the statesmen and politicos. But more treasured was his ability to stay in the background, to be invisible. He was tiny, and although his muletas and unruly hair meant people saw him, he retained a quality of irrelevance, as if one so strange-looking could never move mountains in their world. The other reason they liked him was because they sensed he never meddled with their words. He gave straight translations. He appeared free from ideology and belief and even character, and this they loved.

For years, he worked as much as he wanted, traveling to distant lands and gatherings of politicos, men and women of wealth and power. When he wasn't traveling, they sent him speeches and documents to translate, and he did so with a cold, dispassionate eye.

One day he found himself in Zerbera, a city ringed by endless hills. Sleepless as ever, he went for a late-night stroll. Although he couldn't walk well, he had his father's love of wandering, and on his crutches he could go a mile without strain, sometimes two if the elements and the street paving were in his favor. On this night, the moon was covered by clouds and the city had no streetlamps so he walked in near darkness. He heard the sounds of human revelry and found these sounds guiding his feet in their direction. He came upon a building with no sign or windows, but a door that was ajar, revealing a rectangle of light. He pushed it open and hobbled in on his crutches.

A shebeen, a drinking den. Five tables. Thirty or forty people crowded in, talking, laughing. On the walls were posters of old singers, Fauvist paintings on cork boards, and the skins of flayed cobras and crocs hanging by the nose. West African music was playing over a scratchy sound system, and in one corner a group of men squatting on the floor were engaged in a beetle race. They placed their bugs, fat as Egyptian dates, on the starting line and willed them to the finish, slapping down coins and notes, cheering and shouting.

On one table a woman was reading palms. She was dark-skinned, almost blue-black, and her hair was tied in a top-knot. She wore a black kaftan and strings of beads around her neck and huge hooped earrings of silver, and she looked like a lost princess transplanted to this liquor dive that smelled of whisky and cigars. She was surrounded by men and women listening and laughing as she foretold their fates.

When Nacho entered, she beckoned him over and told the others in Yoruba to make space and give him a chair. This they did, smiling and patting him on the back like a newfound friend. He was surrounded by black Africans speaking Yoruba, Swahili, Amharic, and Afrikaans. A hulking man with scars on his cheeks put a bottle of beer in front of Nacho and disappeared. The lost princess tried him out in a few languages and settled on a mix of French and English, asking him his name and where he was from. Then she took his hand, palm up, and spread his fingers on the table.

The woman peered at his hand for forty, maybe fifty seconds. All around them the others waited and waited until their patience began to collapse.

"Lucille, ni nini kusema?" one shouted in Swahili.

"Est-il un roi ou un pauvre? A king or a pauper?"

"Wat sê dit?" another said in Afrikaans.

Lucille, for that was her name, looked up slowly. Her eyes met Nacho's eyes and broke into a smile, almost flirtatious.

"A special man," she said, then repeated it in four languages. "An unusual man," she said. "You are as rare as a falcon in a glass."

"Come on!" they shouted. "Uliona nini? What did you see?"

"Qui est-il?"

She looked around at them. "Nacho will be a leader of men and women. He works with words now but soon he'll deal in action. A man of action."

She repeated this last phrase in four languages and some of her friends laughed.

"He's lame! Hawezi kutembea!" one shouted.

"You're wrong," said Lucille. "He's more powerful than the rest of you put together."

"Que dites-vous, Lucille? Pouvez-vous traduire? Translate!"

And she said it again in four languages.

"I'm saying he will rise up and defeat armies. He will gather his own army and command men and women and lead them from the streets to a looming tower where he will trick Cerberus into letting him in."

"Qui est Cerberus?"

"Wat sê jy?" said another, in Afrikaans.

"Cerberus is a guard dog," she says. "This man will be a hero to many and an enemy of dictators and oppressors. An unusual man. And yet he doesn't know himself."

"Tell us more!"

"He doesn't know his roots. He doesn't know his parents. He lives in ignorance of himself and his true nature. So I will tell him."

And she did. She told him of the people he would lead and of the tower and of Cerberus and he listened, as always, and let her release his hand, and smiled because he was in the company of strangers. She began to tell him about his parents when suddenly a fight broke out in the corner of the room. Two men began swinging great wide-arced haymakers, and a bottle flew through the air missing its target and smashing against the wall sending a shower of bubbly beer over the fighters. A table was overturned and somehow the scrap escalated into a full-scale brawl with men and women leaping onto tables and hurling chairs. Nacho ducked down and put his head in his hands. He scrambled out the door on his muletas into the cool of the night and hobbled around a corner, as the shebeen echoed with the sounds of glass breaking and lurid shouts and meaty punches thwacking skin. Lucille was nowhere to be seen.

On his way to the hotel he pondered what the woman had said. His father, Samuel, had been a good man, always serving others. That's why they'd killed him. But Nacho felt no calling to lead men and women. As he finally lay down on the floor in his hotel room, the bed having proved way too soft for a night's sleep, he dismissed it all. Lucille was a gifted linguist, too, but as he knew well, that didn't mean she could tell the future. She was a princess all right, but of what? A rusty shebeen where people got drunk and cracked heads for fun. As he drifted off to sleep her face began to fade—her striking eyes, her skin as dark as the night-ocean—until in the morning it was gone, as distant as a dream. But he never forgot her words.

The following evening, he returned to the shebeen, retracing his steps by remembering the cracks in the paving and the exact sounds made by his muletas as he walked—how loudly they echoed, how muffled the tapping. Once again he found the door ajar. He pushed at it only to find the room empty. There was no bar. No tables. No chairs. No posters on the walls. No music. The place had been stripped, gutted, sent back to some kind of original state of grace. He stood at the door and called out.

"Hello? Lucille?"

When there was no answer, he went outside to check that he hadn't made a mistake. Was this the wrong building? But he was sure it was the same. He looked again at the interior, taking in the spaces and reconstructing the layout of the room in his mind— where he had sat, where the crocodile skin had hung, where the fight had broken out—and left.

He made his way back to the hotel, catching a ride with a rickshaw driver who charged him half price, and as he paid up, he thought, 'Zerbera—my lucky place.'

CHAPTER 14

Party at the stone heads—Harry takes

credit—Wolf food, wolf songs, wolf

people—Invincibility—Nacho returns

to work—The quiet life—The brothers

walk to Blutig—A rumor of Torres

At the gates of the city, the damnificados celebrate their victory. In the shadows of the five stone heads, impromptu performances take place by the light of a bonfire constructed from trash. A fakir ascends a vertical rope suspended on nothing. The twins begin a breakdance routine while dozens surround them, clapping in unison. A man in a wolf mask balances on a monocycle while juggling three burning torches.

Groups of damnificados sit around in circles—Harry the baker and his brothers, Raincoat, Dewald the psychologist, and Maria's salon girls. They pass bottles of hooch and homemade wine from hand to hand, taking great gulps as the firelight flickers on their faces.

"Them dogs!" says Harry.

"Wolves!" says one of his brothers.

"Them dogs! Finished off them poor bastards, they did. Mind you, we'd have killed them soldiers anyway. Mark my words. We was well on top."

"Course we would."

"Would've licked 'em," says Harry. "You don't mess with me and my brothers!"

"Not if you want to keep your balls in one piece!"

"I shot two of 'em!" says one of the brothers.

"Me too," says Raincoat. "I haven't lost it. Used to be a sniper, me. Bang bang! Two drop dead. Right between the eyes."

"The doggies just polished 'em off," says Harry. "They was retreatin' already. And did you see 'em runnin' like babies?"

"We should get a medal for this," says another brother.

"It were a massacre is what it were," says Harry. "They come here all rough and ready. Big guns 'n' all, but when it comes to the fightin' they're off! I've always said, haven't I always said, it ain't the dog in the fight, it's the fight in the dog. Haven't I always said that, lads?"

"You've always said it, Harry."

"All it takes is a bit of ticker. That's how you sort the men from the boys."

He looks into the distance, massaging the memory of his heroism. A cry goes up as a belly dancer is pulled up to the top of the middle stone head, where she shakes and whirls to the sound of drummers below.

Emil and Maria walk arm in arm among the damnificados, Emil's free arm in a sling.

"Look at them!" hisses Maria. "Claiming it's their victory. Nacho told me they spent the battle hiding under the bed!"

"Having fun?" asks Emil.

"That's men for you. Always ready to take the credit."

"Enjoying the party?"

"No. Let's go home and make love," says Maria.

"We just finished making love!"

"Let's do it again."

"My shoulder's killing me. And we've only been here two minutes. I want to celebrate a little. Where's Nacho?"

"Nacho this, Nacho that. What about me?"

"He's my little brother."

They walk closer to the fire and feel its crackling heat in their faces. The woman with a dog in a wheelbarrow, now sitting in front of the fire, reaches up and grabs Emil's hand.

"Thank you for bringing food again," she says. "You saved my dog."

"You're welcome," says Emil, with a grin. Somebody noticed. Somebody remembered.

They walk a little further, overtaking Nacho on his muletas, and stop to watch as a woman invents a pagan wolf-dance. She gets onto all fours, wiggles her behind and opens her jaws wide; turns to growling; then leaps. Her friend joins her and they begin a dance of wolf and soldier, call and response.

Not twenty feet away, a man is carving a plank of cedar wood into a two-headed wolf. He concentrates furiously, chiseling away with a bowie knife, the plank laid out on his lap.

At the foot of one of the stone heads, a musician is devising a song—The Song of the Wolves—to commemorate the battle. He carries an ancient lute.

At a drinks stall close by, the owner invents The Wolf—a shot of whisky and soda with sugar and a twist of lime. He then invents The Two-Headed Wolf, which is the same thing except with two shots of whisky.

The owner of a food stall devises the Wolf Burger, a slab of barely cooked steak wedged between two slices of flax seed bread with pickles and dill.

And the people too are become wolfish. Only Nacho sees it. He sees their snouts grow and sharpen to the apex of the wet black nose; their mouths turn muzzle-like and their jaws grow low and powerful. He sees under their collars thick manes dappled with gray. Women laugh and Nacho sees their canines protruding like nuggets of white zinc. As the night unfolds, he sees some of the damnificados slink off in hungry packs. Others stay to howl at the moon. All have turned into wolves, and he wonders if he himself has become one. He looks at his hands, sees they are unchanged, but knows that humans are the last things on Earth to recognize what they have become.

*

Following the floods and the attack by Torres, the inhabitants—returned from their state of wolf-hood—begin to see themselves as the rightful owners of the tower. Once they have overcome the fear that the wolves will come back and attack them, they believe peace and prosperity is theirs, for the first time in their lives.

Many of the adults can now read, and many more work in regular jobs. Some of them begin to state their address with pride. They are the lucky few who live in the tower which was once thought cursed but now seems blessed. They have functioning schools, water and electricity, a famous beauty salon and a bakery where the image of Jesus appeared on a loaf of bread. "What other towers in this city have been visited by Jesus?" they ask. "We are protected by wolves and by a great leader, Nacho, el pequeño lisiado." "An army came to destroy us and left in pieces."

Occasional fights still break out, but fewer and fewer, and the citizens begin to police themselves.

Nacho gets more translating work, hiding himself in his room for hours on end. The work comes as a balm to him, a chance to interact with the outside world without lives being at stake. In the afternoons he props himself up on his muletas and walks the perimeter of the tower, admiring the little plots of land the women are reclaiming, and asking what they are growing.

"Tomatoes, potatoes, mint. Parsley and green beans."

He walks across the plaza and over the road and sees the little businesses springing up in the flood's aftermath: small bodegas reopening under different names, food stalls with grills where the proprietor will roast you a chicken or a cob of corn while you talk about the weather or the new mall in Fellahin or the factory opening in Oameni Morti. They seldom make him pay for anything, and even when he insists, they give him discounts.

Some evenings he plays chess with Don Felipe, running rings around the priest, picking off the old man's pieces one by one, administering slow deaths.

Five floors up from Nacho's quiet life, Emil too is living a quiet life. For six weeks, he does nothing but sleep, eat, tend to his wounded shoulder, and make love to Maria. At first, she takes hourly breaks from the salon to visit him. Whatever he is doing—sitting at table, lying in a bath reclaimed from a tip in Sanguinosa, dozing in bed—she kisses him, hoists up her skirt, and sits on top of him until he is ready. She washes rapidly and is back tending to hair and nails within minutes, smiling at her clients, flashing her dark eyes.

In the seventh week, Emil visits his brother and they take a walk. The sun has already begun to drop so they aren't assailed by the heat of the day and they find themselves retracing steps they took with Samuel many years ago, retelling his stories.

Moving in the opposite direction from the stone heads at the city gates, they come to streets they barely remember, and wonder if their memories are at fault or if everything has changed beyond recognition. Great skyscrapers loom where they remember low buildings of wood and tin. Next to a mosque where there used to be a grassy wasteland there now stands a bric-a-brac store. They peer into its windows and marvel at the random contents: Chinese dolls, Persian kites in the shape of an eagle, jars of olives, jeans.

Nacho feels strong and keeps walking, his muletas tapping on the sidewalks and where there are no sidewalks, on the baked mud and stone that make up the roads. Small parks appear, with acacia trees and birds flitting and rusty swings and slides for children. They reach the river and cross a wooden bridge where banyan plants are germinating on the underside. They pause to look down at the dry creek bed and notice a pair of crows springing from rock to rock. Beyond the bridge they come to an abandoned building site and see the watermarks from the flood way up high on a half-constructed wall.

Never in his life has Emil seen a street without wanting to walk down it. Never has he seen a bridge without feeling the need to cross it, a boat without wanting to sail it, a mountain without wanting to climb it. He says to Nacho:

"Brother, being out here reminds me."

"Reminds you of what?"

"The old days. When I could come and go. I feel trapped in the tower, as if there's some invisible chain holding me there."

"It's not so invisible. It's gorgeous as a beauty queen and running the most successful salon in Favelada."

"And I have to make some money. Maria likes having me at home. She says she earns enough to support us, but a man can't live like that. At least *I* can't."

"Then get a job. You can't stay at home all day. You never could."

"But a city job? I want to sail the seas or go exploring."

"Then you have to make a choice," says Nacho.

"You don't think Maria would want to come with me?"

"Why are you even asking me that? She's the queen bee of the tower. Employs what? Ten people? Last time I saw, she had leather furnishings, Persian rugs on the floor."

"You've been in her apartment?"

"I visited her once when you were gone. She was desperate to see you so I went and talked to her. She won't leave for the life of a hobo. She wants a home, all those comforts. She told me herself, she wasn't born a damnificado. She sure as hell doesn't want to live like one. Or die like one."

Suddenly they are on the edge of a slum. The smell hits them—that bitter tang of rotting fruit and human waste—before they even see the ramshackle housing. They turn a corner and come across the telltale signs: sewage running through the street, trash cans so overflowing you can no longer see the cans, houses built in no order to no pattern, climbing one on the other like rutting beasts, roofs overlapping, wiring tangled. They see people going about their evening business—women emptying brightly colored buckets onto the ground, men lounging outside a shebeen, children kicking a ball.

"Where are we?" asks Nacho.

"Blutig. We must have walked for miles. Anyone you want to visit?"

"No. Let's go home."

They turn and start to walk when a man on a bicycle catches up with them. He is slender, sun-browned and unshaven, wearing stained clothes—all the badges of the damnificados. Nacho thinks the man must be in his sixties, but knows it's impossible to say. The man hops off his bicycle and Nacho and Emil stop to greet him.

"El pequeño lisiado, no?"

"Si, soy yo," says Nacho, and he shakes the man's hand.

"Y quién es?"

"Eso es mi hermano, Emil."

"Mucho gusto," and the man shakes Emil's hand.

"You are visiting us?" the man asks.

"No, we're just walking," says Nacho.

"We hear you make miracles. You tame the wolves and they fight Torres's soldiers. Es verdad?"

"No, it's not true."

"You destroy his army and defeat him. Now he's gone to the hills of Solitario. He . . . how you say? . . . does his penance."

"I know nothing about that. Where did you say Torres is?"

"Solitario. Five days on horse from here. They say he walk there on his knees. He become a monk. Repent his sins. They say you change him. This is truly el milagro de los milagros. I thank you for your time."

And with that, the man mounts his bicycle and does a wide, slow u-turn avoiding a yawning pothole in the road, and clink-clank-creaks his way to the center of Blutig. Nacho and Emil look at each other. Nacho says,

"Do you believe that?"

"Which part?"

"Torres repenting his sins, going off to be a monk."

"I never met the man. But I'd say, with his family history, it's unlikely. They're the biggest bunch of corruptos the city has known. Killers, too."

"I guess we'll find out soon enough. Our enemies are like an onion. They grow from the inside. Don't think you are ever safe."

"What?"

"Something someone told me once."

The sun has gone down so they make their way home in the dark, walking parallel streets to the ones they took on the way. By the time they get home, seen from above they have walked the shape of a long, sharp knife with the blade piercing the tower's entrance.

CHAPTER 15

The Third Trash War—Prison break—

Las Bestias de la Luz Perpetua—

Settlement in Spazzatura—Shocked

and awed—Rodrigo Hellibore meets

his match— Konnichiwa—Truce

THE THIRD TRASH WAR WAS SAID TO BE THE WAR TO END ALL WARS. WHEN IT WAS DONE, the face of Favelada was changed; the trash pile was once again a mountain, inmates from an insane asylum mingled with escaped convicts to take over the running of the city, and a three-hundred-pound pig called Konnichiwa was installed as governor of one of Favelada's provinces.

It all began in Oameni Morti. One drizzly Wednesday, two hundred prison inmates rioted. They hurled bombs made of cleaning products and gasoline at the guards, and set the prison on fire. While the authorities were trying to contain the riot, in another part of the building one hundred inmates bashed down a wall with tools smuggled from a building project, and escaped. By the time the guards realized the riot was a diversion, the countryside around Oameni Morti was littered with convicts tearing through the drenched cornfields.

They hid out in the woods. They survived the predations of wolves and bears by constantly keeping a flame burning, which is how they got the name given to them by the journalists: Las Bestias de la Luz Perpetua—the Beasts of the Perpetual Light. When the rainy season came, they went to the nearest settlement—Favelada—where they camped out in a bus station. They were criminals of the hardened variety: murderers, bandidos, shotgun specialists, heist gurus, and head-mashers of all kinds. In prison, they had been savage. Now, after months of hunting and gathering in the woods, they were feral.

Las Bestias eyed up a patch of wasteland called Spazzatura. There was a river nearby to provide water and a steady stream of boats to use for fishing and transportation. There was just one problem: the land was occupied already. The settlers, also escapees—from an insane asylum in far-off Mundanzas—had built a barrier of trash between themselves and the river, and constructed a settlement of timber and brick. They also built four towers, organized in the shape of a square. Into these towers, it was said, they sent miscreants to live alone for weeks on end.

One night Las Bestias raided Spazzatura. They carried knives, spears, clubs, and a few guns, but in truth they didn't expect trouble. They had heard there were families there, little people living quietly by the river. They got the shock of their lives. Many of the ex-asylum dwellers were paranoid schizophrenics. They fully expected to be attacked at any moment, and when the raiders came, they were ready. The towers weren't solitary confinement after all. They were lookout towers and places from which to shoot at invaders and fling grenades. As Las Bestias flooded in to Spazzatura they were met with a volley of gunfire that dropped ten men in five seconds.

To add to the ex-convicts' confusion, there came a sound at eardrum-splitting volume of Beethoven's Ninth Symphony blasting out of loudspeakers from each tower, followed by a battery of fireworks that rent the sky like bombs and cracked like bullets. Las Bestias didn't know whether it was a party or a war, and only the sight of their comrades bursting open and dying told them. The worst thing of all was that they couldn't see their enemy. In their former lives as prisoners, they had seen their guards every day, given them nicknames, known every trick of speech and angle of gait. They knew who was coming down a blind alley by the sound of their shoes. In Spazzatura, it was as if an alien intelligence was working against them, something hidden and unknowable.

Las Bestias retreated, but vowed to return.

When they did, three nights later, they were doubly armed and ready for a battle. This time they decided to approach from the river. They stole a barge, tying the captain to the mast with a length of nichrome wire, and sailed downriver until they reached Spazzatura. They scaled the wall of trash on all fours, knives in their mouths and guns slung over their backs, but as soon as they reached the top, overlooking the cluster of buildings that formed Spazzatura, the opening notes of Tchaikovsky's Fifth Symphony exploded over the loudspeakers and Las Bestias were met with a hail of arrows. They dived down but still eight men perished.

They decided to fight back this time, and charged the towers. But as they did so, a dozen huge mirrors on springs suddenly jumped out of the trash so that Las Bestias saw themselves attacking, and in the dark became confused. They fired their weapons until the mirrors cracked, but then lost their sense of direction. Stranded, six more were cut down by arrows.

As they regained their equilibrium, three giant screens on pulleys suddenly bounced up out of the garbage, showing scenes from black-and-white films—a Hollywood caper, a Japanese epic, a Nigerian comedy. As Las Bestias paused to see what was happening, another volley of arrows reamed down on them like a rain shower and dropped another four men. On the biggest screen, a celluloid samurai braced himself for seppuku.

Who was orchestrating the Spazzatura forces? What higher power could devise such tactics? The answer, it turned out, was a pig. Along with a madman.

Although confused and disoriented, a group of Las Bestias managed to cut through the movie screens with their knives and shoot down the loudspeakers outside the towers, leaving an eerie silence. After regaining their senses, the invaders hunkered down in a disused brick outhouse from whose slit windows they shot at anything that moved. A small group then set about scaling the towers using crampons and lengths of rope. Once up the north tower they fired indiscriminately, killing the lookouts, and aimed a hail of bullets at the other towers. Meanwhile the men in the outhouse discovered why it was disused. Four rattlesnakes that had been lurking in the corners suddenly began to rattle and uncoil and sent the ex-cons haring to all parts. Exposed once again, another arrow shower picked off three of them.

And so it went on, with Las Bestias massacring the few people they could find while being ambushed by anonymous fire. One of the invaders, Rodrigo Hellibore, escaped from the outhouse and found himself among the buildings. Following the arc of the arrows, guessing at their trajectory, he expected to see a line of archers. Instead, he saw a machine attached to a wooden floor.

At the push of a button it automatically fired a batch of arrows and swiveled on a hinge to change direction. Hellibore knew this ingenious device could be the work of only one man. He saw a confusion of wires, like tangled spaghetti, controlling the device, and followed them until he came to the door of the largest building in Spazzatura. Made of brick and mortar, it had to be the center of operations. He shot away the lock with a handgun and kicked the door open. There in front of him was an old man, all skin and bone, in a patched-up gallibaya, a shock of white hair shooting in all directions: Naboo Lalloo, escaped inmate of Mundanzas Asylum for the Insane, a place he had called home for twenty years.

Naboo Lalloo showed no emotion. He simply sat, head cocked at an angle, eyeing the invader. The sight so astounded Hellibore that he forgot to kill the man and instead started a conversation.

"Chi sei?" he began. "Lalloo? Lalloo?"

Naboo Lalloo looked at him uncomprehendingly.

"Chi sei?" said Hellibore. "Quién es usted?"

Naboo Lalloo began chanting in Persian. Suddenly a pig trotted out of a side room and knocked Hellibore clean off his feet. This was Konnichiwa, Naboo Lalloo's muse.

Hellibore's gun skidded across the floor, and landed at Naboo Lalloo's bare toes. He picked it up.

"You speak English?" asked Naboo Lalloo.

"Yes," said Hellibore.

"Why you attack? We are few people. We don't want fight."

"OK. Can you put down the gun?"

"There is room here. Everyone can live in peace."

The pig began sniffing at Hellibore, nuzzling his midriff.

"OK, can you call off the pig? And mind the gun. It's loaded."

"Who your leader? You?" asked Naboo Lalloo.

"We don't have a leader."

Hellibore was still lying prone.

"Stop the fighting. Why you kill us? We suffer enough."

"We need your land. We have nowhere to live."

"Why you not ask us? Why you kill us first? Is not polite."

Outside, the sound of explosions and screams pierced the night air. Naboo Lalloo shifted in his seat.

"We make deal with you. We live in peace."

Hellibore, who had been a legendary thief with hands as fast as squirrels, looked around. The room was lit by one lamp and a dozen candles, casting shadows on the walls. He had no idea where the pig had come from and no idea why Naboo Lalloo hadn't shot him already.

"OK," he said. "Let's make a deal."

With Las Bestias decimated by arrows, bullets, and grenades, and the ex-inmates of Mundanza Asylum for the Insane weary of battle, Hellibore and Naboo Lalloo brokered a peace. Hellibore staggered to his feet and agreed that there would be no more bloodshed. Facing a madman holding a loaded gun, Hellibore also agreed that Las Bestias would take a plot of land by the river, build their own settlement, and that someone called Konnichiwa could be the nominal governor of Spazzatura. He didn't know that it was Konnichiwa who, at that very moment, was nuzzling his shoes.

In later years, the two men became friends, and Naboo Lalloo explained that the music and the movies that had been part of the battle were the very weapons used in the insane asylum to keep the occupants passive. Beethoven and Tchaikovsky had been their daily diet of music to soothe and calm the blood, and on the occupants' escape they had stolen the equipment used to play it: the loudspeakers, amplifiers, and the ancient scratchy records. They had also purloined the movie projectors and old film reels that had been their evening treat at the asylum. In other words, Spazzatura was a home away from home. Everything else—mirrors on springs, fireworks, and arrow-shooting devices—came from the fevered imagination of Naboo Lalloo, who credited Konnichiwa with the deployment of these, saying the pig spoke to him in Pigg, a language only the two of them could comprehend, and told him where his enemies were and how to defeat them.

Once the peace was brokered, they cremated the dead and sprinkled their ashes in the river, just more waste to add to the world.

CHAPTER 16

More rumors of an attack—Nacho and
Emil discuss their options—Maria's
tuppence—Dog—Conversations with
statesmen—Mayhem—Nacho hatches
a plan—In bocca al lupo—Train journey
to Bieb ta 'Niket—Alone—Nacho's
double lets him in—Johann Stoller

WORD TRAVELS FAST IN FAVELADA. A CHILD HIDING IN A PILE OF TRASH EAVESDROPS ON A pair of off-duty soldiers shooting the breeze. A cleaning lady overhears her boss ranting on the phone through thick walls.

And so it is in these days of tranquility that a rumor goes around the tower—another attack is imminent, and this time there may be no wolves to save the damnificados. The object of the rumor is a monster. Nothing with two heads, but a monster all the same, and with the same name as the other monsters of the past hundred years: Torres.

When one Torres is defeated, another appears. They are like rabbits pulled out of a hat. A sleight of hand, a showman's flourish, and there it is: another! And another! One becomes a monk hiding out in the wilderness of Solitario, but his younger brother then emerges, sounds his barbaric yawp. He is bigger, nastier, meaner, stronger, braver, and, if the rumors are true, hell-bent on avenging the indignities wrought on his family. He knows his brother has become a laughing stock—chased away by a group of damnificados and a pack of puppies, dropping his weapons and running through the streets like a madman, hugging a priest's leg, leaving his troops unattended without orders, every man fending for himself. What humiliations upon the noble name of Torres, worse even than the idiota Rolo Torres, who jumped off the fiftieth floor with a broken parachute, and the cobarde mayor Torres who urinated in his military garb when his enemies lined him up against a wall. The family name must be redeemed, its honor restored.

The rumor comes from Susana's best friend, who cleans the house of a politico. The woman hears the politico discussing the younger Torres, describing him as a man of courage, a likely leader who will stand for office in place of his runaway brother, once he has proved himself by taking back his property in the center of the city. She finishes her cleaning job, returns to the tower, and knocks on Nacho's door. There is no answer, so she tells the priest instead, who tells Raincoat. Raincoat finds Nacho at the gardens of the tower, and tells him:

"We're going to be attacked again. Soon! Torres's younger brother has an army and has sworn revenge on you and all of us. I heard he's already hunted down the wolves and done them in. Now he's making plans to destroy the tower."

"Why would he do that? The Torres family thinks it owns the tower."

"I'm just telling you what I heard. He has tanks, artillery, fighter jets. One or two heroes like you and me aren't going to be able to save us this time. What are you gonna do?"

"I'll talk to the leaders. My brother, too. The priest. And we need to find out more about Torres Junior. I can't make decisions based on rumors. Is he here in Favelada?"

"They're all here except the one we chased off. And they all want revenge."

Later that day Nacho calls on Emil, who is lying half-naked in bed, tossing grapes in the air and catching them in his mouth.

"We need to talk. Hey, is this how you spend your days?"

"Give me ten minutes."

"I'll be in the gardens by the south face. The bench."

Thirty minutes later they are sat together, with a view of the gardeners planting and watering, and beyond them Favelada's traffic coughing up smoke.

Nacho says, "Word has it that Torres's younger brother will attack."

"Oh man."

"I don't know what to do. Do we stand and fight?"

"You saw what happened last time. We don't have any fighters. They're civilians. Families and drunks and working people. Without the wolves, everyone here would be dead or living on the streets. You need to find another solution. Talk to Torres Junior. Cut a deal."

"I don't know him."

"Does he want the tower or does he want revenge? If he wants revenge, we're all dead. If he just wants the tower, we may be able to . . . I don't know. Why am I here? Nacho, this isn't our war. I could be sailing the seven seas or digging for gold or lying under a palm tree somewhere. I never wanted a home here."

"But you're here now. And we need your help."

"What I know about the Torres family is this: the oldest male is the patriarch, makes all the decisions. The others obey his commands, even if he's an idiot. That means the other Torres, the one who ran away, he's the head of the family. If he tells his brother to call off any attack, the brother has to call it off. That's if there is an attack in the first place. You told me it's just a rumor."

"But Torres Senior is far away. He lives in the wilderness."

"Then go and see him. He's a monk, right? Maybe he'll tell his brother to become a monk, too, and all our problems will be over."

Nacho ruffles his hair and mutters to himself, "Go and see Torres. Find him in Solitario. Ask him to call his brother off."

"Got any better ideas? Or do you want to build an army again? Those wild men from Dahomey-Krill have all gone back there, back to the forest. They didn't believe the Trash Wars were finished and maybe they're right. Maybe escaping now is the best thing for everyone, you included."

"Can't do that."

Maria appears behind them.

She says, "Escaping? Who's escaping?"

"Honey," says Emil. "Torres has a younger brother. Might attack the tower. I'm telling Nacho to go speak to Torres the Elder and get him to call off the attack."

"What a stupid idea," says Maria, parking herself on the bench, and crossing her fishnet-clad legs. "The elder one disgraced the family. He ran away, didn't he? Why would anyone listen to him?"

"Because he's the oldest male," says Emil.

"So what?" shouts Maria. "The oldest male ran off crying and became a monk because he lost a fight! What authority does he have over his family?"

"Yeah, you're right, but it's family tradition: the oldest male makes all the decisions."

"Pah," says Maria. "Not in my family."

She gets up and struts her way back to the tower, calling over her shoulder, "Dinner's ready. Get your ass upstairs or it goes to the dog."

"What dog?" asks Nacho.

"She bought a dog. One of those little squiggly things, nips at your feet, barks all the time."

"Why?"

"I dunno. Domesticity? Guard dog? The stupid thing shits everywhere and rips up the furniture."

"What name did you give it?"

"Nacho."

✳

A week passes and Nacho uses his contacts to find out everything he can about Torres the Younger. He asks a statesman, a retired ambassador he traveled with for a month during rainy season in far-off Chuveiro. All those years ago, Nacho remembers, the rain had come down so hard they'd been unable to do anything but stay indoors and talk. And here they are again, in a café owned by the statesman, indoors and talking.

"The younger Torres?" says the ambassador, his genial round face skewed as he chews on a rancid cigar. "The same as the older ones, but worse. He's a gathering storm." The ambassador's trouser legs are rolled up, feet in a bucket of water to soothe his gout. "He already has half the generals in his pocket and he'll run for office soon. It's the Torres way. Put an army behind you and then make a claim for power. He has blood on his hands already and he's not yet thirty."

The ambassador parks his cigar in an ashtray and slurps at an espresso, the cup dainty in his sausage fingers.

"We have an old Ligurian saying: Chi ammazza gatti e chen o no fa mai ciu de ben. Those who kill cats and dogs will never do anything good. I knew the family. Torres the younger was the type of child who pulled the wings off birds and set fire to street cats. If he ever rises to power, expect hell to break loose. His nickname was Mayhem."

The next step is to find out if Torres Junior is planning an attack on the tower. Nacho hatches a scheme to cultivate a spy, a cleaning woman from Oameni Morti who works for a Torres associate and frequents a bar known to the damnificados. But in the end this is unnecessary because a damnificado overhears a drunken soldier boasting about a raid on the tower.

"Two weeks!" shouts the soldier. "And that tower will be empty! The Torres kid's a hustler. He'll be mayor in a year! And I'm gonna be by his side!"

The following day, Nacho is with his brother and the priest.

"I'll go to Solitario," he says. "See if I can find the older Torres and ask him to talk his brother out of the invasion."

"I'm coming with you," says Emil.

"No. You need to stay here and take over the leadership. If something happens, we'll need a leader."

"No way, little brother. How are you going to get to Solitario on your own? It's in the wilderness. There's nothing there but wild animals and monks."

"I'll ask the twins to take me. If they can't do it, I'll go alone. I'll be OK."

"Those twins are just kids. You need me to take you."

"We need you here. Don Felipe, am I right?"

"You're right," says Don Felipe. "Emil, you should stay."

"Dammit," says Emil. "I need an adventure, not a week baby-sitting damnificados."

"I won't be gone a week. I'll find Torres, persuade him to come back with me, and then I'll return. That's all."

In the event, the twins cannot go. Their father needs them to work. Nacho asks if one of them can go, but they look at each other.

"We've never been apart," says Hans.

"Where he goes, I go," says Dieter.

"And where I go, he goes," says Hans. "And our father needs the truck. It's that time of year."

"I understand," says Nacho.

Maria, Emil and Nacho sit around a table examining a map. The yappy dog is silent for once, scratching away at some itch in an absurd canine contortion under the table. Emil traces a route with his finger.

"It's here. See, it's not even named. Solitario is here. I went across the plains here, years ago. It was icy cold."

Maria snorts. "How do you know this map is reliable? It looks about a hundred years old."

"It *is* about a hundred years old," says Nacho. "I got it in an antiques store."

"Your route is this," Emil goes on. "You need to catch a train to Bieb ta 'Niket. There's one every two days that leaves from Fellahin. The train will go through forests, over mountains. Don't get off, whatever you do. That's bandit country. Keep your head down. Once you're in Bieb ta 'Niket, you'll need to go across the plains to Solitario. There's no public transport. It's in the middle of nowhere. Can you ride a horse and take another one along?"

"Emil, I can't even ride a bicycle. You know that."

"That's why I should be going with you."

Maria says, "Why does he need two horses?"

"Because he's trying to bring Torres back and Torres is a fat ox. At least he *was* before he became a monk. If you can't do the last part of the trip alone, you'll need to find someone to take you by horse and cart or you may get lucky if someone has a truck or car. It's rumored that recluses and monks live there, but you'll have to ask around for Torres's whereabouts."

"Last I heard, he was in a wooden hut. No electricity or running water."

"Hey," says Maria, "sounds like a wild goose chase to me. What if you don't find him? Or if he won't speak to you? Or doesn't recognize you because he's lost his mind? Or maybe he moved somewhere else."

"I'll take that chance," says Nacho. "We don't have much choice."

"In bocca al lupo," says Maria.

"That's the second Italian idiom I've heard in three days."

Emil says, "What does it mean?"

Maria replies, "It means good luck."

"But the words mean something else," says Nacho. "In the mouth of the wolf."

✳

Nacho boards the train outside Fellahin. The Chinaman hands him his gray burlap bag and salutes him goodbye.

Emil embraces Nacho and says, "Remember to keep your head down. No one will save you in Bieb ta 'Niket. Solitario neither. It's wild there."

Nacho takes a seat in an empty carriage. The cushion of ripped plastic leaks a tuft of yellow foam, but Nacho is comfortable enough, relieved to be seated and alone for now. Above his head is a luggage rack, and next to him a large window, smeared with patches of grime. He places his muletas under the seat, rests his arms on the table in front of him, and tries to clear his mind.

The train bumps into motion, stutters once, twice, then pulls away at a steady pace. The outskirts of the city move by.

Nacho spreads out the map on the table and plots the route in his mind for the tenth time. He recognizes the names of the towns closest to Fellahin, and tries to remember those places where he has already been.

He looks out the window, seeing the last vestiges of Fellahin: a gaggle of children playing with a ball beside the bone-dry creek, all remnants of the flood having disappeared. A trash pile comes into view, overseen by hovering birds and garbage-sorters picking at the shallow mountain for bits of metal, glass, and plastic. Then the next town.

As he passes Cancello del Dolore he sees men tilling distant fields, backs bent, wide-brimmed hats warding off the sun. Behind them, mountains rise, the deep shadowed crevasses rippling downward, where here and there a trickle of water becomes a cascade. Goats dot the mountainsides, white flecks nosing past clumps of gorse and heather. The sun is rising.

As the morning settles, they pass dozens of villages: Maqsuma, where the great poet Khalid Khamseen went to live in a cave for the last decade of his life; Vojta, where the autumn winds once lifted a house clean off the ground and deposited it in a field; Ti Kras Moun, ruled by a family of dwarves; and Toten Hund, a hamlet where they built a cemetery for dogs on the side of a hill and where they said you could hear ghost-hounds howling at night.

At Pobrea he sees wretches—men and women in tatters, like rag dolls, sitting dead-eyed in doorways or collapsed on the street; shirtless children wandering to and fro; and a man pushing a shopping cart stuffed with boxes and polythene bags. Here there is nothing but crumbling shacks already half reclaimed by the weeds and the owls, with ivy—like the fingers of a lunatic—choking the life out of the walls.

In Caryatid he sees the corpse of a lion abandoned in a cage, all rib bones and discolored flesh, the thing having been picked clean long ago by the vultures and rats. The sight shocks him and then it is gone as the train ambles its leisurely way toward the wastelands.

At Piede di Dio the train shudders and lurches for a moment and stops. Nacho sees agitated figures jogging, hears a hubbub of languages shouted at cross purposes, and ponders every moment of the delay. What is happening? Suddenly the train pulls away again, finding its cadence, opening out onto vast plains, tracts of untouched land.

Later they pass a mine, a great gouge in the earth where hundreds of men are milling, tiny shapes against the louring landscape.

"Ticket, please."

He pulls out the ticket from his pocket and the collector stamps a hole in it with his ticket punch and moves on.

By now Nacho has lost track of time, so he looks out the window again to get a glimpse of the sun high in the sky. Midday, he thinks. The train pulses onward, a slow-burning flame on a five-hundred-mile fuse.

Now they pass the badlands of Hildako Lapur, where a band of marauders once burned a monastery to the ground while fifty monks were praying inside. It is said that, eighty years on, the town still smells of burning flesh, and visitors cannot walk its streets without a mask to keep out the stench.

Outside Pozemek, the train comes to a stop because of cows wandering on the track. An old herder on a donkey chases them off, waving his stick, and the train recommences its gentle chugging across the landscape.

He dozes. He wakes.

The train passes Aokigahara Forest, densely packed with trees, a famed suicide spot where the young and depressed come to speak with the ancestors, ruminating with the spirits of the dead. Through the thicket of trees, Nacho sees sunbeams pinned in thick diagonal wedges to the leafy earth, casting the massive trunks in silhouette.

And when the forest eventually ends, there on the brow of a hill in the distance Nacho makes out the shapes of three crosses. Golgotha in stark relief, three sinners roasting in the sun. Are they real or is he still asleep and dreaming?

'What if Maria is right?' he thinks. 'What if I can't find Torres? Or if the man won't talk to me? Or maybe he is dead. This is wild country. Bandits and bears abound.'

He has never been to these parts before and the territory seems alien. 'What languages are spoken here?' he wonders. 'What cries did those men on the cross utter before the buzzards picked out their eyes?'

He dozes again and when he wakes, he senses immediately the presence of others even before he opens his eyes. Jammed in by the window, he feels a child's stare upon him, and the writhings of beasts, and the stillness of the very old. In his carriage are ten people, a dog and six chickens. An old man with a flat, brown face, wrinkled from the sun, and wearing a paisano's hat, sits opposite, and on his lap, his granddaughter staring at Nacho with a quizzical look. The rest of the carriage is filled with a family of eight, the four boys looking like time-lapse versions of one boy from the age of six to sixteen, all identically dressed in working jeans and checked shirts, faces also browned by the sun.

In a cage besides Nacho's feet the chickens are behaving impeccably. They occasionally nod their heads as if to acknowledge that, yes, they are in a train going from somewhere to somewhere and, yes, this is their predicament in life, this is exactly what they are supposed to be doing and they have no objections for now.

The sun is lower, beaming in on the carriage, and together with the heat of the passengers and the smell of the chickens, it makes the air thick, nauseating.

Nacho opens his bag and eats a hunk of bread and cheese. The little girl watches him so intently he wonders if she is hungry. He offers her the hunk of bread but she hides in her grandfather's tunic and only resumes staring after several minutes. The grandfather smiles at Nacho.

Nacho feels relieved when the family gets off at Zabiják, leaving behind two chicken feathers which hover in the air then float under the seat. He looks again at the map and sees that Bieb ta 'Niket is close, maybe thirty minutes or less.

Now he stares intently at the landscape in which he will soon find himself friendless. He will have to travel the last leg to Solitario in near-darkness, not knowing if there is a floor on which to rest his head. He has a blanket and a knife, a few provisions, but he understands he is entering the unknown, looking for a man who has chosen to disappear.

Outside, as the sun begins to wane, tiny hamlets and settlements with no name pass by. Nacho sees a circle of caravans, like some community of squatter-pilgrims frozen in midsiege against the barbarians. The only moving thing is a whorl of black smoke winding its way up the sky from a cooking fire in the center of the circle.

The temperature drops. Low hills curve on the horizon but the plains here are bare and vast. Small clumps of foliage rise from the land: catclaw and ratany, hopbush and jimson weed, and bulbs of cacti growing one on the other like tumors the size of human heads.

Nacho shivers and covers himself with the blanket. Maria lent it to him. She saw the moth-eaten rag he was taking and handed him a drape of Irish fleece. He thanked her without thinking, but now he is grateful.

He sees a painted sign on a wooden board: Bieb ta 'Niket. The train slows and comes to a stop. He slings his bag over his shoulder, picks up his muletas from under the seat, and walks to the corridor. Two others get off at the station. He negotiates the steps slowly and feels the cold scythe through his jacket and the fleece as the last rays of the·sun descend.

A ghost station. Nobody about. A low building, little more than a wooden cabin, stands beside the track. It bears a sign but written in hieroglyphs, some alphabet Nacho doesn't recognize. He pushes at the door. Locked. He looks around for the two who arrived on the same train, but they have already melted into the dark. He sees another sign, runic, indecipherable, but one line looks like an arrow so he follows it. It leads to a gate in a chain-link fence, the exit. He ambles out, looks both ways, and goes left because there, under a cavernous star-flecked sky, he sees a faint glow of night-lights, perhaps a tavern or some place where he can negotiate a ride to Solitario.

He hobbles along a stone path, sees his breath a corkscrew of blue-white smoke in the frozen air. Flat land all around. No hills. Few trees. Heading toward the light, he stumbles a moment then retrieves his balance. The road is rutted, the shallow furrows of a four-wheeled cart, the light trough of a horse's hooves. He has libros. He can pay for a ride to Solitario, but then will they take his money? Do they even use money? Many of the villages in the badlands still barter for goods. He never thought of this, and he has nothing to barter with except his knife, the fleece blanket and a little food.

As he approaches he sees that the light comes from a dilapidated farmhouse. The roof is patched up with thatch and plastic awnings and as he nears the building, he sees that the stone walls look close to collapse. He stops outside the door and listens. Nothing. Just the glow of a light from within. He turns, looks back along the path, and out to the distance. He sees nothing but the hazy outline of the station. With no other lights or signs of habitation, he knocks at the door.

A moment passes. He knocks again.

He hears a faint shuffling of feet. The door creaks open. And who is on the other side? Nacho raises his gaze and sees . . . himself. The hair unkempt and overgrown like a hedgerow in the barrens, the small-boned figure, barely a feather above five feet tall, the smooth skin of youth giving way to the first traces of middle-age, the same brown eyes and olive skin. They stare at each other for a moment. First the man sees his own face, then he looks down at the body, seeing Nacho propped up on his wooden mulatas. The man's eyes blink rapidly.

"Kdo jste?"

Nacho's heart sinks. He doesn't know the language. The man barks it the second time.

"Kdo jste?!"

Nacho looks him in the eye.

"Do you speak English?"

The man stares blankly at him, still taking in his mirror image.

Nacho tries again. "Spanish? Portuguese? French? German? Italian?"

"Co chceš? Co chceš?! Nemám žádnou hotovost."

The man grimaces, but thinks to himself that this stranger is no threat—he's too small, he's a cripple, and he has the most trustworthy face in the world: mine. The vagabonds and madmen, the marauders and sicarios don't knock gently on doors and stand two meters back. But nonetheless, whatever he wants is his problem. This is the hour when day turns to night.

"Proč si klepat na dveře? Tohle je můj dům."

Nacho thinks fast. He remembers his days interpreting, traveling to foreign lands. Smile. Disarm the man. Find common ground.

"Solitario," he says. "Solitario. I need to go to Solitario."

He plays with the word in as many accents as he can. "Sow lee tario. So LIta RIO. Sore leetriow."

Until the man repeats, "Solitario. Solitario? Ne."

The man points to the wilderness.

"Solitario je támhle. Je to daleko odtud. Solitario je daleko."

The man has stopped shouting at him.

"How can I get there?"

The man stares at Nacho. Looks at his boots. Gestures for Nacho to come inside.

"Pojď dovnitř domu."

The interior is an impossible crush of objects lit by a fire burning in the hearth. In the flickering shadows, Nacho makes out only the miscellaneous shapes, a bazaar of the random and the lost: a matryoshka doll, a Javanese pot, a worm-eaten saddle, a leather suitcase with string handles, a set of British encyclopedias from 1926, a pair of stuffed parakeets in a cage. Something stirs and Nacho realizes there is a dog lying on the floor in front of him. It has the same lines, the same sharp angles, as a wolf.

There is hardly space to place his muletas as he traverses the room, but he somehow clambers over to a spare chair by the fire, where the man has directed him to sit. On the other chair, Nacho sees a half-finished plate of food and realizes the man had been eating.

The man picks up his plate and discards it on a side table. Now they observe each other, like figures in a hall of mirrors. Nacho searches for words, but before he can talk, the man speaks.

"Solitario. Solitario je daleko. Potřebujete koně." He gestures a holding of reins. "Nemám koně," the man goes on, pointing to himself, waving his finger, and shaking his head.

"I understand," says Nacho. "I need a horse but you don't have one. Then how can I get to Solitario? How? Como? What can I do?"

The man goes silent, squints at the fire. Nacho tries another tack.

"Torres. Torres?"

The man registers nothing. A few moments pass. Nacho peers at him, searching his features in profile to see if he and the man really are doppelgangers. Then he sees that the man isn't squinting at the fire at all; his eyes are closed and his breathing has assumed the depth and regularity of sleep. His fingers are clasped on his lap in a gesture of perfect repose.

The dog stirs, shifts its position as the fire crackles. 'How is it possible,' thinks Nacho, 'that a man lets a stranger into his house and falls asleep in midconversation?'

"Solitario," he says, as loudly as he dares. Pleading.

The man wakes up with a start and looks across at Nacho. He gets up and finds a pen and paper and draws a horse and carriage.

"Stoller," he says.

Nacho shrugs his shoulders.

"Johann Stoller." He points at the horse and cart and gestures outside, his hands tracing twists and turns along a path.

The man puts on his boots and a black winter coat, says something to the dog, which gets up and pads to the doorway. Then he ushers Nacho out of the house, and walks with the dog at his side. They take the stony path, turning right and then left, making their way through the dark.

They reach a house and the man bangs at the door and shouts something in the same language he used before. An older man—large, rugged, and bearded—comes to the door. This is Stoller, his voice as deep as an ocean. He peers at Nacho.

"You want to go to Solitario?"

"Yes."

"You have a horse?"

"No."

"It'll cost you one hundred libros. You have it?

Nacho pats his bag.

"Yes. I have it here."

"You have somewhere to stay?"

"No."

"You can sleep in the barn out back. We leave tomorrow at sunrise."

"OK. I thank you. I'm looking for a man called Torres. Came here a couple of months ago."

"I'll take the money before we go. You change the deal, you pay double. You try to trick me, my sons will come after you. You have food?"

"Yes."

"You'll need it. Is that the thickest coat you have?"

"Yes. Yes, it is."

"I have a bearskin you can use. Here. Sleep under this. You'll freeze otherwise and I'll have to dispose of your body."

Stoller closes the door with a nod. Nacho turns to thank his doppelganger, but the man is already disappearing into the gloom, his dog trotting at his side.

CHAPTER 17

In the morning, Nacho is woken by the sound of Stoller talking calmly to the horse in an alien language. It could be horse language for all Nacho knows. Stoller slides the shafts of the carriage through the tug loops and works the tugs until he can lay them flat on the shafts. As he attaches the trace to the carriage, the horse—magnificent beast, chestnut brown with a thick white stripe running the length of its head—whinnies gently and swishes its tail. Stoller pats the animal on the rump and climbs onto the carriage, reins in hand.

Nacho staggers to his feet and brushes the hay from his clothes. He drapes the bearskin over his shoulder and slips the muletas under his armpits. He struggles into the carriage, seating himself next to Stoller, hands over one hundred libros, and without a word the big driver clicks his tongue and the horse pulls forward.

In the light of day, the expanse of the wasteland yawns open, miles upon miles of nothingness. The path soon peters out, turning to rough ground, gorse and bracken, and vortices of dust lifted by the wind, pluming up like geysers. Ahead of them, a wake of buzzards circles in the air.

Stoller weaves the horse and cart around clumps of cactus, but the land is uneven and the cart jolts constantly. Nacho sits rigid, trying to give himself imaginary ballast so he will not be tossed out.

In the distance, from out of the morning haze, a mountain range looms into view. Its orange walls are streaked with horizontal strips measuring out time and erosion. The horse and cart moves parallel to the mountains, and they pass a rock formation that looks like a hooded nun.

Late morning, the weather turns cold. There is barely a trace of wind, but the temperature drops and the sky clouds over as if veiled with a sheen of ash.

Beyond the mountains now, they come to a frozen lake, a scratched plate of reflecting glass. Stoller steers the horse through the middle of it.

"The screaming man," he says.

Nacho looks at him uncomprehendingly, then Stoller points down. They pass a man frozen under the surface of the lake. His face is trapped in midscream, hands raised, imploring. Nacho sees it momentarily, the image blurred by the thickness of ice, and he shudders.

The far side of the lake is ash. A gray flat plain. They pass the remnants of a buried town, the flaked and busted timbers of a hovel's roof cracking in the sun, the spire of a church peeking out of the ash like the blade of an oversized knife. Stoller points at a peak in the distance.

"Volcano. Erupted a hundred years ago. Buried everything."

They move on, no sound but the horse's steady hoofbeats in the dust until, one hour later, the sky ripples, starts to crackle with electricity.

They are arriving at the end of the world. Stoller, bearish in his windcheater and hat, slows the horse and announces "Solitario" like some kind of tour guide. But there is nothing to see. A land without boundaries. No beginning or end.

"This is it," Stoller says.

"How long can you wait?"

"Wait?"

"To take us back."

Stoller looks at him blankly

Then he says, "You want to return?"

And suddenly it dawns on Nacho that people come here to die. Or perhaps to renounce worldly life. From the land of ascetics and hermits, sannyasins and sadhus, there are no return journeys. Stoller takes people here and leaves them, turns his horse around, and expects never to see them again in this world or the next. Nacho wonders how many Stoller has brought here, but does not ask. Instead he says,

"I'm looking for someone. A man named Torres. I have to speak with him and try to bring him back."

"Are you insane?"

"I have no choice."

"No one knows how big Solitario is. It may be one hundred miles, maybe one thousand. You can live here for years without meeting another soul. Somebody's playing a joke on you."

"Did you bring a man named Torres here? Maybe two months ago?"

"I've brought dozens of people here. I don't ask their names and I don't ask their reasons for coming. And I've never, ever brought anyone out of Solitario. At least not alive."

"He was a big man. Big moustache. Maybe still wearing his military uniform."

"I just told you. I don't ask names. And I don't have a head for faces."

"Do you always drop people *here*?"

"Yes."

"If you were a monk, where would you go from here?"

The man pauses, takes a deep breath. This is not his business. The little cripple looks at him imploringly.

"You need a water supply. You need shade. Something to build a fire. Wood. An elevated place to watch for animals."

"Where could I find all those things?"

"I just told you. Solitario is hundreds of miles long. You want to look, you look. I'm turning around. I have to get home before nightfall."

"Can you pick me up again in three days?"

"You *are* insane. How do I know you'll be here? You'll be dead. You don't walk too good. How will . . ."

"If I pay you first."

"What?"

"I give you the money. You just come back here same time of day in three days."

"I can do that."

"Then we do it. One hundred libros. Here. Take it. And if I bring Torres back he can go in the bed of the cart, right?"

"Right."

Stoller looks at Nacho. Then he says, "What happens if I don't return?"

"My sons will come after you."

✳

Nacho once knew a fisherman called Balzac. It was when he was living in Mangingisda where the waves sometimes reached fifty feet and whales would wash up on the beach. Balzac caught fish because he could think like a fish. Stooped and scrawny, he had terrible eyesight, was deaf as a brick, and barely had the strength to lift a barrel. But once in his ropy skiff, Balzac became part of the ocean, a fish among fish, leading them on, coaxing them in.

Now Nacho wills himself into thinking like a hermit. 'Where will I spend my days? What will I wish to see? Where would I position myself if I wanted to touch God?'

As he hobbles on the muletas, he memorizes landmarks and names them, says the words aloud and repeats them so he won't forget. He passes a cactus shaped like a bottle and calls it Spiked Drink; a sharp dip in the land, looking like an open mouth, becomes Jaw Drop. The trees give him shade but the earth is pocked with holes and ridden with duff, and on crutches, the walk is heavy going. He stops again and again, getting his bearings, trying to glimpse a clue, anything made by man—footprints, a torn rag, the ashes of a fire—but he can find nothing that tells him he isn't alone.

Steeped in the sounds of nature, he remembers he isn't looking for God; he's looking for Torres.

After hours of searching, Nacho sits on a rock and eats the last of his bread and cheese. From now on, it will be berries and plants, maybe a fish if he gets lucky. He remembers Maria's admonishment, her calling it "a wild goose chase" and thinks,

'Wild geese would be easier to find than Torres. And what happens next? What if Maria was right? What if I don't find him?' He remembers the words of Stoller, too: Solitario is enormous. It isn't a dot on a map; it's a vast expanse. There are no bounds, no beginnings or endings marked by signposts. There is just wild space, hidden nooks, endless hills, forests, caves, and in Nacho's heart he begins to realize he will never find Torres.

As he sits, his thoughts turn to the tower and all he has left behind. He thinks of the constant noise of the city—children's cries, calls to prayer, traffic, sirens and alarms, the shouts of vendors, and the chattering of TVs. These noises are in his bones now, and the quietness of nature seems alien.

He carries on wearily, wondering whether to call out to Torres. Should he shatter the silence? Would Torres not hide if he heard his name?

The sun goes down. Nacho stops and looks around. He isn't hungry but he knows he must forage for food. A few white-gilled mushrooms are growing at the foot of a tree. He picks at them, sniffs, says "Amanita phalloides," and discards the death caps.

He finds a sandy spot close to a dry stream bed. He pulls the blanket from out of his bag, lies down, and covers himself. He knows he should check his surroundings and build a fire, but a great wave of tiredness hits him. He aches all over.

As always, he sleeps badly. A sense of foreboding comes to him. Something bad in the tower. Nothing here. Invisible paths. Invisible hermits. Madmen come to die. He wakes and sees the sun barely risen. He limps to the stream bed, digs a hole, and splashes muddy water on his face. He sits back down and, for the first time, admits consciously the thoughts that have been nagging at him. What if Stoller doesn't return? Nacho will die here, having abandoned the tower. He will starve or freeze, stranded in this Nowhere with no way out. He will die, and leave the damnificados leaderless.

He pictures Emil lying on Maria's bed, half-naked, half-asleep, giving orders to Hans and Dieter and the Chinaman; now

Emil loading a World War II rifle as an army gathers in the plaza below; now the baker brothers, Harry and his kin, shooting out of the windows with French baguettes, and Raincoat hiding under the bed.

Why did he ever come here?

Nacho wanders all day, stopping only to forage. He picks from shrubs of whortleberries and chokecherries, spitting out the poisonous stones. Under a dead tree, he sees a cluster of black walnuts dropped to the ground, crushes them with his good foot, removes the warty green husks with his fingers, and eats.

He takes refuge from the sun in a hollow and sees a network of small caverns. He peers into them, says 'hello' in six languages. No answer. Still hungry, he fingers a covering of lichen and pulls off a layer of rock tripe, dropping the leathery dark leaves into his bag. He sees a seam of quartz close to a cave and finds a loose stone.

He finds a few spindly trees. He peels thin strips of bark and picks several clumps of dry moss. He adds the down from a growth of milkweed and builds a bed of tinder. He scrapes his knife against the piece of quartz again and again until it creates a shower of sparks that drop onto the tinder, which crackles gently into flame. He puts the burning tinder onto a bed of tamarack sticks and sees the smoke rise. In a tin bowl that he brought with him, he boils the rock tripe and a clutch of nettles.

He kicks the fire down and goes on, seeking out the flat land where his crutches will hold.

He decides to turn back, thinking that if he goto loot he will die. His only hope is to return to the spot where Stoller left him, and wait out the two remaining days. The list of landmarks has grown to over twenty, and he doesn't want to test the limits of his memory because one wrong turn will be the end of him. As he walks, he counts off the landmarks: the Crucifix Tree, the Burning Bush, Hole in the Wall, Jaw Drop, Spiked Drink.

The walk is harder than before, and he stops regularly. He crouches at the river, wondering if he can catch a fish with his hands. He looks around for the materials to fashion a net, but he has forgotten the lessons from his father, the ability to make something from nothing, and in any case his hands have grown soft and useless for making objects. Instead, he kicks open a rotten log, pulls out the white grubs, and eats them alive.

He builds another fire in the evening, eats a bowl of kinnikinic berries and dandelions, and watches the sky. Thirsty, he wanders a while in search of big leaves with accumulated rainwater, but finds none. Instead he swallows the juice of whortleberries and tries to get warm, wrapping himself in the blanket.

The second night is worse than the first. Hunger and cold. He enters a cave but hears the stirring of bats above him and goes back to the woods. He finds a place to camp out, lies down, and realizes it's crawling with bugs he is too tired to catch. He moves again in the dark until he gets to flat land and makes his meager bed there, turning and turning to fight off the cold, but then gets up and collects a bed of leaves for an extra cover. His body begins to shiver and he wonders if he will freeze if he falls asleep. Somehow he doesn't and the night passes, a sky full of stars long dead winking down on him from another age.

In the morning he digs a seep in a dry creek bed, and drinks. He feels the pangs of hunger gnawing at his insides, but while he has strength keeps following his landmarks toward the spot where Stoller left him.

In the middle of the day he is overcome by fatigue and hunger and stops to rest on a rock. He eats some amaranth and cattail and a handful of wild mushrooms and soon his mind begins playing tricks. Psychedelic bushes, talking ferns, a two-headed Torres in a soldier's uniform prancing like a peacock. A swirl of color, projectiles skidding at him like boomerangs of glass, faces hidden in the trunk of a tree. He thinks of the effects of burundanga and levo-duboisine, the hallucinogens Emil told him about, potions used by the bruja of Estrellas Negras. A wave of nausea washes over him. He lies down on the duff and closes his eyes. For an hour he is drifting in and out of consciousness, seeing and unseeing carved stone saints, a yogi levitating, dreadlocked sadhus with talcum-whitened faces.

In his state of half-sleep he wonders if he is dead. The stillness, the silence, it could be Heaven, but then he is returned to the world by a voice singing in a smooth baritone, slightly out of tune: "I was born under a wandering star. I was born under a wandering star. Wheels are made for rollin'! Mules are made to pack! I've never seen a sight that didn't look better looking back. I was born under a wandering star. I was born under a wandering star."

He knows the voice. It rings clean and true in his memory like a hammer striking a bell.

Not twenty meters away, Emil is walking in dappled sunlight, leading a heavy black horse. His eyes alight on Nacho.

"Whoah," he says, and not to the horse.

Nacho is lying on the floor of the wood, so Emil appears to him upside down and though Nacho knows the physique and the swagger and the dulcet voice, some part of him thinks he is still hallucinating. He fights to focus, zooming in and out, trying to locate the figure in space and make sense of this noise-maker in a land of silence. He staggers to his feet and, seeing Emil in three dimensions, lurches forward without his crutches. He falls down again, like a drunk poleaxed by shock and headspin, toppling toward Emil's feet, where he catches a glimpse of a pair of madcap boots—Sicilian pullstraps, hand-stitched Parisian outsole, and an ornate tan shaft with a Greek warrior sewn on.

Emil hauls Nacho up by the shoulders.

"Damn, Nacho, you got skinnier In three days. What were you doing— fasting in the wilderness?"

"It's really you."

"Sure is. Come to take you home."

Nacho stands there trembling. He begs something to eat and Emil reaches into a saddle bag and pulls out bread and cheese, which Nacho devours. Then he takes great swigs of Emil's water.

"Easy, brother," says Emil. "You're OK. We're getting out of here."

Nacho sits on a rock, keeps eating, feels lightheaded as if still hallucinating. Eventually, he says, "I can't find Torres. I can't find anyone. It's a wilderness out here. I walked for two days, saw no one. Not a trace. My food ran out so I've been eating leaves and berries and whatever I could find. It's good to see you, brother. You have no idea. Maria's going to kill you."

"Wrong! Maria *sent* me. She asked me what the hell I was doing letting my little brother go to Solitario on his own, on crutches, on a wild goose chase. I couldn't answer so she answered for me. Packed a bag, stuffed five hundred libros in my pocket, kicked me out of the house, and said don't come back if you don't find Nacho. And I thought it was *me* she liked."

"I can't believe you're here."

"Quit gawping and get on the horse. We don't have much daylight left."

"Help me up."

Emil lifts Nacho onto the saddle, hooking his good foot into the stirrup.

"As for Torres the elder," says Emil. "We'll get no help from him. Not now."

"What do you mean?"

"I'll show you later."

"How did you find me?"

"I'm your brother. I think like you. You remember hide and seek when we were kids? I always knew where you were. Didn't even have to look. Sometimes I even knew one turn ahead where you were going to hide the next time."

"Who's in charge of the tower?"

"No one. They aren't children. But if anything happens I guess Maria will sort it out. You look kind of spooked. Are you OK?"

"I ate a root. Or maybe it was the mushrooms."

Emil leads them past Nacho's remembered landmarks until they are at the verge of the frozen lake. They pause and then cross, Emil walking ahead, leading the horse by the reins. Emil points down under the ice.

"There's Torres. He won't bother anyone anymore."

Nacho looks closer, recognizes the florid moustache.

"The Screaming Man," he says.

"Looks like he's just seen a wolf."

They are still some miles from Bieb ta 'Niket when the sun goes down, but Emil insists they keep going. The sky is smeared with orange strips, bars of flame shredded to wisps, and a massive moon full as a coin, blurred at the edges. By the light of this freak lantern, they find their way to Bieb ta 'Niket in silence, arriving in the dead of night. As they approach the few scattered buildings, they see the faint light illuminating the train station at Bieb ta 'Niket.

"Now what?"

"I have to return this horse," says Emil.

"Where?"

"A stable over there. A couple of miles away. You'll need to wait here."

"Don't tell me you stole it."

"I stole it."

Emil helps Nacho down and mounts the horse.

"If anything happens to me, like I don't return, get the next train from here. Take this." He hands Nacho a bag. "There's money and provisions in here—a blanket, some fruit."

"What do you mean, you don't return?"

"I stole the horse. Out here, they shoot people like me. If they catch me."

"Just get back here. I'll be waiting."

Emil gallops away. Nacho hobbles through the gate to the station. It is deserted. He sits on a bench, and then after a while, lies down. An hour later, Emil returns.

"There's an early train," he says. "Try to get some sleep."

He covers Nacho with his blanket, but Nacho lies awake.

"I met a man called Stoller. He took me to Solitario and promised to pick me up. I paid him already. He owes me a hundred libros."

"Ah, so you met Stoller."

"You know him?"

"Everyone knows Stoller. He was an assassin. One time he found himself out here for a job, to kill a monk who was the heir to some fortune, but instead of killing the guy, he had some kind of spiritual experience in the wilderness. He repented his ways and came to live here. I didn't know he was still alive. He must be seventy, seventy-five."

"He still looks strong. I guess I should get my hundred libros back. And save him a journey, too."

"No. It's the middle of the night. We'll wait a few hours. Get it once the sun is up."

*

Stoller answers the door in his windcheater and boots, as if he sleeps in them, rubs his eyes, hands over the money without a word, and closes his door on the outside world.

Then Nacho and Emil catch the train. They recount their adventures in the wilderness until, overcome with tiredness, Nacho drifts off to sleep. Emil looks out the train window, watching the landscape go by, and longs quietly for the open road, the great lashing sea. Eventually they arrive in Fellahin and take a rickshaw to Favelada.

CHAPTER 18

As they approach the tower, Nacho gets a tingling in his bones, senses something is wrong. In Solitario he had felt a sense of foreboding. Now his premonition—vague and undefined, but connected with loss—returns. A small crowd is gathered at the tower's entrance. Nacho and Emil dismount the rickshaw, pay the driver and walk toward the tower. The twins see Emil and Nacho and go out to meet them.

Hans says, "Come quickly. It's the Chinaman. They shot him."

The Chinaman stays in an anteroom, a boab's chamber besides the entrance. The door is ajar and a dozen people are around the bed in which the Chinaman lies with his eyes closed, a tableau from a sixteenth-century painting, Dutch, dimly lit. The air is thick with the smells of foggy breath and sweat and blood. Among the watchers are Don Felipe, the twins, Maria and two of Harry the baker's brothers. But it is Susana who administers to the Chinaman, mopping his brow with a damp rag. And as she tends to him, Nacho sees in an instant that she and the Chinaman are partners. She seems tiny next to the vast boulder that is the Chinaman's head and the deep mound of his chest that swells and contracts in slow rhythm. His torso is swaddled in a makeshift bandage, stained and heavy with blood.

"What happened?" asks Nacho.

Heads turn.

"You're back," says Don Felipe. "Torres sent his thugs. They were looking for you, but they shot the Chinaman instead."

"When?"

"This morning."

Maria gives Nacho a look. "Back from the wild goose chase? Good timing. The bullet had your name on it."

Nacho makes his way to the Chinaman's bedside. The bed is made of reinforced metal, with a scratched-up cedar wood headboard and legs of heavy iron tubing. The pillow is stained with sweat and grime.

Nacho looks at his old friend. The giant appears to be sleeping.

"How many of them came?"

One of Harry's brothers says, "Maybe six of them. Maybe ten."

"It was twenty," says his brother.

"I heard three," says Don Felipe.

"I thought it was an army," says another.

"There were five of them," says Hans. "One of them called out your name and said Torres wanted to talk to you. When the Chinaman came out to meet him, he shot him. Point blank."

"Everyone out," says Nacho. Nobody moves. "Clear the room, please. You too, Emil. And you, Maria."

They look at one another and, after a pause, traipse out.

"Not you."

He is staring at Susana. She stops, a wet towel dripping in her hand.

"What's your name?" he asks.

"Susana."

"Susana? Is he going to be OK?"

She ushers Nacho out of the room for a moment and into the waning sunlight. She is tinier even than him and looks up as she speaks.

"I'm not a nurse. But the bullet's in his chest."

"Why didn't we take him to a hospital?"

"We tried. No one would see him. We're damnificados. We can't pay."

"There's a free hospital in Fellahin. Why didn't he go there?"

"It was full. They had no beds or doctors. Some kind of massacre happened there yesterday. So we brought him back."

They return to the room and Nacho pulls up a chair and sits while Susana goes to the Chinaman's bedside. Nacho glances around. A gunny-sack in the corner. An open wardrobe with a few clothes, two pairs of shoes the size of duffel bags standing on a box by the wall, a fraying red carpet, and a table with the legs sawn off. On it, a white bowl of soup, half-full, its opaque surface glazing over like a pond.

Later, Nacho leaves the room as the sun goes down. A pair of chasing swallows comes swooping and the call to prayer rises across the rooftops. Nacho wipes his brow, glad to feel the evening air on his skin. Maria and Emil are outside waiting for him.

Maria says, "You need to get the bullet out. Otherwise he'll die."

"Susana thinks it's too late."

"She's a cleaning woman. What does she know? Find a surgeon. And don't take three days over it this time."

"How do we know we need to remove the bullet?"

"You want to leave a slug of lead inside him?"

"I don't know."

Emil says, "Does he have any family?"

"No. They're all dead. Look, there are fifteen hundred people in this tower. Someone must have a medical background."

"We're damnificados," says Maria, almost snorting. "We're the lowest of the low, remember? There aren't many doctors among us."

"We only need one."

"We don't have one. You need to go and find somebody."

"Have *you* tried?"

"I'm a hairdresser. And besides, when they shot the Chinaman, the first thing we did was lock down the tower. We closed the doors and got the weapons ready. We didn't know if they were about to start shooting everyone. We've been hiding out all day. They could still come back."

"If it was Torres, they *will* come back."

"It *was* Torres. One of the soldiers said Torres wanted to speak to you."

"Did you hear him?"

"No. The twins did. The man said Torres. And that he was looking for you, Nacho Morales. When the Chinaman blocked his path, he shot him."

"Torres. He didn't say what he wanted?"

"He wanted *you*. Now go and find a doctor."

But it's too late. Susana calls to Nacho, who goes back inside, alone. The Chinaman's eyes are open and he gestures with his hand for Nacho to come closer. Nacho shuffles to the bedside on his muletas, sits in the chair and leans toward the Chinaman. The giant turns his bear-like head a little, beads of sweat carving runnels in his waxy face, and squints hard in concentration.

"My name is Sato Kazunari Maeda. I am not Chinese. I am from Koizin Prefecture in Japan. My father was Hidetoshi Kazunari Maeda, greatest sumo wrestler of his generation. My mother was Kaori Kazue Maeda, most beautiful woman in province. Open drawer. Yes. There."

Nacho pulls open the drawer by the bedside and finds a black-and-white photo, warped and brown with age, of the Chinaman's mother and father, full-length, standing together, unsmiling. He is a head taller than her and the same build as the Chinaman, which is to say he looks as if he could pick her up in one hand. She has a flat, perfect face, painted white, large eyes, delicate features.

"When I was five years old, I was exiled from province because my father refuse to lose wrestling bout. It all fixed, you see. Gamblers make a lot money. When he refuse, he insult yakuza warlord. His punishment was to never see me again. I grew up orphan. Always alone. Now I don't want die alone. So I tell you my story."

"Why did you stay silent all your life? I've never heard you say more than three words."

"Silence suit me. Fools talk a lot. I live quietly. Work for you. You are good man, Nacho. Good man."

With that, Sato Kazunari Maeda's breathing quickens, then slows again. He closes his eyes and dies, his hand falling open. From the small, high window above his bed—the only window in the room—Nacho sees the last glow of the sun fading to deep orange, and hears the snarl of an evening bus as it turns a corner through the grim-gray streets of Favelada.

*

A day and a half later the cortege begins. They transport the body on a specially made catafalque, a platform of wood and steel which Lalloo rigged up with shining lights and electric horns. It rolls slowly through the streets on wheels purloined from a farmer's wagon in Gudsland, dragged by two Clydesdale draft horses called Samson and Goliath. The mares are shaggy-maned and heavy-boned, their wide, proud muzzles streaked with white.

The crowd is a salmagundi of every street dog that ever raised its nose and sniffed the wind: the shoeshine boys, the hookers, the addicted and the lame. They come in rags, burqas, combat pants, in patchwork suits and miniskirts. Stetsons, pork pie hats, bowlers, beanies, turbans, pakols and patkas, sweating through the midmorning sun, their shadows prefiguring them like prophecies. Past the sleek skyscrapers they roll, picking up onlookers and sympathizers, blocking the traffic on Kaijustrasse, where a street urchin shouts, "The Chinaman! The Chinaman!"

On Perek Avenue, six hookers climb out the windows in fishnets and heels and fancy hats and join the throng, cooling themselves with Chinese fans of bamboo and silk, commissioned specially for the occasion.

A traveling band strikes up a rhythm, banging on lids from garbage cans, ice cream tubs, tambourines of seashells, Nepalese Damphus, pots and pans, and hardwood djembes with goatskin heads, and a voodoo queen with a live python around her neck begins to dance, arms upraised, her long black skirts splaying out. As they pass Molotov Road, the street cleaners sling their mops over their shoulders and take up the walk and a man hanging off a garbage truck removes his hat and does a military salute.

The throng of walkers is a cortege and a party and a protest. A local artist drew a portrait of the Chinaman's face in bold strokes and they printed it up and made placards with the word "asesinado" underneath the image, and now they march to lift up the man from the long history of the corpses of the poor left lying in the dirt and to howl against his murder.

Leading the procession are Nacho on his muletas, Emil and Maria, Susana, and Don Felipe, all dressed in black, and squinting into the glare that bounces off the windows of the boutiques and the high-rises. Past perfumed Bamberlax Avenue they walk, and across the swell of Shiguru with its street cafés and sushi bars, and heads turn and faces appear in windows, and now a trumpeter is picking out a tune above the percussion, laying a high treble that peels into the air, the note as pure as gold.

They stop the traffic on Zalosti Mrtvhi Street. Motorbikes with families of four squashed together, a bicycle cart loaded ten feet high with rolls of wallpaper and cloth, growling cars regurgitating great billows of smoke, trucks with their beds packed full of standing, hollow-eyed damnificado workers—all stop as the cortege moves past.

The noise gathers on Moribondo Avenue, where they pass street merchants sitting on sheets laid out in the road, flogging their wares: bananas, candy, knock-off watches, designer bags, alarm clocks, shoes. Dogs with open sores lie in the street, and the cars and the walkers swerve around them in shallow arcs. The cortege passes a mission and a flophouse and a series of cheap hotels with flickering fluorescent lights. And then the telltale nests of blankets, cardboard boxes, dogs curled up, a bird in a cage—homes of the homeless.

Through all this, Nacho contains his fury, focusing his energy on the long walk. How can it be that a man goes to a tower in broad daylight and kills an innocent? And no one gives chase? The sentries on the high floors see nothing, do nothing. How can it be that his friend is dead and no one pursues justice?

They turn a corner and pass a slum, the land slick with grease and sewage. The horses whinny at the stink of rotten food and the smoky tang of burning plastic.

"Where are we?" asks Don Felipe.

"We haven't left Favelada," says Nacho.

"Is it safe here?"

"Safer than the tower right now."

The huge wagon jiggles on its wooden wheels, now past the riverbank of the slum. Washerwomen emerge from the water, one with a plastic bucket on her head. Squat, dark figures, their pants rolled up to the knees, they stop and stare, taking in the line of mourners and the two leviathan mares that lead them.

Now the wagon crushes stones and kicks up a nimbus of dust on a tree-lined street. Emil hears Nacho's breathing and says, "You OK?"

"Yeah."

And he is, because the music and the surge of the people drive him onward even in the heat.

Maria, in dark glasses and black dress, hair down, stops and pulls off her high-heels and resumes walking in bare feet.

Even the sun has come to pay homage. It glows brighter than ever on the hottest day of the year, paying its respects to the Chinaman who wasn't Chinese, pouring its beams down on the black sarcophagus.

Across the shantytowns of Oameni Morti, Agua Suja, Dieux Morts, Sanguinosa, and Favelada, the people whisper in awe.

"His name will live on."

"He's a legend."

"Biggest man I ever saw."

"I once served him stew. He ate the whole pot."

"Saw him strangle an ox."

"I saw him lift a car."

"He uprooted a tree in Maialino."

"I was there when he broke down the door of the Torres tower."

"He was a gentle soul."

"Never said a word."

They pick up a trio of bongo players, Afro-Cuban boys in bright white shirts and leather sandals, denizens of the mojito bars in outer Favelada, and the drumming escalates as the procession turns to a copse on the edge of Favelada, in blessed relief to be in the shade.

Suddenly the music stops. Emil halts the horses and Nacho is hoisted onto a tall stump between the trees. He tousles his hair and wipes a trail of sweat from his cheek. The mourners crowd around, packed in the hundreds.

Nacho says, "The Chinaman. May he rest in peace."

The crowd begins to cheer and the cheer turns into a roar and for a moment Nacho thinks he can hear an animal in the roaring, a wolf or a lion or a bear, but then he looks down at the faces and sees only damnificados. They wait for him to say more but he doesn't because the Chinaman was a man of few words and his funeral will be the same.

The twins help Nacho down from the dais and some of the drummers strike up a rhythm. A group of teenagers start to dance, and three women in white begin to ululate. Nacho thinks this rhythm and this wailing will take them all the way to the five stone heads at the gates of the city for the Chinaman's final farewell. But first they have to bury the body. Emil clicks Samson and Goliath into motion and the procession moves on toward the burial ground.

"You remember the way to the cemetery?" says Nacho.

"Of course. That's like going home. I hope the road holds out."

A minute later they pass the House of Flowers and Nacho and Emil stare as they walk by.

They arrive at the cemetery and the caretaker, head to toe in black, comes out to meet them. His eyes are watery with drink and he has the face of someone who lives next to the dead.

"We're here to bury the Chinaman," says Nacho.

"You're too late," says the man.

"What do you mean? We spoke to you yesterday."

"The last three plots have been sold. Just now. Someone bought them, paid cash."

"Then where do we bury the Chinaman?"

"Find another place. There's no space here."

"There is no other place," says Nacho. "This is where he'll be buried."

"I sold the last plots."

"Then dig new ones."

"Where? There's no space."

Nacho turns to the cortege and says to Don Felipe, "Please wait here."

Then he beckons Emil over and says, "Walk with me. This idiot just sold the last plots. The people here will kill him. What do we do?"

"Who bought the last plots?"

Nacho turns to the caretaker and asks the same question.

"Someone sent by the . . . the Torres family, I think the name was. I can look it up in the book."

"No need."

Nacho and Emil walk through the cemetery in the full heat of the day, looking for a space—a large space—for the Chinaman. The graves are jammed tight together. Some headstones are little more than blocks of wood with scrawled names and dates; others are carved granite or sandstone with messages etched out and chiseled angel wings, crossed swords, a dove, a torch, a cherub, a star.

On the edge of the cemetery is stony ground, sandy-colored and rutted with the tracks of carts. Now Nacho and Emil walk the perimeter. They pass the graves of their parents, see the inscription and a small pile of dead flowers disintegrating, and keep walking. They are close to giving up when Emil sees a pile of trash in a hole.

"Hey!" he calls out to the caretaker, who has been following them at a distance. "How deep is this?"

"That hole? That's full of trash."

"How deep is it?"

"I don't know. It's been there since the massacre about twenty years ago. But it was never finished and now it's just for trash."

"Where are your gravediggers?" says Emil.

"They aren't here."

"Then give me a shovel."

The caretaker goes to his hut and brings out a shovel. Emil balances down the side of the slope, poking with the shovel at the pile of soggy cardboard, paper, and plastic. He thrusts the shovel in deeper, feeling for where it hits the bottom, and lowers himself, kicking at the trash to check for rats. He starts to shovel out the garbage, making a small pile at the caretaker's feet.

"Hey," he says. "You work here, right? Then get some more shovels. Nacho, call the twins."

Emil and the twins take off their jackets and deepen the hole. The trash is bound fast to the soil, encasing the hole in a layer of mulch that has been there for two decades, but they channel it out and hurl it onto the heap above. They assume a manic pace, throw off their shirts, and dig like fury while the mourners in the cortege stand dumb and watch.

And there, in the same hole he had been digging twenty years earlier, before the gunshots of murderous soldiers sent him running for cover, the Chinaman is buried. The woman with a dog in a wheelbarrow looks on from her place near the head of the cortege, and remembers. Quietly, she says to herself, "I saw him digging that hole a long time ago. He was just a boy."

The casket is lowered on four thick ropes held by twelve of the tower's strongest men, who pause a moment before letting it drop its final inches, and Emil and the twins shovel the dirt back onto the box, and keep shoveling until it is drowned in mud and tiny stones and out of sight.

Then they wipe the sweat from their faces with the backs of their arms. Emil kicks a sheaf of mud from his boots, spits a pearl of saliva at his feet. He flings the shovel hard into the ground and it stands up, vibrates, and settles, erect as a crucifix. He pulls his shirt over his head and takes a final look into the Chinaman's abyss. The land is level, the soil fresh.

"Rest in peace," he whispers.

He picks up his jacket, slings it over his shoulder, and, all bandy legs and fancy boots, walks back with Nacho to the head of the cortege. In silence, the mourners move one by one to the grave, led by Susana, her head covered in a black veil. After her, the mourners toss in mementoes, trinkets to keep the dead man company on his journey, and harbingers of good fortune in the world to come: flowers, candy, coins, paper swans, gemstones, tiny pots of clay, and inch-high marble heads.

As the cortege turns away, Maria mutters to Emil, "What the hell happened? You had to dig his grave here and now?"

"Torres bought the last plots of land. He knew we were coming to bury the Chinaman. There was nowhere left."

"So you buried him in a pile of trash?"

"We removed the trash. You saw us. Every last piece. I checked it for rats and snakes. There's nothing there but worms and the man."

*

The party at the five stone heads stretches long into the night. There are go-go girls in feathered hats and tutus, a trio of break-dancers, and a man in a skeleton suit who pulls out a violin and plays a solo, a long twisting threnody eking its path through the city. Beside the stone heads, a line of chefs in aprons stand at their grills, flipping pieces of chicken and husks of corn, the smoke floating ghostlike, engulfing their faces. At midnight the crowd hoists a whirling dervish onto the middle head and the drummers hammer a rapid tattoo as he twists to a frenzy. They build fires in a rough circle, piling broken furniture from a Favelada warehouse, and in the light of the flames the damnificados dance, heroic in their adumbral glow, their shadows dancing bigger and wilder behind them.

But even as they celebrate him, the Chinaman's visage has already begun to pass from their minds. They see his shape, his mass, but his face becomes a blur. Was he a handsome man? Surely he had a wide forehead, or was it narrow? His hair was always tied back from his face and bunched in a pigtail, wasn't it? Or was it loose with a curled forelock dangling down?

The placards are propped against a low wall, but some have fallen and are now face down on the street and his image is fading fast. If they ever knew, the damnificados, besides Nacho, begin to forget how he died.

And even as they mourn him, what few possessions he had lie in a cardboard box and the first traces of mold begin their cancerous crawl. They burned his bloodstained shirt but the other clothes are badly folded and someone let his tea glass crack when they filled the box and another didn't check his socks for damp and now they begin to fester in the pile. They left his door open to air the room because they said a dying man's breath contains all the chemicals and the carbon dioxide and the argon of everything he ever swallowed and it gives off the stench of decomposition even when the man is still alive. But they let in the maggots and the ants and the insects, and the cockroaches paid a visit, too, fellow travelers on a bloody pilgrimage, and now the Chinaman's room has the woebegone pallor of the dead. Where once wolves bristled and huddled against the cold and rain, and where the Chinaman followed them, reclining on his reinforced bed, sharpening wooden knives with metal ones, now only the lesser beasts flit and scurry and climb his cracked walls.

The moon soars, almost expunged as the light of the new day fires. The last revelers are crumpled on the stone heads, spread-eagled like corpses, or sat with their backs to the city gates, sucking on a final bottle while the man in the skeleton suit plays a lone note on his violin which resolves into a folk song played at an adagio crawl that slows to larghissimo, as if the violin itself is drunk.

Across the land, the day is pulsing into motion. At the heart of Favelada a symphony of car horns begins. An alarm in Oameni Morti emits its ceaseless electronic squeal. In Gudsland a cock crows and a hundred farmers roll out of bed and tug on their boots. At the sea of Kalashli, fishermen shout their greetings to one another across the water and their voices pass through the mist and bounce off the low waves that lap and kiss their barnacled tjotters. In Blutig six fighting bulldogs wake and bark and growl, and nuzzle at the bars of their cage. The sheen of ice that formed overnight in the wilds of Solitario begins to melt, and zigzagged cracks appear on the lake that inters Torres the Elder. In the dense woodlands of Sanguinosa four golden crested mynah birds twitter and babble their call and response and swivel their heads to look eastward at the rising sun.

Across the slums, damnificados turn in their raggedy beds—makeshift pallets, woodchip boards, piles of old newspaper wadded into mattresses—and writhe and groan in the denouements of their dreams as the sun blasts in through the cracks in doorways and the holes in roofs.

In the tower, Nacho sits up in bed in the half-light. All night he has been asking the same questions: how is it a man can be murdered like this and nothing happens to the killers? Where was the Chinaman's protection? How can justice be served when the police don't recognize us, when they think we're less than human?

He takes a deep breath and thinks of the other things he needs to do—prepare a lesson for his half-abandoned students, sort through the Chinaman's belongings, find himself a wife, and work out how to prevent Torres the Younger from decimating the damnificados—and promptly falls asleep again.

CHAPTER 19

When Nacho wakes, he investigates. With a rancid cup of coffee in his good hand, he hauls them all in one by one—the sentries who were on duty, Maria, the priest, the baker brothers.

"What did you see?" he asks a guard called Zaheer. The man is as skinny as Nacho, darker, with a tidy moustache and spidery hands.

"I see the car. Military. I go to ring bell but no. Bell gone. No bell."

"Where was the bell?"

"I don't know. I shout. But no one hear. Or not understand me. Man below no speak English."

Nacho brings in another sentry who was on duty that day. A big pale ham of a man, blue-eyed and bald.

"I'm on the fifteenth floor, I sees the car and the soldiers, I gets out my walkie-talkie, pass on the message like, but the other guards is all gettin' high. S'all they do. Tokin' on blunts all day, no wonder the shit hit the fan."

Nacho talks to the guards on every floor and it turns out that many of them speak no common language so they cannot communicate with one another. He learns that the walkie-talkies don't work, and the bells are missing, probably sold for scrap metal. He brings in Lalloo, who is red-eyed and hungover.

"What about the cameras?"

"What?" says Lalloo, sweating in his jeans and white shirt.

"The security cameras you put up?"

"They're fakes."

"You mean they don't work?"

"Are you crazy? Do you know how much the real things cost? And you need someone to monitor them. That's a full-time job."

"So we have no footage?"

"The cameras are plastic shells. They're hollow."

Nacho talks to the old soldier who set up the system of sentries on the walkways, but the man says he was asleep during the attack, only heard of it the day after.

And so it goes. No one knows anything. Even the twins aren't sure of what they saw or heard. All Nacho knows is that the Chinaman lies buried in the earth and the safeguards were useless.

Eventually, Don Felipe pays him a visit, tells him, "The killer will not be brought to justice until he comes face to face with God. This is the way of the world."

Nacho, sat at his table, is bent with fury. "Why? Why is this the way of the world?"

"Listen. People are saying things about *you*. They're asking why you weren't here when the asesinos came. They're saying you were on some wild goose chase, or on a vacation. A little boy was looking for you, asking if there was school today, and I heard someone answer that you were on holiday, taking a trip on a train. End your inquisition. It won't bring the Chinaman back."

"He wasn't a Chinaman, goddamn it. He was Japanese."

"I don't care to hear the Lord's name used like that. In any case, what does it matter? He's gone."

"It matters because you told me soon after we entered the tower that we had six hundred pairs of eyes to keep watch and keep us safe. Now we have fifteen hundred, and a good man was murdered and these fifteen hundred pairs of eyes saw nothing, and no one had the guts to chase the assassins or identify them or call the police. That's why it matters."

"People are afraid, Nacho. These men had guns. And what use would it do to call the police? To them we're squatters, the lowest of the low. We don't exist. What would the police do for *us*? And if they knew it was Torres who'd sent the assassins, they'd do even less."

"He's running for office. How can a man running for office send out assassins to kill his enemies?"

The priest looks at Nacho for a moment, brings his hands together as if in prayer.

"You have a lot to learn about the world. Men running for office routinely kill their enemies. It's been going on for thousands of years. This is how men achieve power. They take it by killing. You of all people should know this."

"OK, I know it. I know it."

"We can rebuild the defenses for the tower. Bring in new people, reorganize. Do whatever you have to do. But call off your inquisition and let the Chinaman rest in peace."

"For the hundredth time, he wasn't Chinese. His name was Sato Kazunari Maeda. He was the son of a great sumo wrestler."

"Then let's honor his memory and move on with our lives. You are our leader. It doesn't become you to harangue the people here. They are afraid, afraid that more men will return with weapons, afraid they will be made homeless again. They don't have your courage. Or Emil's. Please just let it be. Let the Japanese man rest in peace."

"His name was Sato Kazunari Maeda."

"Sato Kazunari Maeda. Let him rest in peace."

✳

Nacho changes the security routines. He places guards on every fifth floor, finds them walkie-talkies that work, and briefs them on what to do when they see visitors they don't recognize, or army trucks and soldiers. He places guards on the ground floor, twenty-four hours a day, all four sides of the building.

"It's becoming a fortress," says Nacho to Emil. "It was supposed to be a home."

And then something unexpected happens: nothing. For months on end. And the tranquility brings more damnificados in search of refuge.

Slowly, they arrive and become tenants: mule drivers, well diggers, palm tree trimmers, and a host of street entrepreneurs—the types who conjure up a batch of cheap umbrellas as soon as it rains or find the city's hottest traffic jams and walk between the cars selling bottled water at a marked-up price.

The influx continues—hotel workers, artists, migrants, window cleaners, road constructors—until the monolith is full. In lieu of rent they do jobs on the building or the surroundings. The window cleaners clean the windows, the men in construction repair walls and floors with smuggled tools, and others take shifts on the night watch, perched on the walkways of the high floors, binoculars jammed to their faces, or strolling the plaza below, looking out for enemies. Others tend the gardens, clear rubble, or help put water tanks on the roof.

Nacho greets the new arrivals and notices how different they are from his original damnificado army. These newcomers aren't dressed in rags. They aren't pock-marked by the travails of their lives; they are unwrinkled, they walk with straight backs, their hands are steady, and even the middle-aged have a full set of teeth. Nacho talks to them and discovers that few know what it is like to wake up under an overpass, build a cardboard home next to railway tracks, or squat in a tin shack at the end of a runway. He learns that some have years of education, can read and write as well as him. Others have ambitions beyond finding a roof to sleep under; they dream of better jobs, their own house, a place in the world.

The newcomers sleep in hammocks and tents until they can arrange mattresses to be brought in from reclaimed trash piles or used goods depots. They buttress their crumbling walls with stolen cement, and reinforce rusted guardrails on the walkways with cinder blocks.

Emil tells Nacho, "These new people are anarchists and artists. They aren't damnificados. They're opportunists. They're going to blow your little utopia out of the water."

"Why should that be, brother?"

"They're living here, taking advantage of all you've built. But they weren't part of your invasion, were they?"

"Neither were you."

"But I risked my neck to bring you food. Twice. And you know me. But, hey, it's your party. El pequeño lisiado."

"It's not my party. I'm not an elected official. But if we have empty rooms, they should be filled. We've always said the tower belongs to everybody. That's why we came in the first place."

"Yeah yeah. I hear you."

"And you sound more like Maria every day."

The brothers are on the walkway one floor up, standing in shade, drinking coffee that looks and tastes like river silt. Emil has his fidgeting dog on a leather lead. It has been three months since the murder of Sato Kazunari Maeda and the tower has remained unmolested, uninvaded.

"I need to get out of here," says Emil. "Just for a while."

"Can you wait?"

"For what?"

"Mayhem."

"What?"

"Torres Junior. The rumors have died down and we haven't heard from him, but I watch the news and read the papers. He's running for office, opening up businesses. Sooner or later he'll come for the family tower. You can be sure of it."

"It's been ages, Nacho. I think he's forgotten about the tower. Sit down, you stupid mutt!"

"No. He'll come."

"And when he does?"

"That's when I'll need you."

"To shoot those muskets? Fire a water gun? If Torres wants the tower, he'll get it. Unless the wolves show up again, we have no chance of protecting this place. He'll bring an army, and you've got what? Two thousand homeless scaredy-cats. Women and children."

"But they aren't homeless, are they?"

"If Torres comes, they will be. We all will be. And I'm sorry—I'd die for you, but not for a tower. It's bricks and mortar."

Together they look out over the square. Groups of damni-ficados are planting trees, sweeping paths.

"See those people below?" says Nacho. "See what they're doing?"

"Planting trees for this dog to piss on."

"You don't do that unless you want to stay somewhere for a long, long time. It takes years for a tree to grow from a seed. They're in their home here."

"Sure, little brother. But it isn't my home."

"Tell that to Maria."

They stand in silence for a moment, stopping to watch the world from on high. A child chases a pigeon until it flies away. A woman on a bicycle weaves her way through the walkers. Groups of sentries mill about, lighting cigarettes.

"Who's going to replace the Chinaman?" asks Emil.

"He's irreplaceable."

"I said this to you weeks ago. You need a permanent sentry at the gate. Someone has to mind the entrance, like the Chinaman did."

"I'm working on the twins. I know, I know. They're kids. But I'm all out of ideas at the moment. I can't trust any of the others. They like their substances. Or they have other jobs. Let me know if you find a soldier who can do it full-time."

"Get a defector."

"What?"

"Get one of the survivors from the wolf attack—one of the older Torres's men."

"I don't think so. D'you really believe they'll come near here again? Torres himself went crazy that day. The soldiers are probably still in hiding."

"Maybe." Emil shrugs.

"What are you doing for work?" asks Nacho.

"I've got some labor lined up next week in Basura. But there's a boat-building job waiting for me permanently in Ferrido."

"Your old job. Ask Maria if she wants to go mix with a bunch of tattooed sailors in a port. That's no place for a hairdresser."

"She'd adapt. She'd open a tattoo parlor. Or a brothel."

"Don't even think of it."

"You eaten?"

"No."

"Come over later. We'll crack open some wine. Meat and potatoes. Utopia. Want me to fix you up with a girl, too?"

"I'll see you at sunset. Clown."

Nacho teaches his class, but while they write, he finds himself lost in his own little reverie.

He is no longer in Solitario, but a little of Solitario is in him. He imagines life far, far away from the tower, from damnificados, from the Torres family. He is sitting in a swinging chair, drinking a mojito from a long glass, a clutch of fresh mint sitting on the surface. He is watching the sun go down over his land. It isn't the type of land owned by the rich—ten thousand acres ringed by pecan trees, stolen from the peasants—but just a modest leasehold, a patch where a dog can roam and where he can harvest corn, green beans, a little mint for his mojitos, a half-dozen apple trees. On an adjoining leasehold, Emil, rocking gently in a mohair hammock, waves at his brother, raises his glass. Maria, in a peasant smock and no make-up, comes out momentarily to stare at the sunset, trailed by the smell of baking bread.

"Mr. Nacho, how do you write motorcycle?" says a girl of twelve. Nacho limps over to the desk where the girl is sitting and pieces the word together with her, sound by sound.

"What's the mmm sound?" he asks, and she hazards an *m*.

When the class is nearly finished Susana appears, apologizing for her lateness, and he puts her in with a group, one of whom explains their task. Nacho wants to believe that he is now bonded to Susana by her tending to the Chinaman after he was shot, what he assumes was her love for the man, by her presence in the Chinaman's final moments, but she hasn't spoken to Nacho since, nor he to her. At night he ponders how he can talk to her about it, composes imaginary conversations with her, and in the morning wonders how he could ever be considered a leader when he cannot find the courage to talk to a washerwoman. He ponders, too, his mistake in thinking that she was looking at him the way a person looks at someone who they might fall in love with. Instead, she loved his best friend.

As class ends, he stands at the door and bids the students good night, Susana among them. He has trained some of the younger ones to help him tidy the room, and they do so, putting chairs back in place and dropping scraps of paper into a metal basket. Some days they sweep the floor, but not today. He thanks them and watches them disappear up the stairs to their homes, and begins his trudge to Maria's apartment for dinner.

"Where's the girl you promised?" he asks Emil.

Emil laughs. "I didn't see much enthusiasm from you, so I abandoned the plan."

Maria walks in bearing a tray of food. As they eat, Nacho tells them about the newcomers. A group of artists have begun a mural on the north wall of the tower. It depicts the history of the monolith: the two-headed wolf, the Chinaman, a swarm of mosquitoes emanating from a flood, and in the center, Nacho himself, made large and defiant and handsome, his muletas held like weapons, not crutches. The work is half-finished, with parts sketched only in outline, but Nacho tells Maria and Emil that it is a masterpiece that will make residents proud and give them a daily vision of their story. They nod in assent. Only Nacho thinks, 'The story isn't yet finished. Torres will come for the tower. He believes it's his birthright.'

After dinner, the three of them stand on the walkway, leaning against the guardrail, taking in the night air. Behind them is the sign 'Marias Beautty & Hare Salon' in massive black letters against a white background. In front of them the lights of Favelada glow.

CHAPTER 20

Shivarov

ONE EVENING, THERE IS AN UNEXPECTED ARRIVAL AT THE TOWER. UNEXPECTED BUT NOT unknown. A man named Shivarov. He comes wearing black rags and an unkempt beard, and his eyes are ringed by dark circles— mementos of his haunted nights. His face is filthy with the soot of a recent fire. Like the Bruja of Estrellas Negras, Shivarov is a myth, a chimera. His name is used up and down the land to scare children into doing their parents' bidding. "If you don't behave, Shivarov will get you!" "Eat your greens or I'll send you to Shivarov!" His name has even entered the language in an idiom, "Do it now or I'll give you a Shivarov!"

He has spent thirty years living in the same basement room, which is also the room where he does his legendary work. He barely sets foot outside, some say because he is allergic to the light, while others claim he fears to come across the fruits of his labor on the streets of Favelada, where he was born with six fingers on each hand ("It's a blessing from God," said the midwife).

His room at first glance looks like any other shabby squat inhabited by a damnificado—bed, lamp, rusting fan, covered bucket to do his ablutions, upturned crate where he sits to eat. But in the corner of the room is a long wooden box. It could be the coffin of a large snake or a rifle container, but it isn't. It's a toolbox of a very special kind, and when it opens it does so with a creak and a crack, as the hinges need oiling and the two drawbolt latches that keep it closed are imperfectly aligned or at least they are now, for the box is thirty years old and subject to the wear and tear of anything that age that is used with such chilling frequency.

His room is in the basement of an abandoned block and gets so little light that visitors, or rather patrons, because no one visits Shivarov unless it's for business, claim that when they first enter, it's impossible to see, and Shivarov himself is little more than a silhouette against the lamplight. Sometimes the smell of apple tobacco drifts upstairs for it is known that he enjoys a shisha pipe, but other than that he is a mystery. Although thousands have seen his face and experienced his work, the heat of the room and the stench of burning flesh and camphor and the unholy noise tend to trump the memory of what he looks like. And of course barely a living soul has seen him in daylight.

For thirty years, in the Stygian gloom of his quarters, Shivarov has practiced his life's work. He has honed it to perfection, understanding every bone, sinew, muscle, tendon of the human form, for that's all part of his art. Without this knowledge he would not be sought after. He cannot make mistakes, and he never does. They call him the Cripple Maker. An apt moniker, because that is exactly what he is.

Along the streets of Favelada, by the riverbank in Agua Suja, under the bridges of Dieux Morts, in the roads of Sanguinosa and Blutig, cripples abound. They beg in the traffic, sell their wares with their one hand, sit in the streets with their amputated limbs uncovered for all to see. This is how they make a living for their families. But they weren't born that way. They went to the Cripple Maker.

Some families send their youngest child to Shivarov. Others take it upon themselves. He accepts only cash paid in advance. He strips the client ("more hygienic"), gags them with a rag soaked in nitrous oxide, and places a hood over their head. All they hear is the creak and the crack of the box, and then their world changes forever.

And it is the box that he carries as he approaches the monolith. Stooped and spindly, he can barely walk with it strapped around his back. He stops to rest, looks furtively around him at children playing in the fading light. The sentries' walkie-talkies crackle on the rim of the tower. An unlikely assassin, but here in Favelada anything is possible.

One of the guards on the fifteenth floor bites on a sunflower seed, spits out the shell, peers through his binoculars, and says, "Look what Hell dredged up."

He hands the binoculars to his partner. "Then why's he carrying a cross on his back?"

Shivarov limps toward the entrance of the tower, drawing stares from the children as the guards close ranks. He is about to enter their orbit when he collapses. It's a gradual collapse, a staged pantomime in four parts. First his knees go, then his shoulders. He topples sideways and lands with a messy thud-crash-crunch on the ground, woodchips from his toolbox splintering into the dust.

Heads turn. Some of the children stare. Is it Jesus? The guards walk over to Shivarov. They remove the box from his shoulders and pick him up, two lifting his torso, a third gripping his ankles like a man maneuvering a wheelbarrow. He is light, all skin and bones. But when one of the guards sees Shivarov's six-fingered hands, he jumps back with a shriek and drops the stranger's legs.

"Look at his hands! Look at his hands!"

"What of it?" says one of the men gripping Shivarov's shoulders. "I saw a wolf with two heads a few months ago."

The jittery guard grips Shivarov by the ankles again, tries not to look at the hands, and carries him to the entrance. They kick open a door at the foot of the tower and lift him onto the Chinaman's bed. Shivarov gives off such a subterranean aura that when Nacho enters he recoils instantly and his first thoughts are 'this man cannot stay here' while the guards drag the toolbox into the room and leave it by the bed.

"Well, what have we here?" says Nacho, standing above him. "A martyr? Or the bogeyman's bogeyman."

But he doesn't yet know who Shivarov is.

After a minute or so, the Cripple Maker opens his eyes. The first thing he does is close his fists. Then he sees Nacho's withered arm, and he thinks it is not his work. He cannot assemble a masterpiece like that because he only does amputations, regulation slicing and dicing. For a cripple like this, nature must have had its hand on the tiller—childhood polio or arteriosclerosis. His eyes dart around until they fix on his box. Once he has sighted it, and seen that it remains closed, he relaxes again.

"Do you speak English?" says Nacho.

"Yes," whispers Shivarov. "Was fire. My house burn. I come here for to live." His voice is a smoky rasp, a knife scratching on canvas.

"I'm Nacho Morales. What's your name?"

"Dimitri," he says, without a pause. "Dimitri Abramov. I have nothing. Everything burn."

"You have this." Nacho nods at the box.

"Yes. Some things old from my home. You are Nacho?"

"Yes."

"I come here for to meet you. To ask for to stay here some days. They burn my house."

"Who burned your house?"

"I don't know. Smoke everywhere. Flames high."

"Do you work?"

"I am doctor."

"You work in a hospital?"

"No. Private practice. You have glass of water?"

"Yes. Wait."

Nacho goes outside and asks one of the guards to get water. He returns to find Shivarov sitting up in the bed and the box moved under it. Shivarov's hands are gripped together, hiding his fingers.

"I am doctor," Shivarov repeats. "If I stay here, I help people free. No charge."

His face is a daub of black grime, and his eyes puddles of water flecked with red like ink leaking in a pool. Shivarov doesn't look Nacho in the eye and Nacho doesn't trust him. Like an animal, Nacho has a sixth sense.

"What's in the box?"

"Old things. Photos. Some medical equipment."

"Can you show me?"

"Very tired. They burn my house today. I am lucky stay alive. Very tired. I show you box tomorrow please. Just old things. Equipment."

Nacho figures that if Torres the Younger was sending some-one with a bomb, it wouldn't be an aging skeleton of a man covered in soot. And if he wanted to infiltrate the tower, why would he dispatch a ham actor with a fainting habit, unless he was an idiot?

"You can spend one night here, but you won't be alone. The door stays open and the night guards will use this room to nap. They'll go on the floor while you sleep. Do you understand?"

"Yes yes. Very good. Thank you."

With that, Nacho shuffles back to his room, the muletas tap-ping lightly on the stone floor, while Shivarov ponders the asym-metry of Nacho's body—truly a work of art—and thinks about where he can hide the tools of his trade.

CHAPTER 21

The Fourth Trash War—Fernanda

the Garbage Sorter—Panning for

gold—Fernanda gets her revenge

THE FOURTH TRASH WAR WASN'T A WAR AT ALL. SOME HISTORIANS CALLED IT A BATTLE, others a skirmish, and on the famous Zeffekat tapestry that shows all of the Trash Wars, it would later appear as a bloody raid. But the truth is, it was a massacre. Or rather two massacres. They involved a gang of child soldiers high on khat and methadone and armed with Chinese Kalashnikovs, a gold deal gone wrong, a grinning ghost, and a child prodigy in a pink tutu. When it was over it resembled a scene from a painting by Hieronymus Bosch, and anyone who hadn't known it before surely knew it now: Favelada was cursed, the place of devils and demons.

It began with a six-year-old garbage sorter called Fernanda. She was born in garbage, lived in garbage, and all day every day walked through garbage.

When she started she could barely lift the sack, and would tag along behind her mother, also called Fernanda, her father having gone early to that great garbage tip in the sky, borne there on drink and carelessness. Her mother patiently taught Fernanda what to look for, and let her keep the dolls and the teddy bears and the trinkets she found. The latter included a musical box with a ballerina who twirled to the tinkling sound when you opened the box, and from the day she discovered it Fernanda wanted to be a dancer. Years later she would find a tutu and wear it whenever she wasn't sorting garbage.

As Fernanda grew stronger, she began to heave sacks as competently as any of the boys, and because she had been taught well, she excelled at culling the junk from the jewels: the shining diadem, the functioning appliance, the gewgaw inlaid with platinum. By the time she was ten, she had become one of the greatest garbage sorters of them all—better than Deng the Dipper, who could spy a nugget of silver from two hundred yards, better than Rogerio the Rag Man, who once found a diamond-encrusted watch under a pile of newspapers and claimed it had glowed in front of him like a torch, better even than Ruby Kolakashiana, who could fill a gunnysack of recyclable metal in ten minutes, or so the legend goes.

Fernanda was fast. Not limb-swirling, arms-akimbo, sweat-inducing fast, but steady and consistent and with an economy of movement that meant she rarely touched discardables, rarely made a mistake. Others—the hares among them, who flipped over every pile in search of the jackpot—would be collapsed in the shade while she was crouched down or trudging up some garbage mountain, strong-thighed and resolute.

The value of substances rose and fell, so one month she might pick glass—scraping up cullet with a handmade trowel—and the next month it would be tin cans. When a furniture factory opened on the outskirts of Agua Suja, she picked plastic for a year, because it could be shredded to fill seat cushions or honed into cheap chairs. She was adaptable, quick on her feet, and knew the worth of everything.

Aged twelve, she diversified.

At Minhas they were digging for gold. The miners lived in barracks, a line of wooden shacks where they slept two to a bunk. At the end of every day the men showered in the street under a rigged up hose full of holes, and it was there that Fernanda, who was passing by on an errand for her mother, happened to notice flecks of gilt glistening in the runoff water flowing down the street. It was gold dust.

She found out everything she could about gold panning, doing her research by talking to elders and jewel hawkers and passing prospectors, and once, by chance, watching a TV program about it on a recycled black-and-white that her mother had rescued from a tip. She even went to a public library one time, drawing looks because she stank of trash. She was illiterate, but before they kicked her out, she had managed to commit to memory a number of diagrams on panning for gold. It took her two months to figure out how to do it.

Now thirteen, she would take the night bus to Minhas, ignoring the madmen and the muttering drunks, and climb over a fence, knapsack on her back, to get into the miners' village. Silently, on all fours, she swept the street, now dry, where the men showered. This she did with a hand brush until she'd amassed a large pile of dust. All the while she would be listening to the assorted snores of the miners—great isolated honkings, leonine rumblings, and drill-like tremolos.

She panned the dust in water until it became silt. From out of her sack she then produced a bottle of nitric acid, which she poured into the pan. Sitting against the wall of the miners' compound, she heated the pan over a low paraffin fire and then added mercury, mixing the acid and mercury with her hand. She would wipe her hand on the wall immediately after, but still the skin burned, though she knew it would grow back quickly. Ignoring the pain, she would watch the magic of her alchemy as the gold clung to the mercury in an amorphous lump. She picked it out and heated it, holding it in a pair of silicone-tipped tongs rescued from a trash pile. Once the mercury was burned off, she was left with a nugget of pure gold. She packed up her tools and scrambled back over the fence, the gold hidden in the safest place she could find—her mouth.

Every three weeks she would do the same thing, producing a nugget of gold from the dust that fell off the miners' bodies, and she found a dealer who bought the gold at market price: an old man called Reuben, with a crocodile smile but a good heart, who never cheated her once, not even when his foolish son lost a fortune on a wager in a gambling house. Fernanda, meanwhile, gave most of the money to her mother.

Later, during the rainy season, she would break into the drains beside the miners' compound, lower herself with a rope secured to the fence and tied to her waist, and dredge buckets of sludge which contained even more gold to be sorted. The process was different, but the result was the same. This went on for two years until one day her dealer dropped dead and was replaced by the unscrupulous son with a gambling habit. The young man, in Cuban heels and mud-brown Stetson, accused her of diluting the gold with tin.

"You rooked ma daddy for years," he said. "So I'm gonna git me some recompense."

He slapped her down, pocketed the gold, and took off on his moped, tossing behind him a fifty-libro note, a tenth of the value of the gold she had brought.

Fernanda dusted herself off and pondered her revenge.

A day later she visited a group of child soldiers living on the roof of an abandoned train station. War orphans themselves, they were killing machines brainwashed by warlords and other captors. They were the scions of narcotraficantes and murderers, thieves and sicarios, and they spent their days scavenging for food, robbing local bodegas, and chewing khat to stave off hunger.

The following Monday night, on a promise of a share of the gold, they raided the dealer's premises. The episode was short, nasty, and brutish.

The refinery where the dealer and his employees worked and lived, a repurposed mansion now running to ground, was poorly guarded. Two sentries lay snoring in a hut, an overfed Doberman napping at their feet. The child soldiers simply walked in the front door, Kalashnikovs at their hips. They found no gold, but took everything and anything of value—lamps, a vase, a clock, a pair of shoes, knick-knacks. As they turned left to raid the working area of the refinery, they heard a shuffle. Leaping upon them was a group of men carrying spanners, hammers and knives. The refinery, it turned out, was open at night, and these men were in the middle of their shift.

The rat-a-tat-tat of Kalashnikovs and the screams of the wounded echoed in the halls. The dealer himself—Reuben Junior, an ass but not a coward—leaped out of bed and unleashed a two-handed volley of revolver fire until a bullet from a child soldier's Kalashnikov pierced his arm and sent him spiraling back into his room. Shots ricocheted everywhere, destroying the last vestiges of the mansion as it had been. A glinting chandelier crashed to the floor, its icicles of crystal crunching on the carpet, and the glass front of a Georgian cupboard exploded, shellacking the crockery. Two of the boys were hit—one by Reuben Junior and another by a hammer blow—and went down like skittles, but the workers were annihilated. Driven back down the corridor into the refinery, they had nowhere to run, and the boy soldiers killed them gleefully.

The massacre ended only because on the second floor of the house, the ghost of the old dealer, Reuben Senior, tiptoed along the banister's edge, cracked open his crocodile smile, and flew into the refinery, thus spooking the child soldiers enough to make them run.

Urns of molten gold mingled with blood, and the twitching corpses of the workers were draped along the rims of smelters like Dali soft watches. One man lay dead in a riot of glass beakers and flasks and Buchner funnels, and his mate was sprawled by the furnace, helmet still on, skin starting to bubble in the heat.

When Fernanda heard about what the boys had done, she wept for a week. She had told them to get her gold back, not kill everybody.

"That's what happens when you set a wild dog loose," said her mother. "And they didn't even bring you any gold."

The episode would not have been a Trash War if it wasn't for what happened next. The child soldiers lay down their arms. Spooked by the ghost and the thought of their two dead friends, they moved to the dump and joined the garbage sorters. What they didn't know was that Reuben Junior was still alive and after revenge. When he heard the boys were working in the Favelada garbage dump, he vowed to massacre them.

And thus did the Fourth Trash War play out: unarmed former child soldiers cut to ribbons by an army of mercenaries. Fernanda managed to escape by hiding in a drain (for Fernanda had become an expert at opening the covers and lowering herself in an instant), while her mother sat safely in the house she had bought with Fernanda's gold, one mile away from the dump. Reuben Junior, gold dealer, lousy gambler, cowboy worshipper, conman and thief, had his vengeance, but before the day was done he too was dead, crushed by a garbage mountain that collapsed on him. And in it, not a single trace of gold.

When they found him, the garbage sorters took off his belt and boots and sold them for a fortune, pocketed his gun, purloined his father's watch, and gave his Stetson to Fernanda the Elder. The rest they left for the buzzards.

CHAPTER 22

Nacho gets a haircut—Man in a

cage—Trial at the five stone heads—

Jeremiah—Emil and Nacho in a café

NACHO IS SITTING IN MARIAS BEAUTTY & HARE SALON IN FRONT OF A MIRROR. IT IS EARLY morning and the salon isn't open yet, but this is a special assignment. Maria glides over in five-inch heels, white microskirt, and seamed stockings. Stands behind Nacho. Reaches for his hair the way a child might reach for a sleeping snake.

"When was the last time you had it cut?" she asks.

"I think I was about thirty. Maybe five years ago."

"God almighty. Why does it stand up on end?"

"I don't know. You're the hairdresser."

She almost-pats his hair gingerly, checking all the angles, without actually touching it, working up some ideal image of his head in her imagination, designing the architecture of the little lisiado that will (a) make him look more like a leader, and (b) secure him a good woman. But not in that order.

Outside, birds wheel and lark in a sky streaked with salmon pink.

"OK, here we go," she says with a deep breath.

"You're not defusing a bomb. Just cut it."

"I'm an artist. It doesn't work like that."

She picks up a pair of scissors, puts them down, chooses a different pair, puts those down, gets a comb, and runs her inch-long red-painted fingernails along the teeth. Crrrrrrrrrrrrrik.

"What are you doing?" asks Nacho.

"I'm warming up."

"Are you like this with all your clients?"

"You aren't a client. You're my husband's brother."

"Husband? Is there something I don't know?"

"Shut up. I'm thinking."

He waits. Looks at her enormous eyelashes.

Her manicured hands finally touch his hair. It's the first time a woman has touched him in a decade. She begins cutting from the back. She frowns as she works and Nacho sees a deep vertical crease between her eyes that he'd never noticed before, and he thinks, 'She's my age or maybe Emil's. She's lost the flush of youth. She's still beautiful, but beauty never lasts, and hers won't either.'

Gradually he drifts into a reverie, allowing his mind to wander the paths of Bieb ta 'Niket, the shebeens of Zerbera—his lucky place, even the nooks in the House of Flowers where the cockroaches crawled and the sun never shone. Then he runs through chess openings, sending queens on lone sallies and bishops flying diagonally into enemy territory.

Maria takes bunches of Nacho's hair between her fingers and cuts slowly, methodically. The hair drops onto the shoulders of the bib Nacho is wearing. He thinks he looks like a monk in a cowl. All he needs is the hood over his head and he could take himself off to Solitario, go live in a cave, and eat berries for the rest of his days.

"Who's the newcomer?" asks Maria.

"Who?"

"The Chinaman's room. There's somebody there."

"How did you know that?"

"News travels fast."

And Nacho thinks, 'She's right. We live in a tower. A story can get from the ground floor to the sixtieth in about two minutes.'

"Says he's a doctor. His house burned down."

"You believe him?"

"He was covered in soot. And he wasn't a miner, that's for sure. Wouldn't last five seconds in a mine the way he was breathing. So maybe he's a doctor, maybe he isn't."

"I heard he was creepy looking. Like a spider. But it was Layla's kid told me that, and everything's creepy to her."

"How's business?"

"You mean here? If I wasn't cutting your hair now, you'd have to wait two weeks. It's been like that for four months. We're doing well. I want to expand but there's nowhere to expand to."

Her eyes sweep across the room, the emporium. Six swiveling chairs, one desk for transactions, glass fronted cupboards full of beauty products and a hundred baubles on the shelves. She is a collector of clay pots, tiny vases, figurines, tiles, vintage posters. On the wall there's a framed photo of her as a twenty-year-old, posing in a beauty competition, full length, harsh light flooding from above.

Nacho watches his gradual transformation in a state of curiosity. He has never been in front of his own image for such a long period of time, and, not having a mirror in his room, he sometimes forgets what he looks like.

When she is finished, Maria stands back, admiring her handiwork. She whips off Nacho's bib and hangs it on a hook.

"There," she says. "You look good. Now go and find yourself a wife."

*

There is a commotion downstairs. For a moment, as Nacho walks out of Maria's salon, he thinks it may be an attack on the tower. He tries to hurry down the five flights of stairs, but his muletas don't allow him to, and the stairways are busy with people heading to work.

As he arrives on the ground floor, the sight stops him dead. In the plaza, a gang of men and women are carrying a large wooden cage toward the road, holding it by two long struts the length of small trees. A crowd has gathered, jeering and shouting and waving their fists. In the cage is a man stripped naked. He turns and turns in raw fear, gripping the bars. His body is filthy with soot.

"Dimitri Abramov," Nacho says to himself.

Shivarov is screaming now, in Russian, Hungarian, and English, his manic, terrified face a snag-toothed rictus of fear. But his voice is all but drowned out by the baying of the damnificados. Children throw stones and handfuls of dust, and a woman hurls a tomato which bursts against the bars of the cage, pips flying.

Nacho catches sight of Don Felipe walking behind the crowd.

"Don Felipe!"

The priest doesn't hear him.

"Don Felipe!!"

He turns around, his blank face resigned, and pauses to let Nacho catch up.

"What's going on?" asks Nacho.

"Shivarov."

A moment passes. The pink clouds have dispersed and now the sun is beaming down.

"Impossible," says Nacho. "He's a myth."

"He's in the cage. He has six fingers on each hand and a box of tools. It's him. I tried to stop them. I think they're going to burn him at the gates."

"Why burn him? I know he was a Cripple Maker. But people paid him. It was his job."

"It's not what he did or didn't do. It's what he stands for. The people are afraid of him. What do we do with the things we fear? We kill them."

Behind them appears the woman with the dog in a wheelbarrow, but this time she has left the dog behind. And the wheelbarrow.

She calls over their shoulders, "You don't understand. Either of you."

Nacho and the priest turn to face her, and she walks with them.

"He wasn't just a Cripple Maker," she goes on. "He was a government torturer during the Trash Wars. He mutilated people for profit." Then she looks straight at Nacho. "You let the devil into our home."

Traffic stops and the car drivers and the rickshaw boys and the truckers and the cyclists behold the terrible sight. Shivarov railing like a madman, hauled through the heart of the city in a wooden cage, an animal banging at its bars. A pack of wild dogs living on Roppus Street pick up the scent of scandal and lope after the procession.

As Don Felipe suggested, they go all the way to the five stone heads and there begin a mock trial. A tall black man named Jeremiah, with a necklace of snake's teeth, leads the prosecution.

The graffiti artist. Nacho has seen him many times, though the man doesn't live in the tower.

The cage is lowered onto the street. Jeremiah climbs to the flat top of the stone head in the center. His voice is calm.

"Everythin' what you heard about this man be true. He name Shivarov. He a torturer and a cripple maker. The sins this man perpetrated upon humanity be beyond compare. You all heard the stories. He cut people up. In the last war he gone sided with the soldiers and broke people bones. Sure, he sittin' in front of us right now givin' me the evil eye, but I ain' 'fraid. I ain' 'fraid o' you no more 'cause we gone and proved you human just like the rest of us. You have a heart beatin' in yo' chest? Sure you have. You have a mind? Sure you have. The only thing you don' have is a soul 'cause you gone sold that to the devil, know what I'm sayin'? Now I'm sure as a dog is a dog that there are those of you out there who know someone affected by this man's work. Maybe a friend. Maybe a neighbor. Maybe it somebody you don't even know, some innocent guy that you see lyin' in the street. But Shivarov put his hand on him, and cut him up. For all that and mo', Shivarov have to die."

The crowd cheers and there are shouts of "Yeah" and one voice rings out loud and clear, "String 'im up!"

At his insistence, Don Felipe is helped up onto the central stone head and he tells the crowd that they themselves, damnificados and all, are not murderers. Instead, they should imprison Shivarov forever.

And then it's Nacho's turn.

"He did terrible things. We all know it. But for us to kill him for the things he did, that isn't justice. Neither is putting him in prison. He'll be murdered by the other inmates as soon as they know who he is. Instead, we should send him to Solitario. There he'll spend the rest of his days pondering the things he's done. He'll do his penance alone and he'll never return."

"Why should we spare him?" someone shouts.

"Because we're merciful," Nacho replies. "Cover him up! He isn't an animal. He doesn't belong in a cage, whatever he's done."

Someone passes a handful of rags between the wooden bars and Shivarov clothes himself.

"I've said my piece. You've heard Jeremiah and Don Felipe, too. Now make your decision."

The crowd murmurs, whispers, converses in groups. The decision is put to a vote by a simple show of hands and to Nacho's surprise, they agree to his idea. Jeremiah shakes Nacho's hand and touches his shoulder with the other hand and walks away without a word, leaving Nacho to organize Shivarov's departure.

Within twenty-four hours Shivarov is on his way to Solitario. He is clothed and washed and handcuffed. His tools are melted down and resold as scrap metal, and his wooden box is torched at the stone heads. As it burns, those who are present swear they see a thousand souls rising in the smoke—the spirits of those he maimed.

When Nacho returns to the tower his head is throbbing. At the foot of the tower, Don Felipe says, "I thought they would tie him to a stake and incinerate him."

"We're damnificados, not barbarians," says Nacho. "Justice is everything."

He bids Don Felipe farewell, and struggles up the stairs.

"Nacho," Don Felipe calls out. "I hardly recognize you. Did something change?"

"Haircut. This morning."

"Ahhh."

"But it seems like weeks ago."

✳

"Shivarov?" says Emil. "You mean he's real?"

Emil has returned from two days' work in Zerbera.

"Oh yeah," replies Nacho. "Like I said, he was in the tower for one night."

"Were there horns on his head?"

"No, but he had six fingers on each hand."

They are in a café close to the tower. A waitress brings them thick coffee in tiny glasses. Across from them, the snap and clack of a backgammon game—two men sucking on shisha pipes as they play, and a dozing dog tied to the table leg. A fan is whirring on the ceiling and a gang of flies are dancing in its slipstream. The whole place seems half-asleep.

Emil adds a pile of sugar that makes sediment at the bottom of the cup. Nacho puts his hand under his chin, takes in the nineteenth-century portraits on the walls and says, "Do you think Torres will attack?"

"Oh sure. You're the one who knows history, but look at what his father did, and his grandfather and his brother. The whole family. They grab anything and everything they can. And they think the tower's theirs. Some time soon he'll pay us a visit. And then the only question is how long we have left in the tower."

The dog tied to the table leg starts licking its nether parts. Its owner loses the game of backgammon and curses in Arabic. They reset and begin again, throwing the dice like Olympians, with a shake and a flourish.

"It's not like a flood," says Emil.

"I know. 'No more water, but fire next time.'"

"What?"

"Ah, nothing. A song I heard in Zerbera once."

"Can't you use your connections to keep him away? You know some big shots, right?"

"The most I can do is get us free water. Power changes hands all the time. Always has done. One day I'm doing a translation for an ambassador, the next day he's fired and living on a farm in the back end of nowhere. If I knew anyone who could stop Torres, I'd have asked them months ago. And I wouldn't have gone to Solitario."

The backgammon players break into an argument, full of gesticulation and threat. Meanwhile, the dog carries on licking itself, and Emil and Nacho pay up and leave. As they close the door, it makes a rusty clank like a cowbell with a bandaged thumb for a clapper.

CHAPTER 23

Insomniac—The chess days—

Heat—The rationing of power

NACHO LIES IN BED AWAKE. THE GROWLING OF THE MOPED THAT TAKES PEOPLE UP AND down the steps of the tower is silenced. The twins, who came in drunk and singing in German, are long gone, passed into dreamland, mouths open and snoring. The only sound is the whirring of Nacho's fan, a portable white thing that stands in the corner of the room. Like Nacho, it has only one good leg and is constantly threatening to fall.

When he can't sleep, he turns to his translation work—the most boring he can find: a business contract, a technical manual. Once, in the early days, he turned to a book of poems he was being paid to translate, in the hope that it would cure his insomnia. As he started on the original French, he gradually found himself entranced by the poems and stayed up all night to finish the work. He went back to bed as the sun was rising and slept deeply until the first snarl of traffic, the first honking of horns, the first barks of distant dogs awoke him.

It's almost 3:00 a.m. Giving up on sleep, he rises slowly, lopsided, and limps to his table without his crutches. The table is multipurpose—a place to eat, work, converse, entertain, and play chess on the rare occasions he can persuade Don Felipe to sit down and do battle with him.

"You play like a conqueror," the old priest once said. "Always on the attack."

"I learned in the street," Nacho replied.

He had learned from watching the men—always men—in a park in the town of Ajedrez, two hundred miles north of Favelada. They would play with timers that they banged with the flat of the hand every time it was their turn. Each player had ten minutes in total and his timer would run down like a ticking bomb.

Nacho had been sent to Ajedrez to interpret at a business symposium. Because the work was exhausting, the interpreters were given long breaks, and so Nacho would wander into the sun-dappled parks, and it was there that he first saw the lines of men seated opposite one another, at tables, banging their clocks. Small crowds were gathered around the tables. The players seemed barely one step up from damnificados. They wore long greasy coats and fraying jackets in the height of summer, and their faces had the sun-crusted, lived-in look of street people. Their games were played at a slam-bam rhythm and Nacho loved the click of the pieces and then the thump of the hand on the clock.

Chess seemed to Nacho like some strange Eastern religion—its indecipherable rituals, the meditative lulls, the gradual assertions of power. And he loved yet again to be learning a new language, a language of riches such as zugzwang, trébuchet, queening, and patzer. It was only much later that one of the players he befriended told him that the game was feudal, a microcosm of the relations of dominance and oppression that still besmirched the world. The pawns were sent to die first. They were the expendable people, the stooges, the fall guys, with negligible mobility and no chance of glory. They were foot soldiers whose role was to protect the king and queen, the bishop and knight.

"Chess is a bloodless war," said the player he'd befriended.

In that park Nacho once saw the equivalent of hara-kiri, when an obese Romanian raised his gargantuan hand and without a flicker of emotion, toppled his own king in a manner that said, 'This is inevitable. I have reached the end. The king must die and his death shall be the shedding of a feather.' He saw a sly Indian from Chandigarh put the evil eye on his Israeli opponent, who fell to pieces and began weeping. It was no scandal—the onlookers simply shuffled off to another table. He saw, too, a player rise like the furies, midgame, and unsheathe a khanjar, the curved dagger of the Omanis, and threaten to disembowel a spectator who had been shining the reflection from a drinking glass into his eyes.

Nacho thinks about these times, puts his chess set to one side, and fingers a pile of paper—the translations he needs to do: a business report in Italian, instructions for a washing machine in French, and a scientific paper in Spanish. He chooses the instructions. They are artless. There is no human voice in the writing of it—no irony, no curiosity or character—just a straight delineation of how to get a machine working. This suits his 3:00 a.m. mind perfectly. He gets to work and finishes it by hand at 3:45, types it up on his Hermes typewriter, slapping the platen with a thud and a jangle at the end of every line, and goes back to bed.

He dreams of chess.

*

Morning comes to the sound of drilling and traffic. They're tearing up the road across from the monolith, making something new. The piercing rattle is punctuated with shouts from the laborers, a motley mob of swarthy grunts. For the most menial jobs, they form gangs on the corner of Haggalak Street at 4:00 a.m. and hope to be handpicked by the foreman, a gruff ex-damnificado with a snake tattoo slithering up his arm. They work mornings and evenings to avoid the full blast of the sun.

The weather has turned. Under the foggy sky, the heat hangs in the windless air, and in every room in the tower families install fans that are begged, borrowed or stolen from junkyards and dusty stores full of used goods. But when all the fans are on, with the TVs and lights bawling and glowing, and assorted machines burping and puffing, the power in the monolith cuts out. With no warning, the whirring that keeps the place alive turns blank in the blink of an eye and six hundred TV sets are suddenly expunged. Worse, the refrigerators lose their power. Even worse, Maria's hair dryers shut down. She bellows at the tower, at her workers, at all Heaven and Earth.

Fortunately, Lalloo knows how to get the power back, and he does so. Nonetheless, Nacho decides to work out a system for reducing the outages. It involves even-numbered floors abstaining from using too much electricity at certain times of day, and odd-numbered floors doing the same at different times. The damnificados begin their complaining immediately.

"Why should *we* switch off the TV?"

"That's when they show all the best telenovelas!"

"It's a conspiracy!"

"It's not fair! Why doesn't *his* floor do without electricity?"

"They should fix the goddam power!"

"What next? No water?"

"More rules and regulations. *Nacho's* the one with the power problem."

"He's a dictator!"

"He's trying to cheat us!"

Nacho asks the leaders on each floor to explain patiently that on a rota system everyone wins and the power will never go off, that everyone can use their fans all the time and in any case they're getting free electricity round the clock, and that once the heat wave dies down things will go back to normal. And still the complaints echo from the basement to the topmost floor until eventually everyone gets used to the system and forgets there was ever a blackout in the first place because Time has a way of dulling the memory.

Nacho busies himself with his translations because money is running tight, and hangs out with his brother and plays chess with Don Felipe. He works on his cooking, reads when he has time, teaches his class, resolves a dispute over a shared wall that is being shared unequally.

Tired of being cooped up in his room in the terrible heat, he begins to take regular walks in the morning and late afternoon. He sees the garden by the tower beginning to bloom, and the playground frequented by groups of children dashing here and there, their parents sitting at tables in the shade. Emil, loose-limbed, itching for action, accompanies him.

"Where did all these kids come from?" he asks. "Jesus. Some of them even have clothes on."

A few weeks into the heat wave, a rumor spreads that the five stone heads are beginning to crumble, that they burned from the inside and are now disintegrating. Nacho takes a stroll with Emil and Maria's dog to the gates of the city. The stones heads stand as before, faces vacant and flat as kouroi. At their bases are flowers, rags, blankets, the embers of fires.

Nacho doesn't know it and Emil doesn't know it, but these will be the last days of peace.

CHAPTER 24

The unexpected guest—Coffee at sunrise—

Nacho asks Lalloo to invent a weapon

of war—Nacho and Emil make battle

plans—Maria proposes an assassination

ONE HOT NIGHT NACHO ENTERTAINS AN UNEXPECTED GUEST. HE IS FAST ASLEEP WHEN THE guest somehow appears at his bedside. In the dark, outlined against the faint light let in through the slats of the shuttered window, the guest is a silhouette, still as Death. The figure is broad and strong. The man sits at the foot of the bed, which is really a pallet on ministilts, and takes in his surroundings. Sees the modest furniture, the shelf full of books. Smells the air—musty, moldy—says to himself, "Not much for a great leader. A servant's quarters."

Suddenly the Little Cripple is awake and looking at an intruder not three feet away.

"Who are you?" asks Nacho.

"Torres."

"Which one?"

"We haven't met. But you know my brother. By all accounts, you scared him witless. We haven't seen him since."

The man lets out a breath, a semblance of amusement at his brother's fate.

"What are you doing in here? How did you get in?"

"It's my tower."

Nacho is struck by the calmness of the intruder's voice, a warm baritone. They call him Mayhem, but his voice is silk.

"It *was* your tower," says Nacho. "Then the government took it. And then *we* took it."

"Well, I'm not here to discuss semantics and origins and property law."

"Why *are* you here? It's late. Or early."

"Let's say my family has unfinished business with this property. You and the occupants need to leave."

"And if we don't?"

"I'll kill you all. But I'd rather not do that. This area has a history of bloodshed. There's been enough war here, enough butchery. I'd rather you left peacefully. What do you say?"

"No."

"Wrong answer."

"This is our home."

"No, it isn't. This is *my* home, and you're squatting in it. Tell me, Nacho. What would you do if you were in my shoes? If the family property had been stolen and was now being squatted illegally?"

"The property was built illegally in the first place through murder and bribery and enslaving the weak. And the land was stolen. If I were in your shoes, I'd thank God I lived a good life, already had a roof over my head, and I'd walk away and live like an honest man for the rest of my days."

"A beautiful dream. And I admire your courage. But it's not going to save you. I have an army. We'll blast you and your so-called home to smithereens. I'm not my brother. I'm smarter and better-organized."

"Why would you destroy the building? You just told me you wanted the tower."

"The tower is a mess. I wouldn't care if it fell down tomorrow. It's the land. We're in the center of the city. You know that. This will be my base. I'm a businessman and a politician and a general. I'm going to give you two weeks. There are places out in Blutig, Oameni Morti. There's a derelict tower in Fellahin, houses maybe three hundred or four if you live cooped up like animals. Take your people and lead them to another promised land. This one's mine and I'm not sharing it. I don't want to shed more blood. But I'm a Torres, and whatever horrors my family has visited upon the people over the years, it'll be nothing compared to what I'll do to you if you stay."

"You've already shed blood. The Chinaman."

"It wasn't me. One of my officers was out of control. I apologize."

He waits for Nacho to respond. Waits and waits, but the Little Cripple remains unmoved. He sits coolly in his skeletal bed, stays fixed in tranquility. They look at one another.

Torres says, "I hear you're a chess player. This is the equivalent of checkmate."

Nacho stays silent. Torres pushes open the door and leaves with a light step that belies his bulk.

As the last echoes of the intruder's footsteps fade into the night, Nacho wrestles his way out of bed. He tousles his hair, rubs his eyes. The whole exchange took barely two minutes, and he wonders if he was dreaming. But his door is ajar and the faint smell of cigar smoke lingers, the scent of dictators the world over. How did he get in?

Nacho gets dressed, hobbles down the stairs, makes out a few stars in the blackness of the night and looks around. The guards are all gone. Nowhere to be seen. He peers up at the higher floors of the tower. A few lights are on, but where are the sentries, the lookouts with their binoculars? He thinks, 'The heat has lulled us into a long sleep. We've forgotten our enemies. We've forgotten everything. We're in Lethe, the river of forgetfulness, and our boat is drifting miles from the shore.'

He wanders the perimeter of the tower. A mangy dog stares at him and lopes away. A mouse scarpers through a hole in the wall. The children's playground, its surfaces shining in the dark, assumes pure form, like a display of modernist sculptures in bronze and stone.

He goes back to his room, puts a pan of water on the stove, and makes coffee. He drinks it from a chipped mug someone gave him years ago, and sits at his window, watching for the first rumors of light. He thinks of how unutterably beautiful the dawn is, clasps his hands as if in prayer and rests his shaggy head on his fingers. The Torres family again. The great hundred-headed snake in Eden.

*

The day crackles to life but quieter than normal because it's a Sunday and the traffic is leisurely. The first thing Nacho does is find out who was on guard duty the night before. The two men are nowhere to be found.

"Torres must have captured them," says Emil, sitting at Maria's table. They pick at a huge platter of eggs fried in olive oil that Maria brought in, forking them onto their plates and mopping up the yolk with hunks of bread.

"Or paid them off. How did Torres know which room was mine?"

"Maybe he'd been spying on you."

"No. He's a Torres. It doesn't matter that he can speak in complete sentences. If he wants something, he'll just break down the door. So maybe somebody told him."

Later, the brothers hear that the priest has gone missing. Nacho knocks on Don Felipe's door. No answer. He returns to Maria's room and says to Emil, "How did Torres know I play chess? Don Felipe's the only person I play with."

"Maybe the chess set was on your desk."

"It wasn't."

"You think Torres got to the priest? You're full of conspiracy theories today. I thought the old man was your friend."

"No. Not really. I don't trust him."

"Who do you trust?"

"No one outside this room."

In the evening, Nacho and Emil pay a visit to Lalloo. He answers his door looking disheveled. Even with three fans blasting away behind him, he's covered in a patina of sweat that makes his scrawny torso glisten. He wipes his forehead.

"Hello?"

"Can we come in? Get out of the heat?"

"Yes. But there's nowhere to sit. The floor's OK?"

He lives, like Nacho, in one room. Every surface—the bed, a table, and a chair—is covered with wires, springs, widgets, remote controls, screws, nails, washers, metal disks, and cannibalized parts of gadgets, things for which no name has yet been invented. A large rag stained with grease and oil lies in the center of the floor, and Lalloo drags it to a corner and motions for the men to sit on the floor.

"We need you to invent something," says Nacho.

Lalloo looks fearful, drops his gaze to his knees.

"We don't know what it is we want you to invent," Nacho goes on. "We're desperate. In two weeks Torres Junior comes with an army to kick us out of the tower. We have no defense. Few guns. Just the ones the last Torres army left behind and a couple of ancient muskets. Even fewer men who know how to use them. Even fewer with the courage to fight. Your father was Naboo Lalloo, wasn't he?"

"Yes."

"Didn't you want to invent things the way he did?"

"No."

Nacho glances around the room.

"It looks like you're inventing something already."

"This is just a hobby. I'm not an inventor. I really can't . . ."

"We need a weapon of war. Come with us."

The three men walk down the exterior steps of the building, all the way down to the plaza. The evening heat is oppressive, but they ignore it. They walk the perimeter of the plaza and in his mind Nacho sees a chessboard, visualizing the ranks of soldiers massed against him. The infantry at the front, expendable pawns. The big guns ready to boom at the back.

"What do you see?" Nacho asks Lalloo.

"A playground. A piece of land. Some shrubs."

"Look closer," says Nacho. "Think of it as a battlefield. We're inside the tower. They're out here. What do you see?"

"I see nothing. I'm telling you."

"Look harder," says Emil.

"The only advantage we have," Nacho goes on, "is that we know the land better than they do. And we'll be looking down on them. We have gravity on our side. If they attack, we have to be ready and we have to have a plan."

"I'm an electrician," says Lalloo.

"But you have genius in your blood," says Nacho.

"Is there going to be another Trash War?" asks Lalloo.

"Yes," says Nacho. "If we want to stay here, we have to fight."

"I can't. The wars destroyed my father."

"Your father is a legend," says Nacho.

Lalloo begins to shake. "The Trash Wars destroyed my family. My father went mad. Began drinking. He died alone in misery. I'll leave this place."

He seems to be about to break into tears, so Nacho nods to him.

"It's OK. We can come back later. But we need your help."

Back in Maria's room the brothers sit at table and ponder what to do. The little dog wanders in from the salon and begins yapping, and Emil picks it up, tries to soothe it, fails, and kicks it out the door.

"There y'go, hell hound. Run around. Do your worst. Go bite some kids."

"What are we going to do?" says Nacho.

"Make coffee."

"Where's Maria? She may have some ideas."

"She's out shopping or something. Gone to buy new heels or some more pointless trinkets for the sideboard. She's bourgeoisie. Needs all this *stuff*."

"It's Sunday."

"Stores are open on Sundays. You're medieval, Nacho."

"I need to get out more. What are we gonna do?"

"Set up a booby trap," says Emil. "Plant mines. Torres arrives and boom! All his men die and we live happily ever after."

"Our own people would set off the booby traps. We can't cordon off the plaza. Kids play there. People go to work."

"OK. Call all your contacts. Build an army from Fellahin, Minhas, Oameni Morti, Sanguinosa, Agua Suja. There are millions of damnificados. Bring them together."

"Why would they risk their lives for us? Half of them are starving. And how are we going to win a pitched battle against a real army? The streets would run with blood."

"Call your bigwigs. That ambassador you worked for. Ask them for help."

"The ambassador's an old man. He's retired. He sits on his veranda sipping mojitos while his grandkids tickle his toes."

"You have other contacts, right?"

"Low-level bureaucrats. They can't touch Torres."

"What about the cartels? They're armed," says Emil.

"You mean like the Iberians? The guys you stole the horse from? Why would they protect us?"

"OK. How about Las Bestias?"

"Who?"

"Las Bestias de la Luz Perpetua. They're still in Spazzatura, aren't they?"

"They're farmers and tinkers. The sons and grandsons of warriors. Why would they . . ."

"I get it. Why would anyone help us?" says Emil.

The water whistles in the kettle and Emil gets up, makes two cups of coffee. Puts a heap of sugar in both with a wooden spoon. Stirs. Brings them slowly, the steam still rising. Puts them on placemats at the table—Impressionist miniatures, a Degas dancer and a Monet river.

"Nacho," he says. "I can't think of a single way a bunch of damnificados can defeat a trained army. Ask me, we're going to lose. But maybe you should do what you always used to do, which is get over to the library and do some research. Find out how the underdogs beat the odds throughout history. I don't just mean the Trash Wars. I mean all over the world. How did those outnumbered white men beat the Zulus and all that."

"You mean Rorke's Drift?"

"Whatever it's called."

"They had guns and the Zulus had spears."

"I don't care about the details. Just find out how the underdog won."

Nacho sips his coffee and burns his lip.

Emil says, "Lalloo isn't going to come up with anything. What does that leave us with? It has to be you. You're the leader. But then you have to ask yourself, is it worth everyone dying? I have a job waiting for me at Ferrido, building boats. I'm a train ride away from safety. And you can go anywhere—you're a translator. You don't need to be a war martyr."

Nacho blows on his coffee this time and feels the sweet hot liquid on his tongue. His face turns weary, his years suddenly appearing in every pore of his skin where once he was childlike.

"I know. Maybe you're right. I'll think about it. It's the people. Damnificados."

"They're just people. Let them solve their own problems. They'll find a way."

The door opens and Maria prances in like a sixteen-year-old beauty queen, in boob tube, heart-shaped sunglasses balanced on her head and eyelashes like a pair of combs glued to her lids. She flashes a mirthless Italian smile at them, drinks the rest of Emil's coffee in one gulp, kisses him on the mouth, and disappears to the bathroom. She returns a minute later, perfumed and refreshed.

She makes more coffee and sits at the table, her hand on Emil's leg. The brothers tell her what has happened and she shrugs.

"This is Favelada. Everything can be bought. Everything has a number attached, including Torres. Hire a sicario. No. Hire ten sicarios. Tell them the number on Torres's head. The first to bring you Torres's finger with his family ring still on it gets the money. What my grandfather used to say: non c'è niente di più facile che uccidere qualcuno. There's nothing so easy as blowing someone away."

Emil nods.

"Live by the sword, die by the sword."

Nacho says, "How would we get to Torres? He probably lives in a fortress."

"Probably," says Maria, cradling her coffee in two hands.

Nacho shakes his head, thinks, 'I'm not a man of war. I have no gift for it.'

CHAPTER 25

With Emil by his side, Nacho scouts for alternative places to live. They take taxis way out west of the city, beyond the garbage dumps and the disused silver mine, that great gouge in the earth. They wander an abandoned zoo and gaze at the yawning concrete enclosures, rusted cage doors banging against their jambs, layers of ivy toppling over the dens like waterfalls.

"Could we live here?" asks Nacho.

"In cages? This is Hell on Earth."

They walk the cracked stone passageways looking for a base, a center where a man can rest his head. As they walk, they read the fading plaques and the loopy graffiti scrawled on the enclosure walls, and hear the leaves rustling where once monkeys cavorted.

They find the exit and catch a bus to Oameni Morti. They take a short walk through a valley overlooked by a shantytown, the wooden houses all askew but strangely beautiful in the sun. They come to an abandoned garment factory, a giant rectangle with a tin roof. Signs say 'Keep out' in six languages, but they go in anyway, squeezing between locked iron gates. The entrance—a huge door—is padlocked, so Emil vaults a fence at the back of the building, scrambles to the roof and breaks in via a broken skylight. He returns two minutes later.

"It's a bat colony," he tells Nacho. "You can't see the ceiling. That place will be diseased for a thousand years."

They move on.

They catch a ride in a baker's van to Agua Suja, and then another in a farmer's truck to the outskirts and get out at the ruins of a mansion-turned-gold refinery. Weeds clamber up the walls, and the roof is in pieces, great holes through which pigeons flit and flurry.

"Wait," says Nacho. "I've seen this place in books. This is where the Fourth Trash War started. It's on the Zeffekat tapestry."

"So what?" says Emil. "Let's go in."

"This is where the child soldiers shot up Reuben the Cowboy's men."

They push the door ajar and go in. The first thing they see is a catastrophe of broken crystal, a shattered chandelier on the worn-away carpet. They walk around it, seeing ancient bloodstains now turned black on the walls and floor. Animal droppings everywhere. A tree slanting on a diagonal has burst through the wall, grown so strong and thick that it pierces the roof.

They make their way to the refinery at the back of the building. The big smelters have long ago been taken for scrap but their imprints—scratches on the floor where they stood for years—still remain, and the glass from broken beakers and funnels lies where it fell all those years ago.

Emil tries the stairs to the second floor. They creak. He makes it to the landing but feels the floor under him giving way and scampers back down. A pair of birds suddenly takes wing from their nest on top of a wardrobe.

"This whole building is infested with birds," says Emil.

"And it's haunted."

"How do you know?"

"Reuben Senior just walked in behind you. He disturbed those birds."

Emil spins around, feels a gust of air.

"Who's Reuben Senior?"

"Gold dealer. He died fifty years ago."

They catch a bus to Mundanzas.

They get off beside an abandoned nightclub called "the llama's head," an old haven for jazz singers and artists, but all the letters except four are worn away and now the sign says *he ll*. They look through the broken windows and see it has been strip-mined for everything including the floorboards and the roof, and in any case it isn't big enough for hundreds of damnificados.

In Fellahin Emil kicks open the door to a derelict tower, a tip-off from Torres the younger, and it reminds Nacho of the day the Chinaman broke down the entrance to the monolith. This time no wolves but a pack of feral cats bare their teeth, at least until Emil charges them and they scatter and he takes the steps two at a time, pushing open doors, checking for wildlife and residents and the smell of gas. The floors are coated in some kind of toxic gunk, a black residue oozing from the walls. He goes further up, and further still, to the roof, where bird bones litter the concrete and an assortment of objects—single boots discolored in the sun, rusted beer cans, newspapers drenched to a pulp—lie discarded.

"Ten floors," he says, bounding down to Nacho. The cats have disappeared.

"I can count that from here."

"Something rotten about the place. Bad smell."

"Gas?"

"No. Something else."

"Utilities?"

"What?"

"Does it have water? And sockets for electricity?"

"Yeah. I turned a faucet. Some black stuff trickled out. It's a possibility, but ten floors isn't sixty."

"No," says Nacho. "Not even close."

By now, the sun is dipping below the hills in the distance. They hear the honking of far-off horns, the constant whine of rubber on tarmac and snarling engines, and walk toward the sun. They catch a bus to Favelada and a rickshaw to the tower.

*

The following day, Nacho meets with the leaders on each floor. He instructs them to tell the residents they are expecting an attack in ten days, and anyone who wants to leave can leave and anyone who wants to stay and fight can stay and fight, and those in between will have to take the consequences of Torres Junior's wrath and whatever the gods may bring. He spends the rest of his day sheltering from the heat and translating a book of essays by a French statesman. He wonders if he will live to finish it.

A day later Nacho sees the first signs of an exodus. Early in the morning, before the heat gathers and the air closes in, he peers out of his window and sees a family of five hauling their possessions to the bus stop across from the plaza. The children, laden with blankets and furry toys, drag their feet.

At coffee time, Nacho sees others: a young man of fighting age with a rucksack on his back and a battered suitcase in his hand. Later a family of four loads up a truck, the mother carrying pots and pans on her head, walking like a dancer, and the elder of two girls holding a dog in her arms and placing it in the cab of the truck while the younger runs in circles, on an adventure inside her head. An old man walks away in the morning dragging a burlap bag but comes back an hour later via the same path. He does this all day, taking off in different directions and returning, finding no other place to call home. Back and forth he walks until Nacho calls out to him, "Come in, out of the heat, my friend! Try again tomorrow!"

At five in the afternoon, a troubadour arrives at the tower. He is wearing a cloth cap, a white smock four sizes too large and pants like a clown's, held up by string suspenders. He carries a sack over his shoulder and a guitar on his back and his pockets are stuffed with paper and vegetables and coins and shells. He looks up and laughs and says, "La tour! La tour!" and the sentries eye him and raise their guns but at that moment Nacho is coming down the stairs and he welcomes the man, tells him to sit in the atrium and play him a song.

The troubadour sings in French and Spanish, and Nacho applauds before telling him he can come and stay in the tower but in nine days they are expecting an attack to end all attacks, and if he wishes to travel the open roads and bless them with his songs, it will be safer for him. The troubadour takes a room vacated that morning and sleeps on the floor for three days and three nights, his guitar by his side, and doesn't see the sun making great wedges of light that move across the room in slow motion as he snores.

That same evening a wailing is heard ten floors either way and the woman with the dog in a wheelbarrow emerges, bumping her way down the stairs, the dog limp and bouncing on every step. She borrows a shovel from the twins and walks until she finds a plot of unclaimed land behind a school. She buries the dog then and there, digging a hole through her tears, through the waning heat of the evening. Then she fixes a tiny wooden cross in the land, and walks back to the tower. It is midnight by the time she returns.

The following day, Nacho prowls the cavernous municipal library, goes to the section called Military History. Tells himself he must read about warfare and battles and heroes of the past. He sits at a desk and gathers a pile of books, but gets caught up in the tales of Hannibal marching over the Alps and the Pyrenees with a retinue of elephants and forty thousand soldiers, and imagines a herd of elephants with bazookas strapped to their backs defending the monolith.

On his return to the tower, he immerses himself in the French essays, forgetting again the guillotine hanging over the heads of the damnificados, and prepares for his class.

He knocks on Don Felipe's door. Again, no answer. Later he finds the twins and asks them to force open the door.

"Das ist einfach. Easy work," says Hans.

"You do it then," says Dieter.

"No problem. Stand back. Wait. I need to limber up."

"Du kannst es nicht! You're stalling. You've never broken down a door!" laughs Dieter.

"Course I have."

Nacho gets bored of their clowning and turns the handle. To his surprise, the door opens.

"I forgot," says Nacho. "The priest never locks it."

The twins ascend the stairs arguing and laughing, and Nacho sees immediately that Don Felipe has gone, leaving not a wrack behind, save some old newspapers and a half-empty water bottle. 'Betrayed,' thinks Nacho. 'He sold me out for a pocketful of silver.'

✳

The following day, he arranges a visit with his friend Cesare Baldini, the ex-ambassador, this time at the man's home. Nacho comes to a villa on the outskirts of the city, a walled perimeter, Tuscan cypress trees beside the gate. A courteous guard lets him in and he walks a pathway lined with Greek urns. The main house is in front of him, all pastel colors, a two-story chateau that looks like something out of a fairy tale. He turns to ascend the shallow steps of an ornate pavilion of wood and stone, where the old man sits picking at a plate of pasta. His shirt is open at the neck, revealing a thatch of gray hair sprouting from his chest, and his once mighty shoulders sag with the weight of all he has seen and done and eaten and drunk.

"Ahhhh," says Baldini, feasting upon a piece of ravioli in tomato sauce. "Hand-rolled. An old Ligurian recipe. La mia bella signora ha fatto! My old lady. She cooks like a goddess. Used to look like one, too. Sit down. She'll bring you a plate. Amore, portare un piatto!"

An elegant signora in a blue dress comes out of the house minutes later carrying a tray with food on a plate. Nacho thanks her in Italian and places a napkin on his lap. They eat awhile to the sound of birdsong, and then finally Baldini says, "Now. How can I help you?"

Nacho explains the situation and the ambassador's face twists and turns as if someone is prodding him with a tiny dagger in the great rolls of fat under his chin.

"Non c'è niente da fare," he says. "Get out of there. Run, run, run! Run like the wind."

"Not that easy for me."

"Ah, scusate! Then fly!" He wipes his mouth with an expansive swipe of his napkin, and leans into Nacho's orbit. "Torres is a psychopath. I mentioned this before, didn't I? Under his sharp Italian suits there's a big fat snake."

"Do you have any contacts that can help us?"

"Help you with what? I know someone at the airlines. She can fly you anywhere you want to go. I have a reliable driver—he can take you to the train station. Been with me twenty years. You'd like him. Speaks six languages."

Nacho cuts off Baldini.

"Not *me*. *Us*. Help *us*. Two thousand damnificados with nowhere to go."

Baldini shows Nacho the palms of his hands, shrugs.

"If you want miracles, go to a church. I'm an old man living out my days under a veranda. My wife cooks well. I drink a little brandy. Still enjoy a cigar. There was a time when I could move a mountain. Fix an election. Bribe an official or two. It was a pleasant existence and it paid well. But now?"

Show his palms again. Hams it up, with a pregnant pause.

"Me? An old man in a dry month being fed by an old lady."

Nacho finishes off his pasta with a clank as the fork hits the plate.

"Thank you for your time, Don Baldini. I'll always remember your kindness."

"Va bene. My driver is outside. Tell him where you want to go."

"Grazie."

Nacho retrieves his muletas from the low wall of the white-washed pavilion, stops at the house to shout his thanks and farewell, and walks to the gate. Baldini's chauffeur is nowhere to be seen, so Nacho hobbles a half mile and catches a bus home.

CHAPTER 26

WITH ONE DAY TO GO BEFORE TORRES'S PLANNED INVASION OR DEMOLITION, NACHO TAKES a rickshaw to Christ on the Cross, a church in the suburbs of Agua Suja. The morning traffic is the usual honk-yell-skid as pedestrians make hell-for-leather dashes across wide boulevards and the hawkers wander invincibly in the thick of it all.

The rickshaw driver is a young man, maybe twenty, but he has been on a rickshaw for ten years. He has the face of a child and a skinny torso, but calves like a weightlifter's. He keeps to the slow side of the road and waves and grins at pedestrians, water sellers, hookers, tramps, calling out their names or whistling through his teeth.

As they enter the suburbs, the streets thin out, some tree-lined, others looking out over expanses of wasteland. The smell of the river permeates everything. They arrive at the church and Nacho gives the boy a tip and pauses at the building, looks at the roof. Pigeons coo and twitch.

He pushes at the door, a massive wedge of burnished oak, and goes into the hush, the shade, the echo of footsteps on stone. It's the largest church in the region, built by a monster called Resnaut, a gangster who saw the light late in life. The death of his beloved daughter—drowned in the filth of the river a year after his wife had died—turned him to God in his fifties. Resnaut repented of his murderous ways, returned much of the money he had extorted from terrified shopkeepers and families, and gave away his dandyish clothes to the beggars on the street. In order to atone for his sins, he visited church daily, where he would prostrate himself side by side with the damnificados and the indigent. One day he asked a beggarwoman there why she was sweating and could barely stand. She explained that the church they were in was miles away from the slum where the poor lived, and having no money for public transport, she had walked in the baking sun. It was at this point that he had a revelation: build a church on the edge of the slum, where the poor could worship.

Resnaut spent the last twenty years of his life raising money to build his church. It became an obsession. He poured his libros into the project until he had to sell his home and possessions. And even that didn't stop him. He begged and borrowed from former acquaintances, gambled his last hundred libros on black in a casino in Salamurhaaja Street, won, and poured that money into the church. He ransacked his dead wife's jewelry collection, sold everything, pawned her dresses by the yard, gambled again, this time on a vicious fighting dog called Yoyo, who won, and paid off the builders, the contractors, the architects, and the politicians who—he knew all too well—needed to be bribed so that he would get a permit.

Resnaut began to dress like a pauper. He started to smell of the street. His beard grew unruly, a tangle of weeds, and his skin began to shrivel. He lost thirty kilograms and most of his hair. Unable to pay his bills, he moved to a tiny apartment. When he failed to pay the rent for the third month running, the landlord pointed a shotgun in his face. Resnaut moved to a hovel in the Agua Suja slum, coming out daily to supervise the construction of the church. For two months this went on, until one day the residents of the slum recognized him as the thug who had made their life hell, and chased him down the rutted, sewage-filled street.

Resnaut moved to the only place he felt safe—the half-finished church. He slept in the portico. When the builders arrived every morning, he was up and awake. He pretended to be newly arrived at the site, carefully hiding all evidence that this was now his home.

After eating poor food and living rough for months on end, Resnaut became sick. He delivered the final payment anonymously and lived just long enough to see the completion of the church. The following day he was found dead, frozen to death under a statue of Jesus on the cross. Assuming he was a tramp, the authorities cremated his body. A woman who worked at the crematorium was given his ashes in a plastic bag, but the trashcans were full. Not knowing what to do with the bag of ashes, she decided to scatter them in what seemed a suitable place on her way home: the new church that had just been built on the outskirts of Agua Suja. There she opened the bag and, in a sweeping arc, threw the remains of Resnaut onto the side of his church. A freak rainstorm then plastered those ashes to the wall, ensuring that Resnaut would forever cling to his project.

*

And now Nacho looks up at its soaring vault, stops to examine the statues in their niches, and totters down the aisle on his muletas, heading for the altar. There, under a stone carving of the pietà, an emaciated Christ recumbent in his mother's arms.

Nacho sits on a wooden bench and wonders why he has come. He has never been a religious man. He knows the stories and loves the language of the Bible, its grandeur and sweep, but has never felt God's hand touching his shoulder. He is a secular beast. Just like his father, Samuel. Curious and questing, but always earthbound. Nacho believes there is an explanation for everything, that there is no Big Man in the sky dispensing His Magic.

But here and now, with no plan to save the tower, and trusting to dumb luck and blind fate, Nacho falls to his knees and asks for help.

"God give me strength to know what to do in my hour of need."

He kneels there for ninety minutes. No one enters or leaves the church. His lame leg aches but he doesn't move, soaks up the pain, eyes raised to the stone carving. He feels the barely perceptible wind of a breath on his neck, turns and sees no one, but feels the presence of his mother who isn't his mother, wife of Samuel, daughter of Ezequiel and Martha, granddaughter of Zachariah and Jennifer and Antonio and Maria-Elena, and he hears the same message he heard the last time a Torres threatened the tower. "You'll be OK. Everything will be OK."

Only this time he doesn't believe it.

*

Nacho rises from the floor of the church. But his gammy leg has gone numb, and he almost falls. He regains his balance and sits on the bench. He stretches out his legs, berating the left for its weakness, and rises slowly again. He picks up his muletas, takes a last look at the prone Christ, turns, and walks down the aisle.

Outside, he is met by a burst of sunlight so bright it hits him like an explosion and blinds him momentarily. But it isn't just his sight. His ears prick up. Something in the air, a humming that he cannot immediately recognize. A murmur or a thrum. He follows the noise. Walking toward the slums, the sounds escalating to a hubbub. Rubble and patches of cracked earth. Harsh white light reflecting off the sun-seared land. Buildings lower now. Shebeens and lean-tos. Hardboard shacks cobbled together. Mangy dogs. Trash. All the detritus of the poor. And on he walks, drawn by the noise. Toward the river, where he was left as a baby. Agua Suja. Dirty water.

The babble of voices is everywhere now, mixed with strains of music, and he begins to see apparitions, only they aren't. Men, women, children, walking to the river. He follows them, turns a corner, and sees thousands moving toward the sand-silt shore, all wearing white. On the flood plain, hundreds of tents, women balancing pots on their heads, fumes of food cooked in the street, people milling and talking. The troubadour too, also in white, leaning over his guitar, his music drowned in the thrum of the crowd.

As Nacho moves forward he sees hundreds bathing in the river and realizes, or rather remembers, what he is seeing. Years ago his father told him about the Great Cleansing: once every ten years, people came to wash away their sins. They walked into the water, some fully clothed, some in a state of ecstasy, others with their families, yet others—pilgrims from far-off lands—come to achieve communion with all humanity. Here mingled the poor, the wealthy, and all those in the middle.

And now Nacho sees ash-covered ascetics sitting cross-legged in white pants, and men in mundus, white sarongs wrapped elegantly around their waists. And behind them, shirtless boys already splashing in the shallows, and women lifting their skirts a few inches and treading gently into the water. He sees a group of shaven-headed monks in nothing but white underwear holding hands as they enter the river, stepping down from its banks until their feet, then their calves, then their thighs, are covered.

All around him voices call out greetings in a dozen languages. A group sitting in a circle begins to chant, and further down the walkway others sing ancient songs. Nacho comes to a bottleneck of people, hundreds jammed together, and finds himself blending with the throng and moving inexorably toward the water, muletas under his arms, carried along by the crowd.

They take him to the edge of the river. Nacho feels his muletas sticking in the mud, his feet in the mulch where thousands have trodden before him. He puts the muletas down and takes off his shirt and his shoes, rolls up the cuffs of his pants to his knees. Suddenly he finds himself picked up under the arms by two smiling men. They walk him into the water.

"Estas bien, pequeño lisiado?"

"Muy bien!"

And they leave him there, knee deep, among thousands of others. He looks to either side, reaches down and takes two hand-fuls of silt-water and bathes his chest and shoulders. A sense of calm comes over him. Surrounded by so many, he feels safe, as if nothing and no one can harm him. And the stench of the river, for once, doesn't assail him; it is camouflaged by incense sticks burn-ing everywhere and the smell of chicken frying on the riverbank.

Still the masses come as the remains of the sun stain the sky red. Nacho begins to feel himself disappearing, blending in with the crowd. For once, no one is looking to him to make a decision, resolve a dispute, save the day, and so he lets the minutes wash over him until they turn into hours, the gentle flow of the water winding around his knees. Lost in reverie, he barely notices the naked children splashing through the river and clambering out the other side in a madcap race, or the holy man who sits placidly on the surface of the water, or the circles formed by families standing knee-deep in prayer, the slow current forming ripples around them.

Neither does he notice the sunlight playing on the murky water, forming golden stars, or the arrival of a painted elephant on the flood plain, carrying a princess under a huge blue umbrella. On the other side of the river a line of camels approaches, laden with tents and provisions. The masses part to let them pass, and the camels obediently trudge forward in slow motion, all foul breath and slobber. Women in saris begin scattering orange petals onto the water, and a family in white robes stands together and tips an urn of ashes into the river—an ancestor now cleansed of sin after death.

Eventually Nacho goes back to the shore, picks up his muletas and puts on his shoes and his shirt. He walks the riverbank, smells the food, eyes a cauldron of bubbling feijoada and a grill with giant turkey legs, meat charring over the heat. Hungry now, he sees a young black woman in a white kaftan laying out plastic plates of rice and beans on a tray and asks her for one. She smiles and tells him to help himself and refuses money. He finds a low wall, sits and eats ravenously. Rice and beans—the food of damnificados.

He walks a little further down the riverbank and sees a man in a turban stirring two pots simultaneously. Nacho asks him what is in them and the man gives him a bowl brimming with lentils and cabbage stew and a taste of offal and tripe. Nacho eats as if it's his last meal. He shakes the man's hand and moves on, past an empanada seller in an apron. The woman sees him and shouts, "Nacho Morales! My sister lives in your tower!" and she gives him an empanada as if in thanks.

"It's not my tower, but thank you," says Nacho, and he sits beside the woman on the same low wall and eats the empanada.

He watches the crowd and recognizes the poor—their bad teeth, stooped backs, faces prematurely aged, bodies vandalized with random tattoos—and he thinks of something said by the woman with the dog in a wheelbarrow, and says to himself, 'They are us.'

He sees other handicapped people led by the able-bodied toward the water as if this filthy sludge that stinks to high heaven could cure them. He remembers Shivarov and the devil's work that man did for money, and then casts out the thought and watches the carers and their charges descend the riverbank together.

The last wisps of cloud streak the sky, and Nacho wonders if he has ever been happier. All that is missing is Emil, longhaired, bandy-legged, laughing at the world, king of the hobos, the rescuer and savior, the vagabond. For a moment, Nacho also thinks of his mother and father, imagining them there, unchanged by the years. Now they would be in their sixties were they alive, but to him they will always be in their forties, young, unlined. He pictures his father sitting on the wall or peering into the water to find some mudfish or river reed. And his mother smiling at her boys, bringing them food, code-switching in Spanish and English.

As the light fades down by the river, the music swells. All around Nacho now are drummers and singers, people dancing. Figures emerge dripping from the water and go straight to the little groups that have struck up, singing traditional songs, clapping out rhythms, or chanting mantras, eyes closed.

Nacho moves on. His belly full, he cannot sit anymore. But then a man frying anchovies on the river walk catches his eye and calls, "Nacho!" and hands him a fistful of the fish wrapped in paper, and Nacho thanks him and eats again.

The moon comes up and Nacho catches a bus to Favelada. He has no idea that this echoes the first journey he ever made, the bus ride with Samuel to the House of Flowers. From the window, he sees the streets of Fellahin, and the long fence full of graffiti, buildings jerry-built and jammed together. Then past Minhas, its vast holes yawning, where the miners spend their days. And through a No-Man's-Land of brush and scrub and stones, and finally to Favelada.

He climbs down the steps of the bus, and walks across the plaza, past a mural and the children's playground. How peaceful the tower looks in the light of the moon. From the windows the rectangular glow of stolen electricity, and drying clothes flapping in the evening breeze.

"Mr. Morales?"

A child's voice.

"Hello."

Nacho turns and sees a group of boys aged ten or eleven. They are on their knees playing with marbles. The boy who called him is one of his regular pupils, and immediately Nacho remembers what he has forgotten.

"Is there no school this evening?" says the boy.

"I'm sorry! Come tomorrow. If we're still here, I'll teach you everything you need to know."

"Yes, Mr. Morales."

The boy goes back to his marbles, and Nacho walks toward the tower.

Something different. His walk. He feels strong. He looks down. In the place where his left leg should stand—the shriveled bit of string and bone he's propped up all the days of his life—he sees something else. His left leg is whole. He looks at his withered arm. No longer withered. He drops the muletas and leaves them where they land. Begins to run. Takes the steps of the tower two at a time till he's in his room.

CHAPTER 27

Morning dawns—Nacho in stasis—

Torres—A convoy rolls through Favelada—

What the lookouts see—The Fifth Trash War

For once, morning dawns and Nacho isn't the first up. Maria and Emil are knocking on his door. He gets up slowly and lets them in.

Maria says, "I hear you were partying at the river last night while we were getting ready for Armageddon."

"Shut up," says Emil. "Torres is coming."

Maria looks at Emil, scandalized. "Did you just tell me to shut up?"

Her hand is on her hip, so she looks like a lithe and exquisitely coutured teapot.

"No, I was talking to myself. Nacho, we've got to get ready. Word is that Torres is on his way. What are we gonna do?"

Nacho makes coffee. He puts the water on to boil and pulls a filter from a plastic bag. Rubs his eyes. Feels his left arm through his nightshirt.

"Hey, brother," says Emil. "Did you hear me?"

"You want coffee?"

"Nacho! It's today! Torres is coming!"

"I hear you," says Nacho, resigned. He ruffles his hair. "What can we do?"

"You're the leader."

"You trained some of the men, right? To fire a gun. So we'll shoot at them. See what happens. The families need to evacuate before Torres blows us all up. That's about it, isn't it?"

He sits at his chair with his minuscule xicara of thick, sweet coffee. Maria goes to the window. Emil sits opposite Nacho on the other chair. The chessboard is between them.

Suddenly Emil reaches over.

"Your arm."

"I'm cured."

Maria turns around.

"I was at the Great Cleansing yesterday. Something happened to me. I'm cured."

Maria says, "But that's a miracle."

Emil withdraws his hand. "My God," he says.

Maria walks over and feels Nacho's arm.

"Stand up," she says. "A miracle. What happened to you?"

"At the Great Cleansing. There were thousands of people. They took me to the river and I went in. And I just waded a little. An hour later I could walk. And my arm was as you see it now."

That's impossible," says Emil. "Did you go to see the bruja of Estrellas Negras? She's been known to . . ."

"I'm telling you the truth," says Nacho. "I went in the river. I was cured."

A moment later a boy knocks on the door.

"Mr. Morales, I found your crutches on the playground."

The boy hands them over. Nacho thanks him and leans the muletas against the wall.

"I won't need these now."

"Yes, sir," says the boy, his eyes agog, and walks out the door.

✳

Emil touches the chess pieces.

"This is Torres," he says, handling the white king. "And this is us."

"Not really," says Nacho, who, in great handfuls, moves all of the black pieces except the king off the board, and places them on the white side. Pawns tumble and a bishop rolls. "*This* is us. One defenseless tower against an army."

"We have to come up with a plan," says Emil.

"What do you have in mind? Summon the wolves? Get bows and arrows from Dahomey-Krill? It's too late for plans. When he comes, I'll talk to him. Appeal to his better nature and probably get my head blown off for my pains. Then you can start shooting. OK?"

"No," says Emil. "Not OK."

"How many men is he bringing?"

"We don't know."

"How do you know he's coming?" asks Nacho.

"We have people all over the city. It's the word on the street."

"The word on the street?"

"Nacho, do you want to die today? You just acquired a working leg and an arm."

Nacho looks at his brother, sips his coffee calmly. Emil waits for an answer. When he doesn't get one, he speaks again.

"We have to do something."

"I'm all out of ideas. I asked my contacts, I asked Lalloo, I went to the history books. Endless war. That's just what happens around here. People live and die and blood is spilt and nothing ever changes. We fight the good fight or we run away and leave the tower for Torres. What does it matter? How many people live here? A couple of thousand? Let them find other homes. Tell them about the places we scouted last week. The toxic tower in Fellahin, the factory full of bats in Oameni Morti, the abandoned zoo. Move them out. We can't win a war, so let them walk away. At least give them the choice."

Maria turns on him.

"Walk away? My business is here. Thousands of libros of equipment. What do you want me to do?"

"What do you want *me* to do?" says Nacho.

"Get Torres to change his mind."

Nacho almost snorts. "You want me to bargain with a psychopath? See if he changes his mind? He's a Torres."

Maria lets out a snarl. "I'll talk to him myself," she says.

"Be my guest."

"Your body may be cured but you're as useless as every other man."

She turns on a stiletto like a knife and flounces out of the room.

Emil says, "That's not going to work. You're our leader, Nacho. Now's the big moment and you're sitting here drinking coffee, admiring your new leg."

"If you want me to play the hero, I can do that. I can show off my body and say miracles are possible. I can make a big speech about us fighting for our survival. I can preach about justice in seven languages, but it's not going to change anything. Torres is going to kill us. The end."

"But we need to do something."

"At the Great Cleansing in Agua Suja last night . . . like I said, there were ten, maybe twenty, thousand people there, eating, singing, bathing together. It was the happiest and the best thing I can remember. Today that same river may run with our blood, and it'll be a footnote in history. Maybe not even that. Maybe just a scrawl in the margins. Long-term or short-term, we're all dead. There are no happy endings. This is the way the world is. So why don't you get a bunch of cardboard boxes, borrow a truck, pack up Maria's junk, and drive to Ferrido and make boats for the rest of your life. I never asked you to stay or be a martyr."

"Yes, you did."

"Well, I'm taking it back. Get out of here. Take that precious, beautiful, wonderful woman and run for your life. Make a new start. Between you, you can't go wrong. She has more balls than the rest of us put together and you're not so bad in that department either. So go. Go make babies. Start a business. Do whatever you want to do. You have my blessing."

"I don't need your blessing. I'm your big brother. And I'm not walking away. Why do you think I came here in the first place? To rescue you."

"Well, you did it. I thank you. Really I do. But you can't rescue me again. Not from Torres. So don't try."

"I have to try. I'm my father's son. And besides, he keeps coming back to me in my sleep telling me everything will be OK. Mother, too."

He pauses, looks at Nacho. "What? What is it?"

Nacho nods. "I've been having the same dreams. And not always when I'm asleep. Visitations."

At that moment, a cry goes up, and the walkie-talkies begin to crackle. Torres.

❋

The streets of Favelada are closed off. Wooden barriers and orange traffic cones divide up the city and turn it into a maze, pushing the streams of traffic down back streets, under obscure bridges and over roads that are barely roads: trails of rubble, rutted creeks, and dried-up riverbeds. Large signs warn drivers away—flashing lights and upper-case letters. Pedestrians, too, are redirected by men with guns, and even the stray dogs are hustled back into the shadows where they came from.

On the main street—the artery that runs through Favelada—a few soldiers mill about. Electronic messages echo in their radios, and they ready themselves for an arrival, flicking cigarette butts into the road, discarding the dregs of their morning coffee into the drains.

At 8:30 a.m. a rumbling comes, so deep and dolorous that it seems to emanate from under the earth, the breath of some medieval behemoth. The roads, already baked from six weeks of relentless heat, crack under the weight of a convoy of heavy metal.

Along Haggadah Street, the infantrymen come jogging, dressed in khaki, gripping rifles. Some wear helmets customized to their tastes: ostrich feathers or badges that say Death or Glory or stenciled crossbones. Others come unhelmeted, piratical in bandannas or shaven-headed. They run past the old watchmakers and the clothes factory, the smoke and musk of the city hanging in the air, an acrid brume that muffles everything like a layer of snow. In the graffiti-covered tenements, faces peer out over the balconies, and children kicking a ball stop and stare, the ball rolling untamed into the street.

The foot soldiers keep running, wet with sweat in the clustering heat: fifty, eighty, one hundred, two hundred, three hundred, four hundred in all, and a straggler faints, bangs his head on a sidewalk, and is left behind, later to be stripped raw, liberated of his gun and his shoes and his helmet, the last of which will be rinsed clean and used for soup by three generations of damnificados.

Behind them come armored cars, tricked out in spine-like shields, a herd of triceratops. Their drivers wear huge goggles which make them look like insects crouched behind the wheel. The cars come in pairs because the street is narrow.

Seventy armored cars later, the real story reveals itself. A massive clanking. A grinding of gears. A throbbing in the road. Fifty tanks, platinum gray, turrets rotating, aiming their tube-like schnozzles at the shabby bungalows, the moldering tenements, the wastelands off Haggadah where the cats spend their days. The tank tracks crush everything in their path. Dust rises and from the tracks tiny flecks of compacted stone are spat up in whizzing parabolas that clink on the windows of the stores.

The sound is inhuman. A clamor of robot noise, a symphony of iron and gear sticks and metallic coughs and stutters underpinned by a droning baritone—the internal workings of machines of war. Some cries go up, squad leaders bellowing orders, but mainly it's a wordless procession. Faceless, too, until the final tank appears with Torres himself manning the hatch, grinning hugely, his moustache ends twirled for the occasion. Even in the heat he wears a combat jacket festooned with medals he's awarded himself. His hair is slicked back like a '30s film star and he waves at pedestrians who stare, bemused.

Past Milarepa Street, with its bare stone walls and narrow roads, the convoy curves. Here and there an infantryman adjusts to pull out a water bottle or wipe away a bead of sweat. Footsteps echo where the sound gets caught between two high buildings and then the echo stops as the road opens out to the gardens abreast of the Buddhist temple, whose walls are flaking and whose roof is spattered with birdshit and feathers where the pigeons roost.

Down Baldado Street, which is little more than an alley, a collection of shadows and misshapen apartment blocks that lean at angles like drunken sentries, the convoy rolls. Torres waves blindly, at no one, keeping up his actor's grin, and plants a fat cigar in his mouth.

They leave the shadows behind and enter Hollowman Road up a short hill, and the foot soldiers pant and heave and slow down to a walk.

"Get moving there!" shouts a sergeant from his armored car.

The infantrymen make a big show of resuming a jog. The tanks fan out, forming a phalanx three or four wide. By now, the sun has burned through the morning mist and the sky is a bright, bright blue, cloudless and vast.

The tower suddenly looms into view.

And from the tower, the convoy can be seen in all its mass, its impossible heft.

"There!" shouts a lookout on the sixtieth floor. "There!"

Word spreads rapidly down the tower, and the lookouts calculate the numbers.

"Looks like seventy tanks."

"It's at least eighty."

"I make it a hundred."

"How many soldiers? I count a thousand."

"Maybe two thousand! Maybe more!"

On the tenth floor, in a room abandoned by a family just days earlier, Nacho sits calmly at the window, hand under chin.

✳

The Fifth Trash War is a misnomer. No one with his head screwed on straight would possibly call it a war, yet word of mouth has designated it just that, despite the protestations of historians and journalists. For how could it be a war? When seventy armored cars and fifty tanks come rumbling through the streets and find themselves faced with a bunch of scaredy-cat damnificados armed with sticks and stones and cowering under their beds, *war* surely cannot be the right word.

And yet . . . and yet . . . there are those calling for a new tapestry to augment the famous Zeffekat, to depict every movement of that extraordinary day. There are those who say that *this* Trash War, and not the third, was the war to end all wars because from now onward until eternity no one would ever forget the sight, the sound, the stench, as if the world itself were coming to an end.

And it all began with a rat.

*

It isn't the pounding of the soldiers' feet. It isn't the tires of the armored cars. It isn't even the giant tracks of the tanks crowding into the plaza of the Torre de Torres that scare the rat. It is something else entirely, something known only to animals, who have a sixth sense when it comes to imminent disaster. In any case, this rat does something strange. Rather than running away from the largest, heaviest army ever assembled in the streets of Favelada, the rat runs *through* the ranks. It hurtles helter-skelter around the feet of the six hundred soldiers, sidesteps and feints its way past the now stationary armored cars, and jinks past the tanks. Torres sees it and laughs, a deep belly-laugh.

"They've sent a rat to eliminate me!" he yells, and his men begin to chuckle.

The laughter spreads forward to his tank commanders, who have also seen the rat, then his armored car drivers join in the mirthless mirth, and finally a few infantrymen catch the gist of the joke and laugh themselves silly.

"What the fuck are they laughing at?" says Raincoat, trembling on the thirtieth floor, his eyes peeking out the window.

"God knows," says one of the baker brothers.

Twenty floors further down, Emil says to Nacho, "If you're going to go, go now. Go and talk to him. It's hard to murder someone when you're laughing. Go out and share the joke."

Nacho doesn't move.

All over the tower, men and women are looking out of windows. The ex-soldier, carrying a rifle in one hand and a bottle of malt whisky in the other, tries to count the soldiers but his eyes keep seeing double so he loses track. He sees the tanks' guns trained on the building and starts shaking.

Down below, on the plaza, the infantrymen who aren't laughing are panting. Some have put their guns down and collapsed.

One has gone into full calisthenics mode, touching his toes, doing a warm-down. Others are bent double, hands on knees, retching. One is heard saying, "I'm a mercenary, not a freakin' marathon runner."

"Me too," says a comrade. "I signed up to kill people, not go jogging."

"Yeah," says a third soldier. "We get here and what? Nothing. An empty tower block and a rat!"

Meanwhile, Torres wipes his eyes and his sweating forehead with a flowery handkerchief. Then he thinks of another one.

"The rat leaving the sinking ship!"

And his tank commanders howl with laughter again, snorting into the air, slapping their hands onto the turrets, and the armored car drivers can be seen bug-eyed chortling behind their windscreens. This war! What a lark! The rat leaving the sinking ship!

Torres pulls a megaphone from the tank's interior, ready to order the attack, but before he can raise it to his mouth, something strange happens. It turns out there is more than one rat escaping. The one they saw was a pioneer, and it is followed by dozens more, slinking out of holes in the hot concrete or cracks in the walls of the tower and shooting across the plaza. Some of the infantrymen jump, others stamp, and others take swipes with their bayonets, but the rats are too quick.

And then something else happens. A posse of stray cats hiding out around the tower also takes off, skittering past the lines of soldiers and armored cars and tanks. And following *them*, a few normally somnolent dogs rise abruptly from their slumbers and bound away into the streets of Favelada. Up on the sixth floor Maria's dog starts yelping and every other dog in the building does the same till it's a cacophony of growls and barks.

Torres's eyes dart left and right. No one moves. Torres looks up. Blue sky. He looks in front. Four hundred thousand tons of heavy equipment packed into the square, and so far nothing but rats and cats and dogs.

In the tower, too, no one moves.

Zugzwang.

Suddenly, there is a rumbling.

"What *is* that?" says Torres. And those are the last words he utters.

In front of him, all around him, and under him, the ground caves in. It isn't a gradual crumbling of the surface, nor even a crack or a gash as in an earthquake. No. Instead, the very earth drops away, swallowing up everyone and everything in the plaza, sucking them down into one hundred years' worth of compacted, buried trash, and as the tanks and the armored cars and the soldiers drop into the abyss, cries go up like never heard before in Favelada: screams and screeches and hollering as the tanks topple like toys crashing one upon the other, their tracks twisting, wheels flying like Frisbees, whole turrets prized off their rings like the shells of crabs, and the armored cars come apart in a smashing of glass and a rending of metal, and guns twist and snap, and bodies go cartwheeling like clowns, the final cries of the soldiers echoing into the sinkhole until they disappear or are drowned out by the tanks' metal plates clanging and gnashing, and there at the bottom of the sinkhole, one hundred feet down, the bodies and the vehicles of war come to rest, settling in a heap, and the scene is so black, so subterranean, that nothing can be seen by the human eye even with the light of the sun from above, and so no one, not the soldiers breathing their last, nor the few who survive in the tanks, shielded by walls of iron, sees the two enormous crocodiles that seem to come from nowhere to feast on the dismembered limbs and gorge on the pools of blood that lie at the bottom of the abyss, swinging their tails in fat walloping arcs, ramping open their great wedges of jaw lined with iron-hard teeth, those same beasts chased and teased by Hans and Dieter all those months ago, which emerged from the rains and submerged into the dark, feeding on God-knows-what, living in a fetor so foul that it brews gases redolent of the ancient days when the earth was young, and the stench is now augmented by the smells of blood, engine grease, crushed metal and gasoline, and these mingle with the older smells that have bubbled and fomented underground: the odors of mold and rot and decomposing animals, and from the edge of the sink-hole there comes a voice screaming kami ay labanan sa dulo! again and again and it's the ghosted lady of the First Trash War, who in life was tiny and curled like a crustacean but has now grown wings and stands eight feet tall and flew from the roof of the tower and dove to the rim of the abyss like an angel of vengeance wreaking her own brand of havoc in recompense for a hundred years of iniquity and suffering and now with her last wail can fly into the ether, which she does, above the roofs and the tenements and the valleys and the hills overlooking all the broken lives, the ransacked dreams of the damnificados, and from the tower, speechless, eyes agape, *these* damnificados look on, watching the square they have traversed every day disappear before their eyes into a black rect-angle that has buried their enemies so fast and so wholly that the onlookers blink in disbelief and gawp and wonder if they have lost their minds and fallen prey to mass hysteria begetting an illusion of destruction beyond all imagining, and they turn to one another and their mouths open but no words come out because there are no words to utter when hell opens up before your eyes and so they stay silent and one or two stand up and put down their guns and their catapults and their homemade grenades, and look on in homage or horror at the miracle that has unfolded before them to rout their enemies, and finally *down there* when the last scream has been lost to the wind and the last heartbeat thumped in the last chest and the last reshuffle of the last moving tank parts—glacis plates, periscopes, fume extractors, gun mantlets, all sinking into position for posterity—only then does Nacho scramble to his feet, ruffle his hair and announce to the six people in the room the line that will live on long after he is gone:

"We won."

CHAPTER 28

Aftermath—Credit—The damnificados

celebrate—Evacuation—The

damnificados disperse—Memory

THE LITTLE CRIPPLE WHO IS NO LONGER A CRIPPLE IS LAUDED FROM THE MOUNTAINS OF Zaurituak to the mines of Hajja Xejn, from the ice fields of Zaledenom Jezeru to the wastelands of Izoztu. He is the new David, the Goliath-slayer, who used the very strength of his enemy—the sheer weight of their vehicles, the mass of their weaponry—to destroy them, to rid the world of a butcher and a tyrant. The historians construct elaborate hypotheses about how he did it, how he booby-trapped the ground so it would swallow up an army, and the newspapers print detailed diagrams and quote well-respected geologists and anthropologists showing how it's possible to build a sinkhole, a trap that a hunter would be proud of, even in the middle of a city.

And like all stories, this one grows and grows, warps out of shape till it's only half-recognizable: eyewitnesses report that thousands of wild animals were seen evacuating before the Great Drop occurred, and others give interviews claiming they helped to set the trap, digging below the surface of the land and covering it up with just enough soil and stone to prevent the ruse from being discovered. Some even produce the tools used to dig the hole, showing off the shovels they held, the hoes, pick axes and augers they carried night after night to lay the trap that slew the monster.

In the provinces, the name of Nacho Morales becomes synonymous with heroism and ingenuity. He receives notes and telegrams and messages of congratulations and an honorary doctorate from a university in Gudsland. A local bigwig suggests putting Nacho's face on a stamp, and a hack approaches him to write a biography. Outside a museum in Favelada, a statue of Nacho goes up, idealized, with his hair all wrong and his muletas nowhere in sight, so he looks like a Spartan warrior. A chef invents a soufflé that sags in the middle and names it the Grand Nacho.

A movie goes into production, then a children's cartoon to be serialized, and an action figure with crutches that turn into guns or fold out to become wings.

✳

But in the immediate aftermath of the Great Drop, stunned silence reigns. No one is taking credit for anything. Nacho and Emil go outside. Minutes earlier they were facing an army. Now there's nothing but a black cavity six hundred feet by four hundred, a yawning, gaping void where the square used to be. Gone is the mural, the children's playground; gone are the benches where the old men gathered, the tidy lawns and vegetable garden. From the hole in the land, ghostly strings of vapor rise and curl and dissipate in the sunlight.

Emil starts to walk toward the perimeter of the abyss, but Nacho tells him, "Don't get too close. We don't know if it's stable." And Emil pulls back, stays just outside the entrance to the tower and looks on at the scene where the earth has swallowed an army.

"It's like something out of the Bible," he says.

Suddenly they hear shouts going up in the tower, and these signify the realization that the damnificados have won, that the enemy lies buried one hundred feet down, in a mass grave. Nacho and Emil look up at the tower and see people waving in triumph and couples hugging and a woman erecting a flag on the roof. Groups of children begin to cheer, their trebles and sopranos piercing the air. A klaxon sounds and then drums and wild singing.

Nacho says to Emil, "The rats and other animals that escaped—they knew what was coming. They always know before it happens."

Maria appears at the entrance of the tower, tight jeans and big hooped earrings, flushed, almost glowing in wonder. She catches Nacho's eye.

"Che cosa incredibile! You knew all along, didn't you? Sapevi! You planned this!"

"No," says Nacho.

"That's why you were so calm, partying in Agua Suja. Drinking coffee. You knew it! How did you do it?"

"I didn't. We got lucky."

"Bullshit. You buried two Torres boys, one under ice, the other under earth. You're a hero."

And in one sweeping gesture she grasps him by the neck and kisses his forehead, leaving a stain of red lipstick.

The victory march goes as far as the stone heads at the gates of the city and for the first time in his life Nacho leads them with a fast walk, striding ahead while the damnificados do a double take and talk about the double miracle of the victory and their leader's body restored, whole and unbroken. At the stone heads a party erupts, catching revelers returning and still decked out in white from the Great Cleansing at Agua Suja. The dancing goes on all night and into the following morning and some are so drunk by the time they return that they nearly trip into the abyss.

Only when the new day glimmers into motion, clear and sun-soaked, does the truth dawn on Nacho—they need to evacuate.

*

It isn't the stench, though that is terrible. A smell can always be covered up if you bury something deep enough, and Nacho already has in mind filling the hole with sand and stones and debris from the areas around Favelada. The problem is the surrounding land, and that includes the land on which stands the monolith.

"The tower could fall any day. Any minute," says Nacho.

"You're saying we won the battle but we have to leave anyway," says one of the floor leaders.

"Yeah," chimes in one of the baker brothers. "What the hell? I mean crikey, mate, we've won. Let's stay here!"

A few murmurs go around. Nacho is in his classroom. On the board he has drawn a geological diagram of how a sinkhole works, copied from a book he found in the library that morning. Patiently he has explained that nothing now is safe within a two-hundred-meter radius.

"I've told you the facts," he says. "It's unstable land. We're on a precipice. We're living on the edge of a hole a hundred foot deep. The land around the hole is weak. One rain shower and it could all come down, including the tower. Everyone would die instantly. We saw what happened to Torres's army."

"So where do we go?" says Wheelbarrow, who no longer wheels a wheelbarrow.

"I don't know yet," says Nacho.

Raincoat blurts out, "Last week you said there was a factory we could live in."

"Emil told us it was infested with bats," says Wheelbarrow.

"And something about a zoo."

"That's right," says Nacho. "There's an abandoned zoo."

"Zoos are for animals," says a man. "That's not how we want to live."

"If we want to live," says Nacho, "the first thing to do is get out of here. Then we find a place. Or places."

"But this is our home," says Wheelbarrow.

"I'm not forcing anyone to leave," says Nacho. "But you stay at your own risk. And I ask those of you with children: do you really want to live next to this crater? Every time your children go outside you'll worry they'll fall in. Every ball they kick or toy on wheels will roll down the hill and into the abyss where, what, a thousand people died? It isn't safe. I've done the research, looked at geological records, talked to land surveyors and risk assessors. They all say the same thing. Get out before it's too late."

"Then why dya do it if ya knew?" says a voice from the back, a woman with a shaven head and a tattoo of an eye above her nose.

"Do what?"

"Plant bombs under the land so it be cavin' in. That's what they sayin' you done."

"Who said I planted anything?"

"Ever'body. Sayin' y'all with your brother, whassisname, Emilio, done laid a trap."

"It isn't true," says Nacho, "and even if it were, it wouldn't be relevant. We got lucky. Now our luck's run out. We have to leave. I'm telling you what I know. I brought many of you here and now I'm telling you, those of you who want to listen, that it's time to find somewhere else. I'm sorry it didn't work out. We tried. There'll be other towers and other places to call home. We just haven't found them yet."

Nacho walks out of the door and down twenty flights of stairs to his room. He tries to call the twins but they are sleeping off an almighty hangover and in any case their father's truck is nowhere to be seen. Nacho resigns himself to abandoning his books, his furniture, everything that cannot be carried in the back of a spindly rickshaw.

*

"Ferrido," says Emil.

"Bon voyage," says Nacho.

And he's gone with a roar and a shower of dust, Maria hanging onto his back as the rusty motorbike peels away, the head of her tiny dog protruding from a rucksack over her shoulders. She didn't even say goodbye. No looking back. Abandoned her salon. Took trinkets and heirlooms only, and a piece of Nacho's heart.

"I'll see you again, brother," says Nacho to himself. "And you, too, Maria."

Wheelbarrow stands behind him. She looks old now and a little broken, but she has told herself she will follow him till the end.

The baker brothers decide to stay in the monolith, but with most of the people gone and others too scared to enter the building, their bakery soon goes bankrupt and they are reduced to carrying loaves on trays in the street. Within a month they leave.

As for Don Felipe, the priest, it's true he went to Torres, but his reasons were misunderstood. He went on a mission to convert the tyrant to Christianity. Torres laughed in his face, tied him up and threw him in a cell, interrogating him for information about Nacho, threatening tortures that would have made even Shivarov the Cripple Maker pause. The priest was discovered after Torres's death, half starved and delirious in his cell. On returning to his room in the tower, he found that his possessions had been stolen. Shuffling out of the monolith for the last time, with nothing but the rags on his back, he said to himself, "I've made it. Finally, I too am become a damnificado."

The others? They disperse. They slink back into the shadows where damnificados have always lived. They find digs in Fellahin or a hovel in Agua Suja, an abandoned cinema in Blutig or a flophouse in Oameni Morti. They live out their days doing odd jobs, fighting their addictions, looking for a place to call home.

Lalloo finds refuge in Spazzatura, the final resting place of his father. He is greeted like a returning son and put to work in the fields. He invents nothing, nor does he need to.

The twins bound across the regions, working in construction, on farms, in factories, inured from the world by their twin-hood and their wiry strength which pulls them clear of a thousand scrapes and fracases, lets them dodge bullets and dragons.

As for Nacho, he moves into a disused school in Mundanzas and takes twenty families with him. By day he teaches and translates; by night he walks for hours at a breathtaking pace, as if to make up for all those years hobbling on his mulctas. And sometimes he is recognized or half-recognized on the streets and those that see him say, "He looks like the hero Nacho Morales, but Nacho had a gammy leg. It can't be him."

Susana lives in the school, too, but remains loyal to the memory of Sato Kazunari Maeda for the rest of her days. Eventually she returns to Favelada to be closer to his grave. Nacho thinks of her sometimes and wonders what might have been, but eventually his memory of her fades and she becomes just another figure in a fairy tale. And anyway, it was the Chinaman she loved.

Emil and Maria find a place in Ferrido with four apple trees and a view of the sea. In three years they have two girls and a boy, miniadventurers, wild-haired, running helter-skelter along the docks. The port grows and businesses thrive. Maria opens a hairdresser's. And then another. And another. Emil builds boats. Nacho visits when he can, and Emil takes him out on trips along the coast and they talk about the old days, the House of Flowers, the Torres brothers, the wolf.

And some of the damnificados are changed. They are no longer people of the street. And as time goes by, their memories of the tower become hazy. Were they really holed up in the third-tallest building in the city? The one with the incredible views. Free water and electricity. Education. Dignity. Did it really happen that they defeated a wolf pack to get in and were then trapped by a flood so they couldn't get out? Or was it just a story? And did the wolves really return to rout Torres the Elder? And the little man? The cripple? Was he or was he not their leader? He seemed to make all the decisions, but he had a brother who looked more the part.

The tales they tell their children about the tower change according to the teller and the language. When the story is told in Italian it becomes florid, a tale of excess and color and light, and when it is told in Arabic it assumes a formal grace as if it is myth become real, and when told in Xhosa it becomes a poem sung by iimbongi. And the details change every time, the wolves becoming tigers or snakes, the Torres brothers assuming the shape of demons, horned and scaly.

And as the damnificados' memories of the tower begin to fade, the tower itself begins to lose all memory of them. With its last occupants gone, the sounds are erased, the air stilled. The roof is once again taken over by pigeons, and a group of feral cats finds refuge in the tower's lower floors. Clothes left hanging out to dry during the exodus turn into rags, rain-beaten and sun-bleached. Pots and pans suspended on nails or balanced one atop the other are discolored and then swallowed by rust. Abandoned books turn moldy, go brown and limp at the edges, and fall apart. Furniture begins to implode, wooden legs collapsing under the weight of damp leaves that fly in through the windows during storms, and chairs turn rickety in the humid air. Cupboards and wardrobes left standing in the sun blister and crack, and cardboard boxes turn to mulch.

And on the walls and the windows, the doors and the stairwells, nature begins to take over. At the building's entrance, weeds punch their way through cracks in the floor and a dandelion sprouts like a miniature sun. Ivy begins to climb the east wall and it climbs and climbs until it's pulling at the tower, gripping it in stringy hands with a million fingers, tugging at the pockmarked concrete and covering up the scrawls of graffiti.

The tower becomes invisible to passers-by. It is a mark, a stain on the city center, massive yet forgotten by those who walk by or drive past it on their way to elsewhere. A repository of old legends long gone. Occasionally a drunk or a group of partying teenagers wanders into the entrance, lights a fire on the ground floor, but the smell of the sinkhole and the presence of the cats soon drives them away. A rumor goes around that an animal has been seen there—an ancient wolf, its fur clumped and eyes dull as rain, and there was something strange about the creature when seen from a certain angle, as if there were two of them together—but no one can verify it.

And once again, with the glass all gone from the windows, and the doors left flapping and banging open and shut, the wind takes control of the tower, sending its gusts and squalls through the corridors, whistling up and down stairwells, playing arpeggios on the grills of abandoned radiators. On days when the raging rain comes in horizontal, the tower sways, swinging its hips, and the birds rise in unison on a perfect diagonal and fly till they are specks against the gray torrent.

In front of the tower, all the while, the abyss. Here and there, denizens of the wastelands take to throwing their garbage into the hole. Then they start to bring truckloads of it: cardboard, paper, rotting food, the corpses of animals. They come from Fellahin, Oameni Morti and Blutig, Agua Suja, Bordello, and Sanguinosa, and, slowly, slowly, over three decades the hole is gradually filled until once again at the heart of Favelada is a giant dump, a repository of trash covering the bones of the dead soldiers who all those years ago fell in and lost the war that wasn't a war.

And where there is trash there are people reclaiming things, digging in the dirt for a gem, a watch, a doll, a trinket. And as the garbage sorters go about their work, one or two stop to look up at the tower and remember the old songs their parents used to sing—the one about the Chinaman, the one about the wolf.

At the gates of the city the stone heads stand. The authorities build around them, constructing wider, better roads, and all who pass beside the heads are reminded that a city must look for its enemies outside and inside its walls. The rickshaw drivers remember hauling people to the parties there, and they remember the little cripple who ran the show, and they remember the fires and the lights and the singing and dancing, for, however much blood was spilt, commingling with the endless rain, and however long a shadow was cast by the Trash Wars, those were indeed magical times.

About the Author

JJ Amaworo Wilson was born in Germany, the son of a Nigerian mother and an English father, but grew up in the UK. He has also lived in Egypt, Colombia, Lesotho (where he ran a theatre and worked for the anti-apartheid movement), Italy—and most recently the U.S., where he is writer-in-residence at Western New Mexico University. His short fiction has been published by Penguin, Johns Hopkins University Press, and myriad literary magazines in England and the U.S.

"Hard-hitting . . . the kind of language that packs a serious punch!"
—*The Times*, London

ABOUT PM PRESS

PM Press was founded at the end of 2007
by a small collection of folks with decades of
publishing, media, and organizing experience.
PM Press co-conspirators have published
and distributed hundreds of books, pamphlets, CDs, and DVDs.
Members of PM have founded enduring book fairs, spearheaded
victorious tenant organizing campaigns, and worked closely with
bookstores, academic conferences, and even rock bands to deliver
political and challenging ideas to all walks of life. We're old enough
to know what we're doing and young enough to know what's at
stake.

We seek to create radical and stimulating fiction and non-fiction
books, pamphlets, T-shirts, visual and audio materials to entertain,
educate, and inspire you. We aim to distribute these through every
available channel with every available technology—whether that
means you are seeing anarchist classics at our bookfair stalls;
reading our latest vegan cookbook at the café; downloading geeky
fiction e-books; or digging new music and timely videos from our
website.

PM Press is always on the lookout for talented and skilled volunteers,
artists, activists, and writers to work with. If you have a great idea for
a project or can contribute in some way, please get in touch.

PM Press
PO Box 23912
Oakland, CA 94623
www.pmpress.org

FRIENDS OF PM PRESS

These are indisputably momentous times—the financial system is melting down globally and the Empire is stumbling. Now more than ever there is a vital need for radical ideas.

In the years since its founding—and on a mere shoestring—PM Press has risen to the formidable challenge of publishing and distributing knowledge and entertainment for the struggles ahead. With hundreds of releases to date, we have published an impressive and stimulating array of literature, art, music, politics, and culture. Using every available medium, we've succeeded in connecting those hungry for ideas and information to those putting them into practice.

Friends of PM allows you to directly help impact, amplify, and revitalize the discourse and actions of radical writers, filmmakers, and artists. It provides us with a stable foundation from which we can build upon our early successes and provides a much-needed subsidy for the materials that can't necessarily pay their own way. You can help make that happen—and receive every new title automatically delivered to your door once a month—by joining as a Friend of PM Press. And, we'll throw in a free T-shirt when you sign up.

Here are your options (all include a 50% discount on all webstore purchases):
- **$30 a month** Get all books and pamphlets
- **$40 a month** Get all PM Press releases (including CDs and DVDs)
- **$100 a month** Everything plus PM merchandise and free downloads

For those who can't afford $30 or more a month, we're introducing **Sustainer Rates** at $15, $10 and $5. Sustainers get a free PM Press T-shirt and a 50% discount on all purchases from our website.

Your Visa or Mastercard will be billed once a month, until you tell us to stop. Or until our efforts succeed in bringing the revolution around. Or the financial meltdown of Capital makes plastic redundant. Whichever comes first.

Sensation

Nick Mamatas

ISBN: 978-1-60486-354-3
$14.95 • 208 Pages

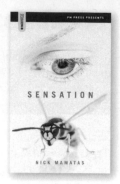

Love. Politics. Parasitic manipulation. Julia
Hernandez left her husband, shot a real-
estate developer out to gentrify Brooklyn,
and then vanished without a trace. Well,
perhaps one or two traces were left . . . With
different personal and consumption habits, Julia has slipped out of
the world she knew and into the Simulacrum—a place between the
cracks of our existence from which human history is both guided
and thwarted by the conflict between a species of anarchist wasp
and a collective of hyperintelligent spiders. When Julia's ex-husband
Raymond spots her in a grocery store he doesn't usually patronize,
he's drawn into an underworld of radical political gestures and
Internet organizing looking to overthrow a ruling class it knows
nothing about—and Julia is the new media sensation of both this
world and the Simulacrum.

Told ultimately from the collective point of view of another species,
Sensation plays with the elements of the Simulacrum we all already
live in: media reports, business-speak, blog entries, text messages,
psychological evaluation forms, and the always fraught and kindly
lies lovers tell one another.

> "Nick Mamatas continues his reign as the sharpest, funniest,
> most insightful and political purveyor of post-pulp pleasures
> going. He is the People's Commissar of Awesome."
> —China Miéville, award-winning author of *Kraken* and *The
> City and the City*

Fire on the Mountain

Terry Bisson

Introduction by Mumia Abu-Jamal
ISBN: 978-1-60486-087-0
$15.95 • 208 Pages

It's 1959 in socialist Virginia. The Deep South is an independent Black nation called Nova Africa. The second Mars expedition is about to touch down on the red planet. And a pregnant scientist is climbing the Blue Ridge in search of her great-great grandfather, a teenage slave who fought with John Brown and Harriet Tubman's guerrilla army.

Long unavailable in the U.S., published in France as *Nova Africa*, *Fire on the Mountain* is the story of what might have happened if John Brown's raid on Harper's Ferry had succeeded—and the Civil War had been started not by the slave owners but the abolitionists.

TVA Baby

Terry Bisson

ISBN: 978-1-60486-405-2
$14.95 • 192 Pages

Beginning with a harrowing, high-speed ride through the Upper South (a TVA baby is a good ol' boy with a Yankee father and a 12-gauge) and ending in a desperate search through New Orleans graveyards for Darwin's doomsday machine ("Charlie's Angels"), Terry Bisson's newest collection of short stories covers all the territory between— from his droll faux-FAQ's done for Britain's *Science* magazine, to the most seductive of his *Playboy* fantasies ("Private Eye"), to an eerie dreamlike evocation of the 9/11 that might have been ("A Perfect Day"). On the way we meet up with Somali Pirates, a perfect-crime appliance (via PayPal) and a visitor from Atlantis who just wants a burger with fries, please.

Clandestine Occupations: An Imaginary History

Diana Block

ISBN: 978-1-62963-121-9

$16.95 • 248 Pages

A radical activist, Luba Gold, makes the difficult decision to go underground to support the Puerto Rican independence movement. When Luba's collective is targeted by an FBI sting, she escapes with her baby but leaves behind a sensitive envelope that is being safeguarded by a friend. When the FBI come looking for Luba, the friend must decide whether to cooperate in the search for the woman she loves. Ten years later, when Luba emerges from clandestinity, she discovers that the FBI sting was orchestrated by another activist friend who had become an FBI informant. In the changed era of the 1990s, Luba must decide whether to forgive the woman who betrayed her.

Told from the points of view of five different women who cross paths with Luba over four decades, *Clandestine Occupations* explores the difficult decisions that activists confront about the boundaries of legality and speculates about the scope of clandestine action in the future. It is a thought-provoking reflection on the risks and sacrifices of political activism as well as the damaging reverberations of disaffection and cynicism.

> "Clandestine Occupations *is a triumph of passion and force. A number of memoirs and other nonfiction works by revolutionaries from the 1970s and '80s, including one by Block herself, have given us partial pictures of what a committed life, sometimes lived underground, was like. But there are times when only fiction can really take us there. A marvelous novel that moves beyond all preconceived categories."*
> —Margaret Randall, author of *Che on My Mind*